VOLUME FOUR

AIRSHIP 27 PRODUCTIONS

Bass Reeves Frontier Marshal Volume 4
"The Hard Ride" ©2020 Ron Fortier
"The Pastor of Lone Hollow" ©2020 Derrick Ferguson
"A Private War" ©2020 Terry Alexander
"Them Bones" ©2020 Mel Odom

Published by Airship 27 Productions
www.airship27.com
www.airship27hangar.com

Cover illustration © 2020 Rob Davis
Interior illustrations ©2020 Howard Simpson
—*I dedicate this art to my Dad, Billy Simpson. Who never told me to get a day job and supported my attempt to start my career when I was only thirteen years old.*—

Editor: Ron Fortier
Associate Editor: Gordon Dymowski
Marketing and Promotions Manager: Michael Vance
Production designer: Rob Davis

ISBN: 978-1-946183-97-2

Printed in the United States of America

10 9 8 7 6 5 4 3 2 1

BASS REEVES
FRONTIER MARSHAL
VOLUME 4

THE HARD RIDE..**5**

By Ron Fortier

After delivering a prisoner to a small Texas town, Marshal Reeves encounters death and savagery awaiting him on the ride home.

THE PASTOR OF LONE HOLLOW..............................**46**

By Derrick Ferguson

Reeves encounters a gun-toting pastor with a secret past. Only by working together can they rescued a kidnapped girl.

A PRIVATE WAR..**89**

By Terry Alexander

Bass Reeves hunts a murderous Indian brave who leaves a trail of bodies in his wake.

THEM BONES...**131**

By Mel Odom

Into his fifties, Marshal Reeves employs his detecting skills to hunt down a professional killer.

THE HARD RIDE

By Ron Fortier

Sheriff Porter Pane, sat on the front porch of the Coleman town jail, the latest Chicago Police Gazette in his hands and his worn McIntosh pipe hanging from his dry lips. His dirty gray Stetson shaded his eyes just enough to allow him to read the print on the brittle, yellowing pages. The issue in his hands was three months old, but then again, the fact that it had survived the journey to this bleak, dried up part of Texas was a minor miracle in itself.

Having finished the article on the raving mad prostitute who had carved several of her more prominent clientele, Pane took in a lungful of tobacco and then exhaled it around the stem of his pipe. It was a quiet summer afternoon and he liked it that way. Nice and peaceful.

Traffic along the town's center road was light with a few homesteader wagons coming and going and an occasional cowpoke or injun riding past. The former most likely making for the Cactus Saloon; the latter for Joe Walters' Mercantile store. This back and forth parade of frontier humanity was so routine as to border on pure boredom.

What was uncommon was the big, tall black fellow riding up the street on an a large white mare. Behind him, following along like a shadow, was a small man wearing a wrinkled suit, bowtie and brown bowler derby that had seen better days. Pane sat up straight and pushed back the brim of his hat. Now he could see the second rider's hands were cuffed at the wrists.

He looked back at the Negro as sunlight glinted off the badge pinned to man's leather vest. Sheriff Pane grinned. Only one black man he knew wore a Deputy United States Marshal badge and sat that tall in the saddle.

"Well, if it ain't Bass Reeves hisself," Pane chuckled getting to his feet. He tossed the magazine onto the chair he'd vacated and stood at the top of the one wooden step.

"Sheriff Pane," Deputy Reeves nodded as he reined in his horse. "Mighty glad to see you as well. Been a long trail and I'm not sad to see it end."

"Who's your prisoner?"

"Surprise you don't recognize him," the deputy said as he dismounted. "Seeing that he embezzled ten thousand dollars from you folks."

Sheriff Pane blinked, moved to the left slightly and shaded his eyes with his left arm. Sure enough, the little gent seated on the chestnut mare was

5

none other Walter J. Williams; former chief clerk of the Coleman National Trust located several blocks north on River Avenue.

"Sonuvabitch, it is the little peckerwood. Where'd you catch up with him?"

"Wasn't me," Reeves clarified as he grabbed hold of Williams' arm and helped him off his horse. "Some bounty hunter recognized him from his wanted flier living the high life up in Kansas. Guess old Walter here was spending his ill gotten gains buying too much liquor and loose women.

"Anyways, this bounty man knocks him over the head one night, throws his sorry ass over a saddle and brings him down to Marshal Higgins in Fort Smith to collect his reward."

"Let me guess the rest," Sheriff Pane offered as Reeves led the captured felon past him and into the jail proper. "Then the same Marshal Higgins gave you the sorry task of bringing him home to us."

"You oughta take up story writing," Reeves grinned broadly. "That's exactly what happened…despite my vigorous objections."

Once in the tiny front room, Sheriff Pane motioned to his deputy, a thin, wiry sort with straw colored hair and rimless glasses busy at a filing cabinet straightening out folders.

"Chauncey, we got us a new house guest," he said indicating the prisoner.

The deputy's eyes widened in recognition. "Hey! Ain't that clerk Williams who ran off with the bank's money?"

"One and the same," Pane chuckled watching Reeves undo the steel manacles. "You go get him squared away in a cell back there. Then go see if you can find Mayor Jenkins and tell him all about it."

"Yes, sir," the young man smiled as he opened the door to the back room where the two cells were located. He took hold of Williams' arm and shoved him inside.

"Hey, no need to get rough," the mousy former clerk squealed. "I'm moving fast as I can."

As the two disappeared behind the door, Bass Reeves took of his dust covered hat and wiped the back of his sleeve over his forehead. "Damn, I need a bath and a good stove cooked meal."

"Maude Wintergreen's hotel and restaurant right across the street should take care of your needs, amigo."

"Alright, tell you what. I'll get registered in, get this trail dirt washed off me and then meet you in the dining room in say…what? An hour?"

"Sure thing, Bass. That should be enough time for my deputy to find the mayor and get him over here so I can fill him in. We still ain't got us a town judge, just a circuit rider. So Mayor Jenkins is gonna need to telegraph him we got Williams."

"Then I'd best be going." Reeves started to pull open the front door, when he had a second thought. "Plumb forgot about my horses."

"You go on to the hotel, I'll have Chauncey take them over to Lem Jacobs stable after he fetches the mayor."

"Sure thing," Chauncey confirmed appearing out of the back room with the cell keys in his hands. "Be my pleasure, Marshal."

"Then thank you both." Reeves stepped out the door with the eager deputy on his heels.

"I'll be sure their groomed and fed properly," he told Reeves before darting off down the street to carry out the sheriff's directive.

Bass Reeves pulled on his hat, turned to his horse and untied his saddle bags. These he threw over his left shoulder. Then he pulled his Winchester carbine from its scabbard with his right hand and started across the street careful to avoid any traffic. Imagining the luxury of the hot bath awaiting him, he picked up his step.

Two hours later Reeves was finishing a tasty slab of apple pie after having put away a two pound juicy steak, mountains of buttered mashed potatoes and a side dish peas and carrots. All of which he'd washed down with several glasses of lemonade.

As he swallowed his forkful of pie, Sheriff Porter Pane, seated across the round table, smiled while taking a sip of coffee. Porter had finished his own piece of pie minutes earlier, forgoing anything more as it would only ruin his dinner later.

"Mrs. Porter wouldn't take kindly to working over her stove all afternoon only to have me come home stuffed," he explained with a knowing smirk.

Reeves acknowledge the sentiment while wiping his lips with a napkin. He kept a thick, black brush mustache and was careful to keep it clean of stray crumbs. He was a fastidious dresser always aware of his appearance.

"Can I get you anything else?" the pretty freckled face waitress asked as she picked up his empty plate and utensils.

"That coffee the sheriff is having smells mighty fine," Reeves commented.

"Coming right up," the girl smiled and disappeared back into the kitchen.

The lunch crowd having come and gone earlier, the dining room section of the first floor was deserted except for the two lawmen. Reeves wore new clothes, having given his soiled pants and shirt to the Mrs. Wintergreen, the hotel proprietor. She'd volunteered to get them washed when he'd registered at the front desk. Now with clean clothes and a full belly, the Arkansas Deputy Marshal felt like a brand new man.

"I guess Jenny would feel the same if I was to snub one of her fine meals," he said picking up the conversation.

"How is she these days?" Pane inquired. "Still giving you more children than you can manage?"

"Oh, yeah."

"Exactly how many you got now, Bass?"

"Four, with a fifth on the way any day now."

Porter laughed. "Damn, you and her planning on populating the entire frontier all by yourselves?"

"Ha. Wasn't the plan when we jumped the broom, but I really don't mind. That horse ranch of mine needs a whole lot of work and having a bunch of strapping sons and daughters is gonna be a blessing as they grow up."

At that moment the waitress returned with a porcelain cup filled with hot coffee and set it down before the Marshal along with a spoon. The sugar bowl was in the middle of the table. "Will there be anything else, mister?"

"No, ma'am. What do I owe you?"

The girl wiped her hands on her apron and bit down on her lower lip as she mentally calculated his bill. "That'll be two bits. Coffee is free."

Bass Reeves dug the fingers of his left hand into his vest pocket and pulled out the correct amount of coins. He handed them to the girl. "Thank you kindly, ma'am."

The girl gave him a big smile and disappeared again.

As Reeves added two spoons of sugar into his steaming coffee, Sheriff Pane drained the rest of his cup. "So, you plan on heading back home tomorrow morning?"

"I do," Reeves concurred before taking a cautious sip of his coffee. It tasted just fine. "I want to get started at first light."

"Any plans for the rest of the day?"

"Naw, just thought I'd mosey over to the saloon and see if I could find a game of cards to keep me occupied for a while."

"Well, if you're at all interested, some of us like to play baseball after dinner, it staying light well into the evening."

"Were at?"

"In the big field behind the Baptist church. You're welcome to join in if you've a mind."

Reeves nodded. "Sounds like fun. I just might do that." He took another sip of coffee and sat back in his chair, at ease and at peace. This trip to Texas had turned out just fine.

As he'd planned, Deputy Marshal Bass Reeves was up and on the trail a good hour before the sun rose. He took the road out of Coleman going east so that he was able to witness the majestic sunrise. As the purple skies above gave way to the encroaching pink and yellow colors, the bright orb climbed the heavens spilling forth a blue sky decorated with giant, puffy white clouds. Doves, grouse and pigeons erupted from the brush and took to the air, all of them singing their own individual songs.

Having always loved the outdoors, Reeves felt a part of the nature around him. He cherished the taste of the sweet fresh morning air that filled his lungs. He kept his horse to an easy gait while loosely holding the lasso that was affixed to the brown mare's bridle. He'd raised both animals on his ranch and they were strong, dependable creatures. This early in the day, he hadn't expected to meet many other travelers and his assumption was correct. He had the road to himself.

Eight miles out of Coleman, he left the main road and started north. An hour later he crossed the Red River and left Texas behind as he rode into what the maps labeled the Indian Territories. He would gradually veer north-east moving along a diagonal line that would cross several hundred miles of wilderness and bring him to the Arkansas border and the rapidly growing town of Fort Smith.

The terrain before him was flat, hard scrabble dirt dotted with prairie dog holes. Reeves let his mount choose its path, knowing it was smart enough to avoid the treacherous holes before them. The brown mare did likewise.

As he rode, he sang gospel hymns his mother has taught him as a child.

By mid-afternoon he was weaving his way through shallow ravines in which babbling creeks were found. Towering over these was a range of gently rising hills made up of thorn bushes and red hued boulders. The sun had warmed the day nicely so he made a point of sticking to the shade of the water gullies. In one particular spot, access to the water's edge was clear and he decided to rest a bit. Both horses stepped up to the creek and dropped their muzzles into refreshing water. At the same time, Reeves retrieved his canteen from his saddle, went down one knee and dunked it into the racing stream. Once filled, he took a swallow and then dipped it again to fill it completely.

After securing it again, he walked over to a fallen ponderosa pine that stretched across the sand, its bark nearly completely peeled off after years of exposure to the elements. Wary of rattlers, Reeves checked both ends of the hollowed log carefully. Satisfied it was devoid of snakes and other mischievous critters; he sat down with his shoulders and head against the dead tree, pulled his hat down over his eyes and proceeded to take a siesta.

Later, the sound of falling gravel awoke him. Alert instantly, Reeves made no sudden motion, but rather lay silently to see if the sound would repeat. When it did, he deduced it was coming from the cliff's edge over the far end of the gully. Slowly, he reached up and pushed the brim of his hat off his face.

Three Indians on horseback were riding along the ledge in single file. From the painted symbols on their horses and their feathered attire, he recognized them as Chikasaw. That was no real surprise as this was their territory. He knew them to be a peaceful people and these three were most likely out hunting. Still, he was glad they hadn't seen him or his horses. Even peaceful tribes didn't like strangers on their lands.

As the last Indian brave vanished from view, Reeves sat up and looked around. Both mares were behind him nibbling the sharp leaves of a mesquite bush. Using the log to balance himself, Reeves stood and then brushed the dirt off his jeans. It was time to get going again. With any luck he could make another thirty miles before nightfall.

Another thirty miles closer to home.

By the end of the day, Reeves had left the hard barren ground behind him and entered into wide open prairie grasslands. The ocher colored tall-grass reached as high as his stirrups and the thin blades slid under his boots as he rode along. With the sun quickly setting back over his shoulder, Reeves began to scout out a decent site to make camp. He found it in a small copse of Pinyon pines that rose out of the earth before him just as the darkling sky blanketed the world.

After tying his horses to a clump of thick green bushes, he removed their saddles and set them on the ground in an open spot between the trees. Using old towels from his saddle bags, he rubbed down both mares then fed them oats. Once they were taken care of, he gathered up broken branches as kindling to start a decent campfire. Next he retrieved his small blue steel pot and set it on a big flat rock next to the crackling flames. In this he poured a little water from his canteen and then added crushed coffee beans. Soon he could smell the aroma of the ground beans.

Removing his neck bandana, he carefully wrapped it around the hot handle of the pot and poured the black brew into a small tin cup; careful to stop before any of the coffee grinds escaped. Despite not having any sugar, he still enjoyed the taste. He sat down cross-legged on the ground to eat his simple meal. It consisted of several pieces of dried deer jerky and a couple of sweet corn biscuits he'd bought back in Coleman and his coffee.

Brought up a slave until he was in his early teen years, Bass Reeves had often gone on far less vittles. The jerky and biscuits were both tasty and filling. "A person should appreciate what they has, instead of crying about they don't have." It was one of his mother's favorite sayings. Now he reflected on what a truly wise woman she was.

He looked up and was pleased to see the black carpet of night sprinkled with so many shining stars. As he watched them, a flash of yellow-orange streaked across the sky, like some kind of celestial fox with its tail on fire.

Damn, he thought to himself. That was sure pretty.

It was almost high noon the next day when Bass Reeves came upon the massacre.

Most of the morning he'd been riding across a flat, grassy landscape with little or no trees. Then as he continued north-east the ground began to rise up into a series of small hills dotted with white pines and evergreens. He saw animal signs but paid them no mind, as most of the tracks were of nocturnal critters that wouldn't be about during daylight.

Then as he was moving down one steep hillside, he heard the screeching of birds and looked up to see a half dozen vultures circling overhead. Where they were flying, a thin plume of black smoke spiraled upward.

Something over the next hill was burning and it wasn't a campfire.

He spurred his horse onward and as he crested the hilltop, he saw the cause of both the smoke and the agitated birds. Approximately a hundred yards ahead of him was a dirt road and there stood the charred, smoldering remains of a covered wagon. There were no horses hitched to the wagon's front and at first Reeves couldn't see any people.

Then, as he rode carefully down the slope, he was able to see around the ruined cart and there he beheld a sickening sight. Several mangy coyotes were chewing at three lifeless bodies while at the same time fighting off a half dozen large vultures who were brave enough to challenge them for the easy meal.

From where he sat, Reeves made out that the bodies were of a man, a woman and a small child. The last looked like a little boy. One of the wild dogs was biting at the boy's face while two others tore at his legs.

Reeves pulled on his reins and his mare made a whinnying noise. Several of the startled carrion feeders jerked their heads around to see what had interrupted their meal. Spotting Reeves and his two horses, they barked loudly. A few dared to growl warning him off from their prize.

The marshal pulled out his Winchester, chambered a round and then bringing the stock to his right shoulder, he sighted and fired. The nearest coyote was kicked into the air with a yip and fell to the ground dead. Now the others started barking again and Reeves shot another as easily as he'd done the first. The shot echoed across the open land and the vultures jumped like rabbits. Unnerved by the loudness, they began to fly off.

When Reeves shot and killed a third coyote, the others wasted no time abandoning the corpses and raced off in the opposite direction. Holding his rifle with his right hand, he tugged his reins with his left.

"Go on," he told his white mare.

Skittish from the gunfire, the stench of the black smoke and the smell of the dead, the horse reluctantly move forward, it's big round eyes battling the fear that threatened to override its senses.

"Easy, girl," Reeves' voice calmly urged her forward. "It's alright now."

Of course that didn't stop him from carefully surveying the immediate area. Something…or someone…had killed those folks and there were no guarantees they might not still be nearby. Close enough to have heard his gunshots and return to investigate. He wasn't about to be ambushed like this innocent family had been.

He rode around the wagon side away from the bodies. Although the fire had destroyed most of the frame, somehow only one of the rear wheels had collapsed and in doing so titled the bed. This had caused various goods to tumble free. He ignored these and continued to the front. The box seat had collapsed and the heavy canvas covering was history. Only small fragments still clung to the bent steel bows. Now blackened by the dying fire, they looked like the ribcage of a mammoth beast. He'd heard tell of the mighty buffalo that at one time had roamed the high plains country. They were said to have been gigantic. Maybe even as big as this now broken wagon.

Coming to the tip of the wagon's long wooden tongue; its tip resting the dirt, Reeves dropped to ground and tied his reins to heavy beam. In doing so, he read the tracks. Two big horses had been tied there; mostly likely farm draft horses. Someone had set them free. Walking past the tongue, Reeves looked down at the earth intently.

He'd spent a good part of his youth among the Indians of the Five Civilized Tribes. Among the many things they had taught was how to read signs. As he carefully studied the disturbed dirt, information filtered into his mind's eye.

Two men had ridden up to the wagon. They were riding horses shod with steel shoes so they weren't Indians. Only white folks put shoes on their horses. The riders had obviously stopped the wagon. He made out the footprints of two men. The shoe sizes were about the same.

Careful not to disturb those tracks, Reeves approached the body of the man and woman lying only a few feet apart. Both appeared to be in their thirties, were dressed in simple garments and seemed like ordinary sodbusters. Each had been shot several times, blood splotches were visible on their bodies, along with the missing pieces torn away by the coyotes. Looking into their faces, he saw nothing but horror. Of course, their last vision in this life had been of their own doom.

In his career as a lawman, Bass Reeves had seen a whole lot of killing. He had witnessed first hand the cruelty of men, and some women, and he still could not fathom how a person could commit such heinous acts.

Lastly he walked over to the dead boy. Having sons of his own, he figured the child to have been seven or eight years of age. He too had been shot several times.

"Sweet, Jesus," he gasped, rubbing the back of his hand over his eyes as if to wipe away the image before him. Looking down at that dirty,

"Sweet Jesus!" he gasped.

ravaged little face, he vowed to hunt down the men who had committed these killings and bring them to justice. Either by the Judge Isaac Parker's hangman's noose in Fort Smith, or from the end of his own Colt .45 Peacemaker. They would be made to pay.

A light breeze kicked up several of the clothing items on the ground and ended his mental reverie. There were graves to be dug. But Reeves felt uncomfortable having the family's belongings scattered all about. It didn't seem right. He set down his rifle against the leaning wagon and began picking up the scattered shirts, pants and dresses.

Once he had an armful, he inspected what was left in the burned out bed and discovered an open chest set atop a bunch of loose tools. He managed to lean in far enough to start stuffing the clothes he gathered into the chest. As he did so, he spotted a framed photograph stuck between the chest and wagon's side. He pulled it free to examine the image. It was one of those family portraits taken in a professional studio. Half the glass was cracked and missing but he could still recognize the people captured in their frozen pose. But there were four of them, not three.

The father and mother sat side by side, with the little boy on his mothers lap. Standing awkwardly stiff behind them in the middle was a young girl with long dark hair draped over her shoulders.

Marshal Reeves sighed. He looked back at the corpses and then the area all around them. He didn't have to guess what had happened to the girl. She had been taken by the men who had butchered her family.

For a moment, he debated whether to drop everything and see if he could catch up to the outlaws. If the girl was still alive, he might still have a chance to rescue her. But there was no guarantees he could find the killers' trail or even reach them before the end of the day. Meanwhile he would be abandoning the bodies to the coyotes and vultures again. When he weighed both alternatives, common sense won out. He had to do the decent thing by the three lost souls. Then, if the Good Lord was willing, he would find the others.

Reeves put down the photograph. There was a shovel among the man's tools and he pulled it out of the wagon. It was time to go to work.

Thirty minutes later, Reeves stopped to take off his shirt and vest. His barrel-like deep-brown chest was covered by sweat as he went to fetch his canteen. He took a long swallow and then went back to digging. It was his thought to make a hole large enough to bury the family together. He made sure to keep his hat on. The last thing he wanted was heat stroke.

He'd been at it another ten minutes when he heard the sounds of horses approaching. Lots of horses. Looking up from the depression he had made, he saw a troop of blue clad cavalrymen approaching. All of them were colored except for the Indian scout who rode a brown and white pinto in the lead beside a grizzled looking Negro with sergeant chevrons on his sleeves. Even though Reeves was illiterate, he didn't need to know his numbers in regards to the red and white pennant being held aloft by the honor guard.

This was the 10th Cavalry, known throughout the territories by the name the Indians had bestowed upon them; the Buffalo Soldiers. Riding two by two, in a military fashion, they wore black boots, dark blue trousers with yellow piping down each leg, a lighter blue cotton shirt and yellow kerchiefs. About their middles was an army issued leather belt with a US embossed bronze belt buckle. Each man wore a white hat though several of them had the brims folded up and tacked to the crowns. They looked much as their reputation claimed; a bunch of rough and ready soldiers.

As the troop reached the remains of the prairie schooner, the sergeant held up a white gloved hand and shouted out loud, "COMPANY, HALT!"

Reeves put down his shovel and climbed out of the unfinished grave.

"Howdy gents," he greeted amiably looking up at the sergeant; clearly the man in charge.

"Sir," the army veteran nodded. His skin was a light mocha and he had a three day old stubbly beard wrapped around his face. "I am Sergeant Cornelius Morand. Who might you be and exactly what are you doing here?" The sergeant swept an arm towards the hole and the three bodies lying near it.

The lawman picked up his vest and turned it over to show his silver badge. "I'm Deputy Marshal Bass Reeves, riding out of Fort Smith, Arkansas, for Judge Isaac Parker."

"I've heard tell of you, Marshal," Sgt. Morand nodded again, his eyes looked tired. "What happened here?"

"I can only guess," Reeves shrugged. "I just rode up to this here massacre less than a few hours ago. By what tracks I was able to read, this poor family was set upon by a couple of murdering varmints. I figure they was robbers looking to see if these homesteaders had any money stashed away in their belongings.

"So they shot the parents and the little fellah, then after tearing through their belongins, torched the wagon and took off with the daughter."

"Daughter?"

"Huh, huh," Reeves pointed to the pile of clothing visible at the back end of the cart. "I found a picture that showed the four of them. Girl looks to be about fifteen years old.

"I'm thinking those killers are looking to have their way with the poor girl before they is done with her."

Sgt. Morand pulled at his chin looking over the site while he digested Reeves' account. "Our scout, Gray Eagle here," he tilted his head towards the Indian, "came across some signs of two riders about ten miles north of here. They might possibly be the ones who did this."

Reeves turned his attention to the scout and easily identified him as a Chiricahua Apache by his dress. Soft moccasins covered his feet, then sturdier deer-skin leggings wrapped his white cotton pants to the knees. Under his military belt, which held a pistol holster and knife sheath, was draped a traditional white apron. The burly, bronze skinned brave wore a blue Union jacket over his bare torso, a yellow kerchief about his neck and a wide, dull red head scarf. Long black hair fell over his shoulders and his face was sharply defined as if chiseled from granite. His eyes were a hard slate gray and seemed to drink in his surroundings with restless attention.

Bass Reeves swept his right hand across his chest and then outward in a sweeping gesture that was regarded as a peace greeting amongst most of the tribes in the territories.

Gray Eagle returned the sign.

"What happened to the team pulling the wagon?" Sgt. Morand asked Reeves.

"Whoever done this, cut them loose. I figure the fire would have spooked them and God knows where they is at now."

"Hmm. Hopefully some Indian tribe will find them before bears or big cats do. Hate to see fine animals wasted like that for no good reason."

"I agree, Sergeant." Reeves was thinking of his own horse ranch back home.

Sgt. Morand stood in his stirrups, twisted around and looked back at his men. "Privates Wilkins and Alright, grab your shovels and relieve Marshal Reeves here. The rest of you dismount and get busy. We'll camp here tonight."

"Thank you," Reeves said as the sergeant climbed off his horse. "That's kind of you."

"Seems you've done enough already," the cavalry sergeant pulled off his leather gloves. "You should rest up a little."

As the two privates singled out by their sergeant hurried over to the grave, the other men set about seeing to their horses and preparing a proper campsite.

Gray Eagle nudged his horse forward. "I will ride west. Maybe find new signs of the war party."

"Very well," Sgt. Morand approved. "If you spot anything get back here pronto."

The Indian merely grunted and spurred his horse into a gallop. As he did so, Sgt. Morand cupped a hand next to his mouth and yelled, "Get us a few jackrabbits while you're at it."

He turned back to the marshal, who was looking at him questioningly.

"You're not just patrolling, are you?" Reeves asked.

"No, Marshal. A group of about twelve to thirteen young Comanche bucks went on the warpath about a week ago. They been raiding settlements and homesteaders up and down the Texas border.

"They've left a trail of bodies behind them."

"And you was sent to catch 'em."

"Yes, sir. When we first saw this wagon we thought it might be their work, but apparently, we got us two different sets of raiders on our hands."

"It would appear so."

Both men were silent for a few minutes as the Indian Gray Eagle disappeared over the far horizon.

Without being asked, privates Wilkins and Albright dug three graves instead of merely continuing the one Reeves had been working on. When they were done, other soldiers helped them wrap the bodies as best they could with the clothing the marshal had collected. Then they reverently laid each in their respective resting places before replacing the mounds of dirt. After the graves were completed, several troopers made simple crosses from the remains of the burnt wagon and shoved them into the ground in front of each mound.

As it turned out, Sgt. Morand not only could read and write, but he also owned a battered church bible. The company, along with Reeves, assembled before the freshly dug graves as the grizzled sergeant read solemn words about this fragile life and how all things made of dust must one day return to dust.

While he read, Bass Reeves, his hat in his hands, head bowed slightly, felt the last rays of the sun warming his backside. Soon night would fall, ending their impromptu service.

Finished with his prayer reading, Sgt. Morand and his men returned to their duties. By now they had two blazing fires crackling.

"You're welcome to share our camp and spend the night," Morand offered Reeves.

"Thank you, Sergeant. Considering you say there's a band of angry Comanche out there somewhere, I'm happy to accept your kind invitation."

Sides, them bushwalkers won't be traveling at night either, he thought as he went to see to his horses and fetch his sleeping blanket. *Plenty of time to pick up their trail in the morning.*

By the time Gray Eagle reappeared, with four fat rabbits, twilight had fallen and half the sky was filled with bright silver stars.

The next day, Marshal Reeves enjoyed a cup of hot coffee with Sgt. Morand before bidding him and his men farewell. Astride his white mare and pulling his second horse, Reeves tipped his hat in farewell and rode off northward.

The sun quickly dispelled the morning chill he rode along appreciating the new day the Good Lord had set before him. Before leaving the cavalry troop, Gray Eagle had described the landmarks he would encounter so that he might locate where the apache had spotted the horse tracks the previous day. There was no guarantee they belonged to the men who had murdered the homesteaders, but seeing that they were within a half day's ride from the scene of the attack, Reeves thought the odds were in his favor.

The Indian Territories were, for the most part, still untamed, unsettled lands containing thousands of acres of emptiness. Since the end of the Civil War, a few settlements made up of runaway slaves had sprung up scattered among the Indian villages. Reeves was familiar with most of them. The fact that these frontier communities were unfriendly towards whites was one of the principle reasons he had been recruited by Judge Parker. A black marshal had a far better chance of surviving out here than his white counterparts.

Even though he did miss his wife and children, there was a beauty to the landscape he had come to love and riding along, he felt at ease. This is where he belonged. As if reading his thoughts, a soaring golden eagle screeched its approval as it swooped overhead. Reeves watched its graceful light and envied the regal flier.

When he arrived at a wide gap bordered by hills to his right and dozens of large gray boulders to his left, he slowed his horse. He had been riding over the same trail the cavalry troop had trampled over. The rocks stretched into an open forest glade. It was here Gray Eagle had seen the twin sets of horse tracks. Reeves directed his horse off the main path while his eyes scanned the ground by the boulders. It took him less then ten minutes to find the duel set of prints.

He studied them intently. One set was deeper than the other as if the horse that had made them was carrying more than a single rider. That could be the kidnapped girl. He urged his horse into the trees and continued to follow the tracks. Eventually the tracks became faint as the ground was hidden by a layer of detritus. Trusting his instincts, he continued forward in a straight line. After a few miles, Reeves heard the sounds of running water. A herd of five deer appeared through the trees ahead and then quickly dashed out of sight.

Minutes later he emerged on the banks of a swift flowing blue river. Sunlight glistened off the water as it cascaded southward over a zig-zag course strewn with treacherous rocks. The roar of the water muffled any other forest sounds.

His animals both snorted loudly at the smell of the wet air and he casually rode up to the bank where he dismounted and let them both drink. Moving away several feet, Reeves knelt down on the hard ground, removed his hat and then scooped water up to splash over his face. It felt cold and refreshing. Then he put his hat back on, leaned over and using two hands, quenched his own thirst.

He was thinking of refilling his canteens when something across the river caught his eye. There, barely visible beneath a thick bush was a blue something. Reeves stood and squinted his eyes to peer harder. It looked like a piece of cloth.

He looked about cautiously; all too aware that the men he was tracking could be anywhere. With one hand on the butt of his right hip pistol, the marshal walked behind his horses, his left hand patting their rumps to keep them calm. He seemed to be alone with no one visible up and down the river. Satisfied with that, he then looked to see how deep the moving water actually was. From his perspective, it didn't seem any deeper than two or three feet. Still the speed by which it flowed would prove to be a problem should he try to bring the horses across.

No. He would have to cross on foot and hope for the best.

Bass Reeves tied both his horses to a tree and then set off across the river. The chill of the river soaked his pant legs immediately causing him to gasp. No way he was about to lose his balance and take a bath in that water. With each step forward, he held his arms out to keep himself steady. The water's tug was powerful and he fought it with each new step. At the same time he never took his eyes off the piece of blue cloth.

After what seemed an eternity, the marshal reached the opposite bank, took a deep breath and forced himself out of the river's grasp. On dry land, he stomped his boots several times and then walked over to the thick bush now only a few yards before him.

The blue cloth now revealed itself partially. It was a gingham dress and from it a shoeless leg was visible. It was dirty, heavily scratched and appeared to have blood on it.

Carefully Bass Reeves approached the thicket, reached down with his right hand and pulled the branches back. There, huddled in a fetal ball, was a young white girl, her dress ripped in several places like an old used rag. Ants and other bugs crawled over her. For a second he couldn't tell if she was alive or dead.

Then the girl moaned.

Not knowing how badly the girl was injured, Reeves kept his voice soft in the same way he would approach a skittish horse.

"Hello, there, little miss." The girl's face turned upward at his words. "Don't be scared now."

Her round face was dirt smeared and bruised. He knew those marks were made by fists and he felt his stomach tighten.

As the girl gazed upon him, her sky-blue eyes widened fearfully and she brought up her arms defensively.

"NO! Please...don't hurt me no more." Her feet kicked at him and Reeves back away.

"Whoa there," he kept his voice unthreatening. "I ain't gonna hurt you none. I promise."

The girl stopped thrashing. She looked at him again, hands balled up in front of her face. "You're just like them," she blurted out fearfully.

"Like them? You mean the two fellahs that took you?"

"Yes…like them."

"How so? I don't understand."

The girl tried to catch her breath as she fought back tears. "You're a brown man like they was."

Her words cut into Reeves as if someone had stuck a hot poker into his heart. All the while he'd envisioned the family massacre and fate of the kidnapped girl; he'd not given a single thought to the possibility that the raiders were colored folks. A voice in his head reprimanded him for his naïve mistake. As a marshal he'd gone after and apprehended men, and women, of all races: white, red and black. Still, the fact that the two murderers were black upset him.

"Well, I ain't them," Reeves stated simply. "In fact, I'm deputy marshal and it's my job to stop men like that."

The girl sniffled and wiped her nose with the back of her sleeve. Reeves sensed she wanted to believe him but the recent harm done to her was an emotional wall between them.

"You do?" Her voice trembled. "Is a marshal..like a policeman?"

"Indeed it is, little miss." Reeves reached up and touched the silver badge on his vest. "See, I even have a real badge. I is just like a policeman."

"Papa always said we should listen to policemen. That they are suppose to help us all the time."

"Your Papa was right. Say, my name is Bass….Bass Reeves. What's yours?"

"Mary." The girl pushed up off her elbows and sat up. "Mary Louise Anson."

"Well, that's a right pretty name, Miss Mary Louise Anson. I am very happy to meet you." Reeves held out his hand.

The girl looked at it for a second, then shyly reached out and touched it carefully. Then she grabbed with both her hands and grasped it tightly as she began to sob. Reeves leaned forward on his knees and wrapped his free hand around her shoulders.

"There, there, Mary. It's alright now. I got you and I ain't gonna let no one hurt you no more. I promise."

After a few minutes her crying stopped and she let go of his hand. Reeves looked back over his shoulder at the river and mulled over how he was going to get them back to the other side and his horses.

"Mary, when you was a little girl, did you ride on your Papa's back, you know, like he was a horse and all?"

"You mean piggy-back?"

"Ah..right, piggy-back."

"Huh…huh. All the time. Papa would stomp his feet and race us all around the house. Me and my baby brother…." The thought of her sibling abruptly ended the girl's pleasant recollections.

Reeves saw it and pressed on quickly. "Alrightee, then. I got some deer jerky back there in my saddle bags. I suspect you must be mighty hungry."

Mary nodded.

"Good, then you're gonna climb onto my back and I'm gonna carry you back across the river. Is that alirght?"

"Huh…huh."

"Then let's go." Reeves took hold of her hands and pulled her to her feet. In doing so he could see dried blood on the tops of both her thighs. He did his best to ignore, though he felt anger heat his blood. Mary's blue dress was torn and barely covering her four foot lanky frame.

"Alright now, you climb on," he said as he turned his back to her and rose up on one knee. Mary draped herself across his broad back and wrapped her arms about his neck. He stood up slowly and reached back with both hands to take hold of her buttocks and heave her up higher. "Go on and wrap your legs about my middle, dear." She did as he suggested and he walked over to the water's edge.

"Hold on tight, Mary. The water is a might cold and we're gonna get a little wet crossing over. Just don't be afraid and don't let go."

"I won't, sir. I promise."

"Good girl. Here we go now."

Bass Reeves stepped into the flow of water and set his foot down solidly. He held his balance bringing down his second foot and instantly water splashed over them. Mary cried out and instantly tightened her hold on his neck.

"That's it. Hold tight." Reeves took another step and then another. The sound of the water hitting the rocks was deafening as he plowed onward. With determined steps the marshal continued moving forward fighting the current that threatened to topple them. As he neared the opposite shore where his horses were standing, his eye caught an odd motion to his left. Reeves turned to see a thick broken branch rushing towards them.

He took a deep breath, clutched his precious cargo firmly, and lunged forward. Now it was a race. There was no time to worry about balance. Step, step, step. The awkwardly shape tree limb seemed to swell in size as it raced at them.

Reeves pushed harder…

Reeves pushed harder. Throwing all caution aside, he ran the final few yards and climbed up out of the swirling river just as the branch tore past them. He dropped to his knees and took a long, deep breath. Mary Anson's face was still buried in his back.

He touched her elbow. "It's okay, Mary. You can let go now."

Reeves retrieved one of small horse towels and handed it to the girl. At full height, the top of her chocolate brown curls came to his chest. Then he dug back into his saddle bag for his extra pair of pants and socks. The marshal was all too familiar with life on the road and always carried extra clothing. He suggested she take the towel and wash herself as best she could at the river, then pull the pants up over what remained of her dress. He didn't have an extra shirt, but there was enough of the garment to cover her up decently.

"What are you going to do?" She held the rough cloth, jeans and white socks in her hands.

"I'm gonna cut up some branches and get a little fire going so's we can warm up while we eat. How's that sound?"

"Fine, Mr. Reeves."

"Mary, you can just call me Bass. Everyone does."

"Why did your mother name you after a fish?"

The question caught Reeves by surprise. In that moment, Mary Anson reminded him of his own small ones.

"Darn, Mary, you know what? I never once asked Ma that question. Now that is a puzzle, ain't it? I'm gonna have to ask her that when I see her again."

A tiny smile emerged on the corners of the girl's mouth. Even with her face layered with dirt, the smile brightened it warmly. With that, Mary turned and walked over to the river bank where she carefully set down the pants and stockings. She put the towel over them and then bending over, began splashing water over her face and arms.

Reeves set about gathering brittle bush limbs and stacking them in a clear spot. He placed fist sized rocks around the stack and then using a wooden match, lit the kindle and started his fire. Once it was burning, he threw in bigger pieces of wood. That done, he went and retrieved his food from his second saddle bag.

He was putting down his burlap sack of vittles when Mary reappeared. She walking clumsily like a duck because of the oversized pants she was drowning in. With both hands, she was valiantly trying to hold them up. Her feet were now clothed in his socks and the tan horse towel was wrapped around her wet hair. With her face washed cleaned, there was a rosy flush to her cheeks.

Reeves couldn't help but laugh at the sight of her.

"Ha, it does seem like we's got to some adjustin' here. You hold on a second now."

From his saddle he fetched his lasso and then cut off a long strand with his hunting knife. With this, he returned to the girl and carefully slipped the chord through the pants loops.

"You keep holding them pants up," he chuckled before dropping to one knee before her. He took hold of each pant cuff and quickly rolled them upward. As he did so, the pants lowered considerably until he was able to tie the improvised rope belt into a snug knot about Mary's middle.

Though it looked like she was wearing giant balloons on her legs, the pants themselves stayed up and her feet were free to walk without tripping.

"That's much better," Reeves approved smiling. "Come sit by the fire and let's get some food into you."

Once seated Indian style before the fire, the marshal handed the girl one of his remaining corn biscuits and she tore into it ravenously.

"Whoa there, slow down a bit," he cautioned her. "You swallow that biscuit too fast and you'll end up with a belly ache for sure."

Mary looked at him shyly and then nervously wiped the crumbs off her lips with the back of her hand. "Sorry."

"No need to be sorry, child. You're just hungry is all. Here, this is deer jerky. It's tough, so chew on it carefully."

The girl nodded and took the dried meat. She bit off a piece and began to work on it with her teeth. Reeves did the same with his own strip.

After each had finished swallowing, they took a drink of water from one of his canteens.

"Want another one?" he asked holding out a second biscuit. Mary nodded and he gave it to her. As she began to bite into it, he reasoned it was time to have her tell him of her experiences. He'd deduced most of it from the evidence at the site of the burned wagon, but her personal account is what would matter to Judge Parker.

"Mary, I don't mean to upset you, but can you tell me what happened to you and your folks?"

There was a moment of hesitation, then Mary Aston began her tale. As she recalled, the two men of color had appeared two days earlier shortly after high noon. They looked harmless riding up to their wagon, one of them even waving a friendly hand. Both her parents greeted them accordingly; her father halting their twin draft horses so they might converse with the riders.

Mary told Bass Reeves she and her brother, Joseph, had been in the back of the wagon at this time. Upon hearing her Papa calling out, Mary had climbed up behind her mother to get a better look at who it was he was talking to. Then, without any warning, the two men had pulled out their hand guns and shot her both her parents. Mama had cried out and fallen against Papa, who in turn fell off the wagon seat and onto the ground.

Mary remembered screaming at the horror she had witnessed and then she rushed back into the wagon yelling to her brother to run. Poor Joe was too confused to understand what she was saying. Scared, he started to climb over the tail gate and then jumped to the ground. One of the killers told the other not to let the children get away.

By now Joe had gone only a few yards when she heard another gunshot. Joe was knocked to the ground never to rise again.

Mary Anson began to tremble as the memories of what she had witnessed overwhelmed her emotions. Reeves leaned over and gently touched her shoulder.

"Take a breath, Mary," he said softly. "You're doing just fine. Can you describe the men? I mean what did they look like. What were their names?"

"Huh…huh. There was the big one who was black….like licorice candy. He had a thick beard. He was called Sam and he was a monster. He laughed all the time the other one tore through our things in the back of the wagon."

"What was the other fellah called?"

"Rufus. He wasn't as dark like Sam and he smaller."

"How much smaller?"

"About like my Papa."

Reeves recalled Mr. Anson having been shorter than his own six feet.

"Was there anything different about this here Rufus?"

"Well, he had a front tooth missing and his hair was really long. Like a girl's. He was very happy when he found Mama's silver pieces of jewelry. He waved them at Sam and told him they could get lots of money for them."

So they were nothing but murderers and common thieves, Reeves thought. Killing innocent folks for a few trinkets.

"Where was you during all this, Mary?"

"After they killed Joe, I jumped out of the wagon and ran over to where Mama and Papa were lying on the ground. I fell on Mama and cried so hard I couldn't stop. Even when I got her blood on me."

"Then what happened once they had the silver pieces?"

"Sam told Rufus to cut our horses loose and then he chased them off. After that he got off his horse and picked me up. I tried to punch and kick him. But he was too strong and he put me up on his horse before getting on behind me.

"That's when I saw the wagon was on fire. And then we rode off."

Mary took another drink from Reeves' canteen before finishing her story. That night, the two men had made camp in a ravine which offered them some small shelter from the elements. She thought of trying to run away before Sam had tied her hands and feet together. The girl was sure they were eventually going to kill her as they had done to her family. Instead, once they had a fire going, Sam dragged her away from the light so that they were hidden in the dark. Then he untied her feet, he pulled up her dress and then savagely tore away her undergarments.

"He…raped me, marshal. All the time he was so heavy on top of me, then when the pain came I sort of passed out for little while. When I came to, it was Rufus' turn. I passed out again and didn't wake up until the next morning.

"They was still sleeping and I saw an empty bottle of whiskey in Sam's hands. He was snoring as loud as a freight train. That's when I run off into them woods back there. That was yesterday. I must have got lost. When night came, I found the river here and hid in those bushes where you found me."

"How old are you, Mary?"

"Be fifteen come September."

"I think you are the bravest girl I have ever met."

"I ain't brave, marshal Bass. Not me. I couldn't help Mama and Papa or Joe. All I was doing was trying to stay alive."

Reeves reached out and held the girl's hand and smiled kindly. "Sometimes staying alive is the bravest thing of all."

Once they had finished their cold lunch, Reeves doused the fire and they saddled up and rode on. He was pleased to see that the girl was a natural rider and handled the brown mare with ease. They backtracked through the woods and upon reaching the flatland trail turned northward. It was early afternoon and Reeves hoped to cover a lot of ground before the end of the day.

As they rode along side by side, the bright sun and blue skies set a vista before them that was breathtaking in its natural simplicity.

"What's gonna happen to me now?" Mary Anson inquired, holding her reins loosely and letting the horse trot along at a relaxed pace.

"Been thinking on that," Marshal Reeves admitted. "You got any kin in these parts, Mary?"

"I have an aunt and uncle in Arkansas somewhere, but I'm not sure exactly where. I never met them. Uncle Ira was Papa's younger brother. They wrote to each other at least once a year."

"Mmm, that's good to know." Reeves scratched his chin. "When we get to Fort Smith, I'm sure Judge Parker will be able to help us trace them down for you. In the meanwhile, you can stay with me and Jenny on our horse ranch."

At that news, the girl's face brightened considerably and she began asking Reeves about his ranch and his family.

The day passed peacefully.

By the time twilight was on them, Bass Reeves and his charge were dropping down into a valley. With the terrain rising up to either side, they would soon lose the light. Reeves had started thinking where they would camp for the night when he spotted a tiny light in the distance. It was a campfire maybe two miles ahead of them.

He stopped his horse and the girl did likewise. He pointed to the yellow glow.

"They may be the varmints who killed your folks and hurt you," he said somberly.

A look of apprehension crossed her face. "How can you be sure? Maybe it's somebody else."

"That's possible, I suppose."

"Then why don't we just ride around them," she suggested.

Her idea made sense in its own way. The last thing he wanted to do was drag the poor girl into another meeting with the savages who had raped her. He could avoid that contact easily enough. The valley was large enough that they could ride miles around whoever had set the fire.

Yet even as Bass Reeves considered doing just that, another though rose up in his mind. One that he simply could not shake. What if the villainous duo, Sam and Rufus, were indeed before him and he let them go? Even if he came back days later, after taking Mary to safety in Fort Smith, there were no guarantees he would find the pair before they murdered someone else. Maybe even another helpless family. And then those deaths would be on his hands.

No, Bass Reeves had sworn an oath to both uphold the law and to capture any who broke. He really had no choice in the matter.

"I'm sorry, Mary, but if it is Sam and Rufus up ahead, then I got to go after them. It's my job."

The girl looked at him and gradually resigned herself to his decision though it was obvious she wasn't happy with it.

"I promise," Reeves continued. "I ain't gonna put you any danger. As we get closer to that fire, I'm gonna set you someplace where they won't be able to see you and then I'll go brace them…alone."

"What happens if they kill you?" Her voice trembled.

"You need not worry about that, sweatheart," Reeves grinned. "Lots of others have tried and I'm still here ain't I?"

His smile was infectious and the girl returned it.

"Alright, now this is what we're gonna do," he explained.

Thirty minutes later, Marshal Bass Reeves walked quietly towards the blazing campfire. He had left Mary Anson and the horses behind a clump of boulders out of sight from the main path through the valley. The sun was gone and night had fully descended leaving him clothed in darkness. Unless he made a noise, he would remain undetected until he was within the radius of the fire's light.

He heard the two men conversing before he was close enough to make them out.

"Wish you hadn't drank all the whiskey," one reedy like voice complained.

"Stop your cryin' Rufus," a deeper, heavier voice retorted. "Will get more next town we come to." That had to be the one named Sam.

"Which is exactly where? You don't even know where's we at right now."

"I know we're ridin' north and that way is Arkansas. Plenty of towns up there."

Reeves moved the way he'd been taught by his Seminole Indian friends; each step slow and deliberate. He was a weightless ghost moving over the ground. When he was near enough to see the campfire and the two speakers, he reached across his body and pulled the gun on his left hip out of its holster. He held it pointing forward and continued forward.

Lying to either side of the small crackling fire, the two men were exactly as the Mary had described them. To the right sat the gangly thin fellow with coffee complexion and the long, wild hair. The other, seated with his back against his saddle, was a bearded giant with ebony skin the color of ink.

Rufus and Sam: cold blooded killers both.

Behind them, tied to trees, were their horses.

This close, Reeves carefully examined each man and his weapons. Both of them wore a gun-belt. From his position, the marshal could see a rifle next to the big fellow's saddle. He assumed skinny Rufus would have one as well though he couldn't see it.

"You men by the fire. Put your hands in the air!"

Startled, both campers began reaching for their guns at the same time looking around wildly.

Reeves fired sending his bullet into the heart of the fire. It kicked up burning embers everywhere and the men fell back from it.

"Pull those guns and you're both dead," Reeves warned. "Ain't gonna tell you again."

"Hey, now," Sam yelled loudly. "Whoever you is out there, this is some kind of mistake."

"Yes sir," Rufus chimed in. "We're just a couple of cowhands on our way north to look for work."

Reeves fired a second shot. This one hit the ground near Rufus.

"HEYYY!"

"I said put your hands up in the air!"

Realizing they had no other options, both men lifted their empty hands skyward.

"Good, now get on your feet and keep them hands where I can see them."

Sam and Rufus eyed each other for a second and then awkwardly stood facing the spot they surmised Reeves was located.

Bass Reeves stepped out of the night keeping his gun aimed at the two killers. By the reactions on their faces, he had a fair idea of what they were thinking.

"What da hell!" Sam declared. "You one of us!"

The lawman tapped the ornate badge on his vest with his empty hand. "My name is Bass Reeves. I'm a duly appointed U.S. Deputy Marshal and I's arresting you boys for murder and rape."

"Now I seen it all," the big man shook his head. "A black law-dog."

It was Rufus' turn to speak up. "Marshal, you got it wrong. Like I says, me and Sam here is just going north to find honest work. I swears, we ain't done no murder or raping."

"Shut up," Reeves snapped coming around the fire towards Sam. "You turn around and keep those hands high."

Sam glared at Reeves but the determination he saw in the marshal's face canceled any further resistance and he did as ordered. "So, what you think you're gonna do now, law-dog?"

Reeves came up behind Sam and using his gun barrel, clubbed him across the back of the head. The big man coughed a stifling cry and dropped face down like a fallen timbre. Reeves his gun on Rufus before he could do anything but gasp at the sight of his companion knocked unconscious.

"Now you come over here," Reeves said. "And hurry it up."

The shaken Rufus hurried over, his eyes wide with fear. Reeves told him to draw his pistol from its holster and toss it to the ground. Rufus complied. Reeves then leaned over the sleeping Sam and extracted his gun and threw is aside.

"Alright, fellah, you take hold of this hombre's feet. Then I want you to drag him over there by those trees."

For a second Reeves prisoner looked confused and the lawman waved his gun at Sam's feet. "You heard me. Move!"

Reeves backed away from the unconscious killer and watched as the skinny Rufus bent down and took hold of his partner's legs. Then, with a heave, he began to pull the heavy man around.

"Sheet, marshal, he's too damn heavy," Rufus complained.

"Just keep on pulling. It's only another twenty feet or so."

His face breaking out into a sweat, the slim outlaw gritted what teeth remained in his mouth and unceremoniously dragged his pal over the hard ground. Ten minutes later, he had Sam next a sturdy white birch and he released his legs. With a heavy sigh, he leaned back against the tree.

"You got some rope?" Reeves asked next.

"Huh, huh," Rufus replied between gulps of air. "We got lassos by my saddle over there."

"Go fetch them."

Keeping his eyes on his prisoner, Reeves holstered his gun, then took hold of the Sam's shoulders and lifted his body so that he was in a sitting position with his back to the tree. In doing so the marshal was grateful for just how strong ranch life had made him over the years.

When Rufus returned with the two coiled lassos, Reeves directed him on how to hog-tie Sam. Taking one of the twenty foot chords, he began with tying the man's legs together, then he brought the rope up to encircle his hands. Once done, he wrapped the heavy rope around Sam's chest and the tree tightly. The final restraint was looping the lasso about the big man's neck and the birch.

Reeves reckoned that should the outlaw awaken during the night and attempt to shake himself free of the rope, he'd start choking himself at the same time. That should be deterrent enough for him quit and accept his fate.

"Alright," Reeves, holding the second rope, pointed to the next tree in line. "Go on over there and sit down with your back against the bark."

"Please don't crack me on the head like you did Sam."

"Don't give me any trouble and I won't."

Rufus dropped down and positioned himself as Reeves had directed. The marshal tossed the rope into his lap. "Go on, tie your legs together."

Once that was done, Reeves dropped to one knee and wrapped the lasso about Rufus' hands. Satisfied they were snug, the then circled the upper body.

"Mister Marshal, please don't tie up my neck. I ain't gonna try and escape. I promise."

Bass Reeves studied the squirmy murderer and against his own better judgment, finished tying off the lasso.

"You listen up good, fellah," he said dropping to a crouch before his prisoner. "I'm a light sleeper. You so much as sneeze loudly, I'm gonna know it. And if I sees you tried to get loose, I'm not gonna just hit you on the head.

"I'm gonna shoot you between the eyes."

Rufus gulped. The look on the lawman's face was a reflection of a sure and certain death.

"Do you understand that?"

"Yes, sirree, Mister Marshal. I do."

"Please don't crack me on the head…"

Reeves nodded and stood. He went over to Sam and double checked his bonds. Then he went and collected the discarded pistols. He slid these into his own belt before getting the killers' rifles. With these in his hands, he gave the site a final look and then disappeared back into the night from where he had first appeared.

Later, when he rode back to the campsite with Mary Anson in tow, Bass Reeves wondered what her reaction would be at seeing the two men that had raped her. What he hadn't expected was the effect the girl's appearance had on Rufus.

"Oh, sheet, sheet, sheet!" he sputtered as Mary rode up to the now dwindling fire and stared across it at him. A cold mask descended across her lovely features.

"Those the men who hurt you?" Reeves asked as he got off his white mare.

"Yes, marshal. It was them. That one's Rufus. The other is Sam." As the big man wasn't moving, Mary inquired, "Is he dead?"

"No. I just had to knock him out so I's could get them both tied up proper." Reeves walked his horse to where the other horses had been tied. Mary dismounted and brought over the brown mare. Reeves had bound the captured men's rifles to the back of her saddle and stowed their pistols away in his own saddle bags.

As Reeves took the reins from her, he said, "We're leaving their saddles on. I want us back on the trail at first light."

The girl nodded trusting Reeves knew what he was doing. As she walked back to the fire, she did her best not to look over at Rufus and Sam.

"They ain't going anywhere," Reeves assured her as Mary sat down by the fire and held her hands palms out towards the warming blaze.

The marshal then picked up one of the saddles on the ground and carried it over to where Sam had been resting. He placed both side by side and pointed to both of them. "You can use one of these to rest your head Mary. It ain't no pillow, but it will have to do.' The girl looked up at him and smiled. "I'm use to sleeping on the ground, marshal Bass. Daddy took me coon hunting in the spring. Lots of times we slept under the stars like this."

Reeves nodded appreciating the girl's grit.

Rufus was still mumbling to himself and Reeves turned to him annoyed.

"I gonna hang…just like my Ma always said. Rufus…you no good, you gonna hang some day."

"Hey!" Reeves yelled. Rufus stopped his ranting. "You shut up and get some sleep or else I'll come over there and conk you on the noggin' like I did the big one."

It was enough to quiet the scared outlaw.

Reeves gathered more twigs and fed the fire to keep it going. Once satisfied it would last the remainder of the night, he sat down next to Mary Anson and crossed his legs Indian style. Across his legs he held his Winchester.

"You go on and get some sleep," he told her. "Sun up will come quick enough."

The girl lay back, her head and shoulders against the hard saddle and within minutes was fast asleep.

Bass Reeves looked skyward. Clouds hid any stars and somewhere far away an owl hooted. His gaze turned to the snapping yellow flames and he longed to be back home.

Big Sam started yelling and cussing the second he awoke. The first rays of the sun were slicing the heavens above and dew had settled on the ground. Frustrated by the ropes that bound him to the tree, the killer tried in vain to shake himself free all the while cursing Marshal Bass Reeves.

"I'm gonna kill you, lawman," he bellowed as he tried to push his massive torso through the horsehair restraint. "Kill you good and slow and then leave yah for the buzzards to chew over."

Bass Reeves had been half awake and about to rise when the hollering set in. He got to his feet, pulled one of his hip guns and without blinking fired it at the Big Sam. The bullet struck the tree inches above the man's bald head sending chips raining down on him.

"Want to yell some more?" Reeves asked waving his smoking pistol. "Next one will be through that big mouth of yours."

Sam was silent for a moment but the anger in him only continue to swell. Then, in a softer tone he growled, "Y'ain't got nothin' on us, lawdog. No proof we done…"

It was then that Mary Anson stood up behind Reeves and stepped forward. At the sight of her, Sam's eyes widened and any further words died in his throat.

"You was saying?" Reeves chided.

When Sam didn't say anything else, the marshal nodded. "What I thought. After this young miss tells a jury what you two done, Judge Parker's gonna see you both dance at the end of a rope.

"Now me, I'd just as shoot you both here and now and make my job a whole lot easier. But that ain't what the law says I gotta do. So we is gonna make the ride up to Fort Smith and both of you varmints are gonna do exactly as I say. Or I'll bring you back across your saddles."

Having finished his directives, Reeves told Mary to go around the tree to which Rufus was tied and undo the knots. Bass's gunshot had awakened Rufus and he'd witnessed the exchanged between Sam and the marshal. He wasn't about to give Reeves any trouble at all.

Freed of the rope binding, the gaunt outlaw used the tree to get to his feet.

"Good," Reeves commented. "Now you step back, Mary and go fetch all our horses."

"Yes, sir, Mr. Bass," the girl hurried off.

Reeves pointed his Peacemaker at Rufus. "Now you are gonna untie your partner. Then you will collect the rope and step away from that tree. If you do anything else it will be a mistake."

Rufus couldn't hide his fear and he hurriedly complied with Reeves' orders. Once freed, Sam got to his feet and massaged his arms to get the circulation flowing in them again. All the while he continued to glare are Reeves. The marshal knew the man was nothing more than an animal on two feet and if given the opportunity would charge him. He kept his gun steady, his own stare letting the other know he'd be ready.

When Reeves could hear Mary moving around the cold campfire leading the four horses, he ordered Rufus to approach. "I want you to tie Sam's hands together, then bring the excess rope around his chest and tie it off in the back. You understand me?"

"I do," Rufus replied.

Reeves backed away by several yards, knowing Sam would be tempted to act the second Rufus came between them. "You try anything and I'll shoot both of you where you stand. Go on, tie him up."

It took Rufus less then two minutes to tie the big man's hands and then wind the rope about his body. When he was finished, Reeves ordered Sam to get clear. Looking over his shoulder, he told Mary to get his carbine. She did so and brought it to him but he didn't take it. Instead he told her to chamber a round and point it a Big Sam.

"I'm gonna tie up the other one. If Sam moves an inch, you shoot him down. Can you do that?"

Mary Anson looked at Big Sam then jerked the carbine grip and smoothly chambered a 30.30 bullet. She brought the stock to her shoulder and sighted along the barrel. "Go on, Mr. Bass, this one ain't gonna be no bother."

Slipping his gun back into its holster, Reeves bent down and snatched up the remaining rope. Then wasting no time, he circled the rope about Rufus's hand then about his body giving it a tight pull before tying it off.

That done, he relieved Mary of the rifle and told her to mount up. As she did so, he pointed the carbine's end at his prisoners. "Alright, time for you boys to get on your horses…nice and slow."

Although awkward with their hands and arms constrained, both Rufus and Sam managed to climb into their saddles. Reeves was the last to swing up onto his white mare keeping the rifle in his grip.

"Alright, we're gonna start heading north with the two of you in the lead," he explained. "I'll be right behind you all the time. Don't forget it."

"Ain't we gonna have no breakfast?" Rufus whined. "I's hungry."

"Jim Bywater's trading post is twenty miles north of here," Reeves said. "Sooner we reach there, sooner we can all eat. Now get the lead out."

Neither prisoner said another word and together they started off down the trail riding side by side. Bass Reeves gave them a thirty yard lead and then followed along with Mary Anson joining him.

He hoped this last leg of his journey would be an easy one.

The day warmed considerably during their first hour on the trail with only a small breeze from the west to cool them off. The terrain was flat, hard scrabble dirt with little vegetation except for a few thorny cactus and the occasional mesquite bushes. Balled tumbleweed rolled past them, spooking their horses while prairie dogs poked their heads up in curiosity as the quartet rode past. High above them crows screamed at their uninvited presence.

East was to their right and there a chain of small hills jutted out of the earth like a series of connected lumps in a batter of wheat flour.

Marshal Reeves could see Rufus and Big Sam jawing though he couldn't make out their words. He hoped they weren't foolish enough to try and escape. It would be easier on him delivering live prisoners rather than having to haul two dead bodies. But one way or another, he would deliver them to Judge Parker.

"They are gonna hang, aren't they?" Mary Anson queried softly. She was uncomfortable with the topic and yet determined to face it head on.

"Yes, Mary," he kept his eyes on his captives. "Once you've told what happened to you and your folks, ain't no way they is gonna go free. Judge Parker is a fair man and he will do what is right by the law."

"Will I have to…ah…be there?"

The question surprised him and he turned to look at her remembering just how truly young she was.

"No, little miss, you don't have to see it. You done seen enough bad things to last a lifetime I reckon."

As Reeves was turning his head frontward he caught a sparkle in the hills. He peered at the spot and saw it a second time. Someone was up there watching them. Then he made out several riders coming down a winding path in single file.

Indians!

They were still too far away to get an accurate count, but he guessed at least ten or more. They had begun shouting which definitely wasn't good.

"Mary, I need you to ride as fast as you can. We got us some Indian trouble!"

The girl looked past him and nodded. "I'm a good rider, Mr. Bass."

"Good, then let's go and don't look back!"

He kicked his horse and charged forward; the girl keeping up with him. As they neared Rufus and Sam, Reeves rode around them. As he went past them, he turned in his saddle and pointed rearward. "Look alive, we got us an Injun war party on our tail!"

Both Rufus and Sam looked back, saw the Indians and then spurred their own horses into a full gallop.

Rifle shots rang out and Reeves heard the whine of bullets passing them. Crouched low over his saddle, he glanced back at the oncoming braves. They were yelling and waving their weapons high in the air, creating a cloud of dust behind them.

Comanches, he thought. This had to be the renegade group Sgt. Morand and his company had been hunting. What the Buffalo soldiers had failed to do was now his misfortune. Morand had described them as wild bucks looking to collect scalps. Letting themselves be caught would mean certain death.

Marshal Bass Reeves wasn't going to let that happen.

More shots were fired at them and Reeves was pleased to see Mary Anson folded down over her own saddle. Smart girl.

As they raced across the open plain, Reeves' two horses had no problem maintaining their speed. The years of love and care Reeves had given them was now paying off and he was damn proud of both animals. Whereas Rufus and Sam weren't as fortunate. Having neglected their own horses except for basic feeding and watering, they now rode two quickly tiring creatures whose breaths were labored.

Marshal Reeves was all to aware that he and Mary were swiftly outdistancing the two black men and unless he could find some kind of respite soon, they would quickly succumb to the rapidly closing Comanches.

Reeves scanned the land ahead silently praying for any kind of a break in the open ground that left them exposed. Then when he'd almost given up hope, he spotted a dark black line approximately two hundred yards before them. The line was actually the lip shadow of a long winding ravine cut into the prairie. He didn't yet know how deep it was, but at this juncture, even two feet would be enough for them to take cover and make a defensive stand.

"There!" he yelled to Mary and other others pointing to the sharp depression. "Make for that gully!"

More shots rang out and one hit Rufus' horse in the neck. The animal collapsed sending its rider sprawling. This brought about more enthusiastic shouting from their pursuers.

Rufus, dazed, scrambled up onto his feet and saw the screaming braves descending upon him. Their faces were painted various colors and they continued yelling at the top of their lungs. Some fired more shots. Rufus turned and called out, "SAM! HELP ME!"

But Big Sam had no intention of stopping. He'd seen his partner fall. Looking back, he realized that if he went back to help Rufus then he too would be lost.

Rufus couldn't believe his eyes. Sam was leaving him; abandoning him to his doom. Fear raced through his veins and he began to run as fast as his long skinny legs could carry him.

Another shot barked and the bullet plowed into Rufus' back tearing through his heart. His body's momentum took him several more steps before it shut down completely and he fell dead on his face. His last conscious thought was the fact that he wasn't going to hang after all.

Coming up to the sharp ravine, Reeves and Mary tugged on their reins to halt their horses. At the bottom of the sloping depression was a dried up creek bed.

"Get down and hide as best you can," Reeves instructed the girl.

She nodded and urged her horse forward. It carefully descended the steep sandy wall and once on the bottom Mary Anson dismounted.

Meanwhile Reeves had turned his own horse around in time to see Big Sam charging towards him; the Comanche party almost upon him. Not seeing Rufus, he assumed the worst as he raised his rifle. Even during the wild chase, the marshal hadn't let go of his weapon. Now he sighted it at the oncoming Indians, his eyes targeting the warrior who was the closest.

Reeves squeezed the trigger and hit the Indian in the chest toppling him backward off his running mustang. He took a breath and immediately aimed at a second brave. He fired again and was rewarded with his second hit.

Big Sam was now at the edge of the ravine and doing his best to maneuver his horse down into it. The animal lost its footing, neighed loudly and fell over onto its side. Sam was sent sprawling on to the ground and rolled over once before coming to his feet.

Mary Anson had already dismounted and stretched out on the sandy wall keeping her head below the lip. Her horse was standing still behind her not knowing what it should do next as banging gunshots overhead continued.

Bass Reeves wasted no time riding down into the protective gully, his white mare recklessly sliding down the loose rocky side. He leaped to the ground just as Sam's own horse managed to regain its footing.

"Give me a gun," Big Sam said. He held up his bound hands. "No way you can fight them off on your own."

Bullets whizzed over them. Reeves had only a second to decide. He called out to Mary Anson. "Untie him…fast!"

For a second the girl looked from Reeves to Big Sam, clearly not happy with the marshal's command. But she had come to trust him and shaking off her own doubts, she ran in a crouch towards her rapist. Sam dropped to one knee as the girl set about unloosening the knots at his back.

Reeves now climbed carefully up the ravine wall to a position where he could see the raiding party. Still howling and screaming, they were less than twenty yards away. As he fired his carbine a third time, his eyes took in their number. His bullet missed and he fired another. This one hit one of the horses and it crumbled taking its rider with it. The man didn't get up, though Reeves didn't have the luxury of waiting to see if he would or not. He simply kept firing.

Even with the three he'd taken out, he estimated another ten were about to fall on them.

"Marshal!" Big Sam shouted above the noise. He was standing to Reeves' right slightly lower on the wall. He was free, his hands out.

Bass Reeves always wore two Colt .45 Peacemakers, both in reverse fashion on each hip. Holding his carbine with his left hand. With the right he yanked the gun from his fight holster and tossed to Big Sam.

Even as the outlaw was grasping the weapon, a charging Comanche rider suddenly materialized above him; the horse's hooves barely missing his head by inches. Big Sam twisted around and grasping the gun in his right hand, shot up at the Indian. The bullet caught the brave in the ribs and as his horse sailed over to the other side of the cut, the Indian's body fell off.

Desperate to stop the assault before they were overrun, Reeves climbed up several feet and rapidly fired into the attacking horsemen. Systematically like a well oiled killing machine, he dropped the four nearest Comanche. So devastating was his shooting that the Indians in the rear of the attack were forced to veer off to either direction instead of their own horses crashing into the rider-less animals now frozen in place.

As they did so, Big Sam also climbed higher on the wall and fired at several receding warriors. Two of his three shots hit their targets in the back while the third went wide. Watching the remaining braves scatter, Bass Reeves counted the dead strewn before them. In a matter of minutes, he and Sam had halved the Indians number. But would that be enough to deter from attacking again.

He stood on the slope, balancing himself as best he could in the loose gravel. He reached into his vest pocket and pulled out more bullets with which he reloaded the carbine.

"You think they'll try again?" Sam asked as he too tried to keep their enemies in site.

"Can't say," Reeves replied honestly. "They got to know if they come at us again, odds are lots more of them will die here."

"Yeah, damn right."

"Look," Mary Anson called from where she was still hiding under the ravine lip. She'd lifted her head and was pointing to the now gathering remnants of the war party.

The two smaller groups had formed up and seemed to be arguing among themselves. Finally one of them raised his hand and the others were quiet. Whatever they had decided was settled.

The Comanche braves then rode back towards where Reeves, Sam and Mary waited. They stayed at a distance out of rifle range and eyed the three defenders. The young Indian who had apparently taken command raised his rifle over his head and gave out another war cry.

Bass Reeves held his rifle across his body and waited.

Then the new leader of the Comanches turned his horse and he and his fellows rode off towards the horizon.

"Well I'll be," Reeves mumbled to himself. It appeared they weren't going to die after all.

"Put the rifle down!" Big Sam cocked his pistol and pointed it at the marshal.

Reeves slowly turned to face the outlaw. He'd taken a gamble and now he'd lost. Strange that he would survive the encounter with the Comanche only to be shot by this lowdown varmint.

"Drop it," Sam snapped. "Ain't no way I can miss this close."

Reeves shrugged and tossed his carbine onto the ground. There was nothing he could do. Except maybe die like a man. Still, he thought about Jenny and his children. He wondered how they would fare without him.

"Told you I wasn't gonna hang," Big Sam chuckled. "So long, lawdog."

Mary Anson threw a handful of dirt in the Sam's face. He cried out, one hand going to his eyes, while the other fired his gun.

But Bass Reeves had twisted away while drawing his left gun. In one smooth motion as he dived he brought it up and fired. Hot lead slammed into the outlaw's chest and knocked him off his feet.

Sam lay on his back, blood spilling from his lips, grit covering his face. Mary Anson looked down at him without pity. There was a gurgle in his throat and then his body shook one last time as death embraced him.

Marshal Bass Reeves came up behind the girl, his smoking pistol at ready. Seeing Sam was dead, he holstered his pistol and put a hand on the girl's shoulder.

"Thank you, Mary."

She came into his arms and started to cry.

He held her tightly knowing the long, hard ride was almost over.

THE END

THE BACKGROUND

After the Civil War, many people found themselves displaced from the lives they had known before the conflict. Many freed slaves saw no future in remaining in the south despite their finally being granted emancipation. They packed what little belongs they had and headed west beyond the Mississippi. Thousands settled in what was then known as The Territories located north of Texas in what would eventually become the state of Oklahoma.

Now these open lands were not uninhabited as there were half a dozen Indian tribes living on them. Most of them had established villages or towns with their own police forces. Freed slaves soon established their own all black towns and for the most part had no quarrels with their Indian neighbors, though they rarely interacted with each other. It was pretty much a let and let live atmosphere that suited both people fine.

Sadly it wouldn't remain that way long. As ever when a civilization expands it also attracts the criminal element: drifters, con artists and outlaws eager to steal what others toiled so hard for. Seeing that The Territories had no real law, outlaws who raided such states as Texas and Arkansas realized they could find safety and shelter out in this frontier wilderness. Some raised up actual outlaw towns as their own deadly sanctuaries.

Eventually the Federal Government in Washington decided it was time to bring law and order to the expanding west and their first step was to establish a Federal Court in the border town of Fort Smith, Arkansas. The man they sent to rule over it was Judge Isaac Parker who would all too quickly become known as the Hanging Judge. Parker wasted no time in recruiting marshals and giving them the authority to ride into The Territories when hunting outlaws. Unfortunately the first group he deputized were all white and they found it nearly impossible to serve their warrants in black and Indian towns, never mind avoiding the outlaw enclaves altogether. Many of these badge wearing fellows never came back from their assignments. It was dangerous to be a lawman in The Territories.

Thus Parker took the bold step of deputizing blacks. One of the first of these was a horse rancher named Bass Reeves. Having lived with the Seminole tribe during the Civil War, Reeves had been taught how to track, shoot, hunt, etc. Skills that would hold him in good stead during his thirty years as a U.S. Deputy Marshal riding for Judge Parker. In that time he brought in over three thousand felons, was in fourteen major gunfights and never wounded once.

One of the things Parker and Reeves had in common was their love of justice. In Parker, Reeves found a man who, when meting out the law, was color blind. Parker dispensed justice equally to all, regardless of race, sex or creed. It was something Reeves emulated during his entire career.

In writing "The Hard Ride" I wanted to show that quality in the man and at the same time hopefully describe the landscape in which this amazing lawman toiled for so many years of his life. I hope my little story has given readers a glimpse at what it must have been like to ride those prairies and hills in The Territories along with Deputy Marshal Bass Reeves.

RON FORTIER – Comics and pulps writer/editor best known for his work on the Green Hornet comic series and Terminator – Burning Earth with Alex Ross. He won the Pulp Factory Award for Best Pulp Short Story of 2011 for "Vengeance Is Mine," which appeared in Moonstone's The Avenger – Justice Inc. and in 2012 for "The Ghoul," from the anthology Monster Aces. He was awarded Pulp Grand Master in 2017 by the Pulp Factory. He is the Managing Editor of Airship 27 Productions, a New Pulp Fiction publisher and writes the continuing adventures of both his own character, Brother Bones – the Undead Avenger and the classic pulp hero, Captain Hazzard – Champion of Justice. (www.airship27.com)

THE PASTOR OF LONE HOLLOW

By Derrick Ferguson

The groaning old man creak of the wagon wheels provided a soothing, near musical counterpoint to the soft, almost delicate clip-clopping to the hooves of the five horses. Four of those horses pulled a wagon. A contraption of solid construction. Made for one purpose only. To hold desperate men prisoner. Tom Lucky drove the wagon and he didn't much care for it. The wagon he preferred to drive was little more than a cage on wheels. Because he preferred that whatever prisoners kept inside be exposed to the elements. It kept their minds from thoughts and plans of escape when they were thinking more of staying dry, warm or cool. This prisoner wagon was more like a box with the only ventilation for the prisoners being barred windows in the sides and the door. There were three other wagons of the kind Tom Lucky preferred but all three were signed out and in service. Other Deputy Marshals had need of them and while Tom Lucky would have cheerfully waited until one was available, Bass Reeves had no such notions.

Bass rode on a few feet in front of the wagon on his white stallion Cisco. As always, keeping his eyes watchful for any signs of approaching trouble. Not that he expected much on this trip. This was a simple case of picking up prisoners being held in jail in the town of Stark Butte. Judge Parker had asked Bass to ride on over, bring back the prisoners to him for proper sentencing. There were no murderers, bank robbers or violent malefactors in the bunch of seven prisoners. These prisoners would serve another requirement since the town of Fort Smith was a booming one with plenty of construction going on and need for unskilled laborers with strong backs. Judge Parker would put it to the men that if they were to "volunteer" their time serving on one of the many construction gangs currently working in Fort Smith for say, ninety days, why then, Judge Parker could see his way to dismissing the charges against them and send them on their way. It was none of their business that Judge Parker received some small gratuity from the bosses of those construction gangs.

So, it wasn't as if these were vicious desperadoes who had equally desperate friends that would seek to help them escape. Or who would want to make themselves a fast reputation by killing Bass Reeves. Still, Bass learned long ago that oftentimes it was the very same jobs that you didn't think would amount to much were the ones that turned out to be the most trouble.

But the prisoners had been no trouble at all so far. They followed orders without the grumbling, complaining and cussing that most prisoners indulged in. It also didn't help that most of the time whatever prisoners Bass transported were of a hostile disposition. But these men didn't appear to be that sort.

"We gonna stop and make camp soon, Bass?" Tom called down.

Without turning around, never taking his eyes from the terrain ahead, Bass replied; "There's a river somewhere nearabout if'n I recall correctly. Been a while since I been through this part of the country."

"Ain't there a town as well? Why not push on until we get there. Be nice to sleep in a bed for the night."

"Yeah, there was some flea ridden town around here somewheres. Name of Lone Hollow, I believe. But I don't recall them having a sheriff or marshal. I'd rather not have townies gawkin' at the prisoners or keepin' you up all night buying you drinks so you can tell them tall tales about how you captured these desperadoes. It won't kill you to spend another night out on the trail."

"Damn you, Bass Reeves. I'm an old man. My bones can't take sleepin' out on the trail like I usta could do."

Now Bass did half turn in his saddle to give Tom a knowing grin. First off, Tom Lucky wasn't that old. He was maybe ten, fifteen years older than Bass which still made him a relatively young man, considering that the life expectancy of a lawman in the Indian Territory wasn't a long one. But Tom has been smart enough to resign from the Chickasaw Lighthorse before he got himself killed. Secondly, as a full-blooded Chickasaw Tom had spent more days sleeping out on the trail than he ever had in a bed.

"Tell you what, Tom. You put up with sleepin' out one more night and we'll push on until we get to Grimworth. That's a town of some size with a jail big enough to hold this bunch here. We'll lay up there for two days, have us some real food, get us a couple decent night's sleeping in real beds before we make the final push to Fort Smith. What d'ye say to that?"

"I say that you should have said that right from the start. Would have saved my breath doin' all that complain'."

"No, you wouldn't have. I ain't never met a grown man love complainin' more than you do. Specially not no Chickasaw man. I know your wives must be glad to see you go when I need you to posseman for me."

Tom filled the air with his cackling laugh. "Yeah, they glad to see me go, awright! But not for the reason you're sayin'!" And now the rich warm laugh of Bass Reeves joined that of his friend's.

After about another hour of travelling they did indeed come to a river. More like a stream, actually. Bass climbed down off of Cisco and kept his Winchester trained on the prisoners as Tom climbed down from his seat, opened the door of the wagon and led the prisoners out. All of them wore heavy leg shackles, designed to slow a man up should he take a notion to make a run for it. They permitted a man to take normal steps but that was all. The prisoners also wore wrist shackles. Tom lined them up in front of the wagon while Bass spoke.

"Okay, boys...we done spent a couple nights on the trail so you know how this goes. Y'all been behavin' yourselves on this trip and I do 'preciate you not being a bother to me or to Mr. Lucky here. Continue to do so and we won't have us no unpleasantness I got to repent for when I goes to church next with the missus and the family. Just like the last couple of nights, Mr. Lucky will take off your shackles. You got ten minutes to take care of your personal needs and if'n you want to jump in that there stream and wash, be my guest. Long as you take ten minutes to do whatever it is you got to do. When everybody is back in their shackles, Mr. Lucky will fix us dinner and then everybody go on straight to sleep. We got a long push t'morrow."

Bass eyed the seven prisoners for a few seconds before speaking again. "And once again I feel duty bound to remind you that I don't chase no prisoners and I don't fire warnin' shots. You take it in your head to do something foolish and it's on your head as to what happens when you do. Mr. Lucky, you go on ahead and unlock the first man and let him go on to do his business."

The night passed without incident. Once the prisoners were fed, Bass allowed them to sit around the campfire for an hour and smoke. Then he returned them to the wagon and locked them inside. He left off their shackles and handcuffs so that they could sleep more comfortably. In the morning Bass awoke first as he usually did. He roused Tom from where he slept near the horses and indicated that he should get breakfast started. Bass tossed him the keys to the wagon. "You wake 'em up, tell 'em to get ready to move out. We'll be on the road right after breakfast." Bass headed toward the stream to wash up. He would be glad when this job was over. Not that he didn't appreciate how quietly and calmly it had gone. More often than he liked to recall his forays into the badlands resulted in horrendous bloodshed and death. A lot of it he caused. Not that he had any regrets. Bass had long ago resolved to set his feet on this path and once he did so, he never looked back or wondered what might have been. This was his life.

Bass hunkered down at the edge of the stream and vigorously washed his face with the cold water which along with the cursing, shouting and gunfire he heard behind him served to snap him into full wakefulness. Bass whirled around, drawing one of his matched pair of Colt Single Action Army revolvers. He looked at the wagon. Most the prisoners stood around it, looking scared and confused. One of the prisoners was legging it downriver, arms and legs pumping madly. Tom Lucky lay on the ground, cursing up a storm.

Bass ran over to Tom, keeping his revolver trained on the prisoners. "Get back in that wagon! Close the door behind you!"

"Don't shoot us, Marshal! We didn't know Rowland was gonna jump your man!"

"Get in that wagon!"

The prisoners scrambled inside the wagon, slammed the door shut. Bass reached down his free hand to help Tom to his feet. "What the hell happened, Tom?"

Tom got up, angrily adjusted his buffalo hide coat. "My own damn fault, Bass! I must be gettin' too old for this work. Rowland jumped me just as easy if I was a green kid just starting out. Slugged me and while I was on the ground grabbed my gun. Rowland shot at me while I was laying there and missed. Son of a bitch can't shoot for shit 'cause a blind man coulda' hit me. He was smart enough to take off, though, knowin' that shot would bring you runnin'."

"You okay?"

"Yeah! Yeah! Just mad I let myself get took so easy. Damn, I'm sorry, Bass."

"These boys been easy as pie up until now. No reason for you to think one of 'em was gonna make a try for it. You sure you're okay?"

"Yeah, yeah! Get after that son of a bitch! I can handle the rest of these boys."

Bass nodded and quickly saddled Cisco and took off in pursuit. Rowland wouldn't get far as he took no pains to cover his tracks. Bass had no trouble picking up his trail and set his horse at an easy trot along the bank of the stream. Rowland had a loaded gun and so Bass didn't want to run up on him just in case he decided to lie in wait in the shrubs and brush alongside the stream and take a chance on bushwhacking Bass. Rowland had to know that Bass would be after him soon.

Bass didn't know much about Rowland. He had been just as easygoing as the rest of the prisoners up until now. Bass realized now that the man played docile from Day One, biding his time, waiting for just the right opportunity to make his move. Bass had to grudgingly give the man his due. It was a wise wolf who knew how to play the sheep when in the company of other sheep. He hadn't given Bass or Tom the slightest hint that he was capable of such calculated cunning.

Bass heard yelling, shouting, splashing up ahead. He nudged his horse into a faster trot, rounded a slight bend in the stream. Standing in the middle of the stream were two dozen black folks. Rowland was in the middle of them. He wrapped a wiry arm around the neck of a young girl, looked to Bass to be no more than fifteen. "Git back!" Rowland yelled. "Alla you git back!"

Bass slid off Cisco, took his Winchester out of the scabbard and stepped forward cautiously, raising the gun to his shoulder. "Ain't nobody been hurt yet, Rowland. You let that girl go, drop that pistol and come on over here peaceable like and we'll forget all 'bout this."

One of the women, probably the girl's mother struggled ferociously in the grip of three men clearly having a hard time holding onto her. With good reason. The woman was big enough and muscular enough to be a blacksmith. "You men keep a'hold'a her!"

"We're tryin', dammit!"

"I'm a Deputy Marshal and that man is my prisoner! Everybody just stay back and let me handle it! Rowland, I ain't gonna tell you again! We can end this peaceable right now!"

"Drop the gun! Drop it in the water and stay where you are! I'm taking your horse!"

"No. You ain't. You let that there girl go and surrender. This is your last chance." Bass tried to get a solid bead on Rowland but the man was canny and knew how to use a hostage to shield him to his best advantage. Both he and the girl were thrashing around so much that there was no way Bass could get a clear shot at Rowland. Apparently, this was not the first time Rowland used an innocent as a shield.

A man dressed all in black separated from the cowering group, approached Rowland and his frantic hostage. "Son, I don't know what you done but this ain't the way to go about solvin' your issues with the law. Best to give yourself up and let this man take you in."

"Git back! I'll kill this bitch!"

The man kept on approaching, his hands up, palms facing Rowland. "I ain't got no gun, son. I just want you to let the child go and give yourself up."

Bass snarled in frustration. That's all he needed, some well-meaning preacher getting in the way and-

Then Bass blinked in surprise. The preacher suddenly moved as fast as a rattlesnake. He lunged forward, seizing Rowland's gun hand, forcing it up and away from the girl's head. A single gunshot rang out. The preacher's free hand balled up into a fist that he drove into Rowland's throat. Rowland stumbled backwards, letting go of the girl.

The preacher yanked the gun out of Rowland's hand, expertly flipped it around with a speed and dexterity that bespoke of long years handling revolvers and placed a bullet squarely into the center of Rowland's chest. Rowland yowled, toppled over backwards to splash into the water and lay floating there, calling on God and his mother to save him from death and damnation.

Bass ran into the stream, seized Rowland by a leg and hauled him onto dry land. Rowland coughed up water and blood. He was still alive but there was no way of knowing how long he would stay that way.

The preacher joined Bass, holding out the revolver, butt first. Bass silently accepted it, stuck it in his belt. "Mighty fine gun handlin' you displayed there, pastor."

"I'm the spiritual leader of these good folks but I have not been properly ordained." He stuck out a hand. "Joseph Dell."

Bass shook his hand. "U.S. Deputy Marshal Bass Reeves at your service, sir."

"I thought so. It's gettin' so you're as infamous as the owlhoots you hunt, Marshal." Both Dell and Bass looked down at the dying man at their feet. "You want to bring him to town and have our doctor look at him?"

Bass sighed. "I suppose I better. An if'n you can scribe I'd be obliged if'n you'd write out a statement I can take with me back to Judge Parker so

he can have a record of this here incident."

"Can't you just say that you shot him?"

Bass looked up from Rowland, back to Dell. "Any reason why you'd rather I not say it was you? You ain't did nothing wrong. You saved that girl's life. Yeah, you took a chance but if'n you hadn't, I'd have had to take a big risk and I'm obliged you spared me having to do that."

Dell shrugged. "No. No reason. I just thought it would be simpler is all. We got us a wagon we can put this man in and tote him on back to town. We came out here to do some baptizin' but I don't reckon nobody is in a baptizin' mood now."

"You do that. I got to go collect my posseman and the rest of my prisoners. I'll meet you in town. How exactly do I get there?"

In answer Dell raised his voice; "Jubal!"

A painfully thin boy with a head that looked to Bass to be two or three sizes too big for that scrawny body, about twelve years old dashed over. "Yes, Pastor?"

"Do me a favor and go with Marshal Reeves and show him the way to town. We're gonna take this man here to the doc's. Bring the Marshal there when you get to town." Dell looked up. "Okay, Marshal?"

"Fine. You just be careful with this one, hear?"

Joseph Dell looked down at Rowland. The man's eyes rolled wildly and he wheezed hoarsely as he fought to draw in air. Air escaping from his chest made the blood bubble. "Somehow, I don't reckon this here boy is gonna give anybody much more trouble today, Marshal. Israel! Michael! Come on over and help me carry this man to the wagon. Lively, now!"

Lone Hollow didn't appear to have grown much since Bass rode through there four, five years ago. It was a town where poor blacks, whites and Indians lived together, worked together and got along right well. Being poor was the greatest unifier of all. One didn't have time for prejudice when one worried about putting food on the table from sunup to sundown.

Bass turned in his saddle to call back to Tom Lucky, following him with the wagon. "Find yourself someplace to secure the wagon. I'll find you. And mind you keep those prisoners in the wagon and chained up."

"We staying here the night, Bass?"

"Might as well. What we do next depends on what the doc tells me. If he can pull Rowland through, we'll stay until he's well enough to travel. If not, we'll bury him here. If he's got kin wants to claim his body, they can come dig him up and tote him theyselves."

Directed by the boy Jubal sitting behind him, Bass made his way to the doctor's. He helped the boy down first then climbed down himself. "You know how to look after a horse, boy?"

"I do, Marshal. Want me to take care of yourn?"

Bass fished up a silver dollar from a pocket and flipped it through the air into the boy's eagerly waiting palm. "I do. You see to him good; you hear me?"

"Yessir!"

Bass strode up to the front door and knocked, waited until he got a "Come on in!" and went on inside. The doctor's office was just one room where he apparently lived and did his business. Rowland lay on a table. The doctor had cut his shirt away and already cleaned the wound, taken out the bullet and in the process of bandaging up the wound. He looked up. "Howdy. You'd be Marshal Reeves. I'm Tibbett White. I do the doctorin' for the folks here."

"Howdy." Bass peered at him closely. "Seminole?"

White grinned. "You got a good eye, Marshal. Yeah, my mother's Seminole. My father's Canadian. Come down here 'cause he got a wandering foot. Had a couple of kids with my mother then lit out back for Canada."

"How's my prisoner?"

"If'n I was him, once I got my health back, I'd take up gambling for a living because there's no luckier man that this bastard right here. There ain't many men could take a shot in the chest at close range like he did and still be alive."

"You could tell he was shot at close range?"

White nodded. "Could tell from the powder burns."

Bass nodded in appreciation. He admired and respected professionalism. "How soon until he can travel?"

White regarded the unconscious man gravely for a few minutes before answering. "If'n it was up to me I'd say give him a week. But judgin' from the look on your face, you don't want to wait that long."

"I would not. But I don't want him to die either. I intend to see that he gets back to Fort Smith alive so that Judge Parker can hand him down a stiffer sentence. This boy would have gotten off light if he had behaved himself. But he tried to escape and threatened the lives of innocent, law abidin' citizens. He got to answer for that."

"Tell you what, Marshal. You agree to compensate me fairly and in two or three days we'll set out for Fort Smith. I got me a wagon I can tote this man in and I'll keep him alive on the trail. Been a while since I've been to a real town and I could do with some decent drinkin' and whorin'."

"You do that for me and I'll see to it that you're paid fair." Bass stuck out his hand and they shook on it over the unconscious Rowland. "Whereabouts can I find me Pastor Dell?"

"Go on out back to the street, turn right and keep on goin' until you hit the church. Pastor lives in the back. He'll be there. Pastor's pretty much of a homebody. Not that there's much of anyplace to go here in Lone Hollow. We got one saloon that ain't hardly worth the name."

"He seems a capable man. Shot this man like he shot men before."

"He come here about a year ago. Just rode into town and stayed on. Took up with Melissa Brookings, our blacksmith."

"Big ol' muscular woman?"

"That be her. The church was built by a preacher man that liked to drink and it was by drink he died. Heart just bust from him drinkin' so much. 'Bout two months after he come here, Dell took over and it wasn't too long before we callin' him pastor although he ain't never represented himself as a man of the cloth."

"He preaches good, though, right?"

"He does. Right powerful words you can feel come straight from his heart. Sometimes he does his sermons from The Good Book but I likes the ones where he just speaks what's on his mind and in his heart. I don't know where he come from but he's a man who's done some livin'. I can tell."

"Bet you done some livin' yourself, I dare say."

"Let's say I got around some when I was younger and leave it at that."

"You'll be okay bein' alone with Rowland?"

"Him? Marshal, he ain't gonna cause me no trouble with that hole he got in his chest. When he comes round chances are, he'll be in so much pain he'll beg me to give him something to knock him out again. Believe me when I say he ain't gonna be no problem. And if he does take a notion to act up?"

"Defend yourself as you see fit and don't worry about what happens after."

White nodded and bent back to finish his work while Bass walked back out into the street and following White's directions soon found himself walking up a short flight of steps into the cool interior of Lone Hollow's church for it's colored populace.

Bass took off his wide brimmed bolero hat and paused on the threshold. The diffused light streaming into the church was caused by the greased paper covering the windows. The calm and quiet of the church seemed to envelope Bass. He smiled slightly. He walked down the center aisle past the rows of pews, his bootheels softly thumping on the floor.

"Who's out there?" The voice came from deeper inside the church.

"Bass Reeves, pastor."

Joseph Dell emerged from a shadowed doorway, pushing aside the blanket covering it. He held a revolver in his hand. Bass raised his own hands. "Whoa, now, pastor. You done got to cultivatin' an appreciation for shooting men?"

Dell uncocked the weapon, grinning sheepishly. "Apologies for that, Marshal. What with all that's happened today I'm just a mite jumpy. What can I do for you?"

"Just wanted to tell you I spoke with your Dr. White. He's going to be bringing Rowland back with me to Fort Smith, keep him alive so's I can see to it he hangs proper and legal like. But we won't be leavin' for a couple of days so you got time to write out that statement. I would appreciate it if you'd have it ready by then."

"Of course, Marshal. Be glad to. Tibbett would be right tickled to hear you call him a doctor. He ain't no more a proper titled medical man than I am a pastor."

"If'n you and he provide a service to the people of this here community and they accept you as such then what's the difference?"

Dell tucked the revolver into the small of his back, underneath his coat. A gesture that was not lost on Bass. The man was keeping his weapon close at hand for a reason. "Let me ask you a question in return by way of answer, Marshal. What if you took off that badge but continued to hunt down bad men and bring them before Judge Parker. Would there be a difference?".

"The difference is that I'm lawfully deputized. Bounty hunters got their place. I ain't disputing that. But I'm legal authorized to bring men in to be sentenced to justice by the law. Bounty hunters ain't so discriminatin'. They tend to bring in their prisoners anyway they can. Some think it's easier to bring 'em in dead."

"You don't bring in prisoners dead?"

"You saw how I work today at that stream. I give Rowland every chance I could to turn himself in. You yourself saw no way out but to shoot him.

"You don't bring in prisoners dead?"

How does that sit with a man who preaches the gospel?"

"I saw a need and I handled it the best way I knew how. These are good people. They don't deserve violence to be brought to their community."

"We see eye to eye there, pastor. That's why as soon as my prisoner is able to travel, I will be leavin' your town and trouble the good folk here no more."

Dell nodded, walked closer and gestured to the door of the church. "Fair enough, Marshal. And now, if you have no otherwise pressing business, can I invite you to partake in the hospitality of Lone Hollow's one and only saloon? The whiskey ain't the best but it'll get you drunk, that's for sure."

"I'd be right proud to pull a cork with you, pastor. Lead the way."

Dell nodded. "Just give a minute to fetch my hat and coat." he turned and went back through the doorway which Bass presumed led to Dell's personal living area. Hearing footsteps at his back he turned to see the same big muscular woman who had to be restrained by three men at the river coming into the church. She slowed up some upon spying Bass and her eyes narrowed with alarm and suspicion.

"Where be Joe? What you done to him?"

"I haven't done anything to the pastor, ma'am. I'm just waitin' on him so's we can have a friendly drink together." Bass placed his hat over his heart and bowed slightly. "U.S. Deputy Marshal Bass Reeves at your service, ma'am. You'd be Melissa Brookins?"

And now anger joined suspicion in the woman's eyes. "What bizness you got knowing my name?" She looked over Bass's shoulder. "Joe! Where be you?"

Dell emerged from the doorway, now wearing a coat and his hat in hand. "Right here, Melissa. I swear your voice rattles the roof. What you bellowing about?"

"I didn't know where you were, that's why I bellowed. You okay?"

Dell chuckled. "Sure. Why wouldn't I be?"

Melissa turned her hostile gaze back on Bass. "Why he still here? And how come he knows my name? You tell him?"

"No, I didn't tell him. But the way you carry on there ain't many who don't know who you are fifteen minutes after they come to town."

"It was Doc White who told me your name, ma'am. It come up in conversation."

"Why you still here? Why you ain't take that man what grab my daughter and leave? Ain't you supposed to take bad men to Fort Smith and hang 'em?"

"That was your daughter Rowland grabbed up back at the stream?"

"That be my Sally, sure."

"She okay?"

"She's fine. I took her home, give her some cabbagestalk tea and sent her to bed."

Dell gestured with his hat at Bass. "You might want to thank the Marshal here for seein' that Sally is safe."

Melissa snorted. "Why? You shot that man, not him."

Dell sighed mightily. "Melissa..."

"Naw, pastor, naw. She right. You were the one shot the man threatening her daughter, not me. Any credit due goes to you. I don't believe in takin' the praise for another man's doin's."

"You still ain't said why you ain't take that man and leave."

"Doc White said it'll be another day or two before Rowland is fit for travel and even them Doc White has to come with me to make sure he doesn't die on the trail. You make me curious as to why you're so powerful bent on me leaving, ma'am."

"It's peaceful and quiet here. We don't like gunplay. And then there's you."

"Me, ma'am? I'm a peace officer of the law, duly and properly sworn in by the honorable Judge Isacc Parker himself."

"The only thing worse than a white man with a badge is a nigger with a badge."

"Melissa! You be standing in God's House and I will not have that language in here!" Dell roared, plainly outraged.

"My apologies, Joe. An' I beg forgiveness of the Lord. But I seen what happens when the white man gives colored men badges and tells them they lawmen. They start actin' like they done forgot all the times white men spit on them, raped their women, killed their chirren."

"I ain't forgot, ma'am." And though his tone was still respectful, an added measure of something dark and dangerous gave added timbre to Bass's words as he continued, "I freed myself from slavery. If'n I knowed you better I would show you the scars I got on my back from the whip. Don't you be presumin' to tell me what I forgot. Long as I live I ain't never gonna forget those days."

"Then why you wear that badge? Why you do the white man's job for him?"

"The law is supposed to be for everybody, ma'am. Black and white alike. That's the only way everybody gonna be free eventually. And for the law to work for black and white alike it got to be enforced by black and white alike. That's why I do what I do. Now, I ain't sayin' that there ain't some truth in what you say. I done seen black men given a badge and abuse it just like white men who wore the badge. But they ain't me. Pastor, I do believe I'll wait for you outside. And I'll bid you a good day, ma'am."

Bass walked past Melissa and continued out of the church and into the strong midday sunlight. He could hear the angry whispering going on between Dell and Melissa. There was something going on with those two. After a few years of being in the business of hunting down malefactors and murders, one developed a certain instinct or else one didn't last those few years. But he resolved to just ignore it and let it be. He had more than enough on his plate with his wounded prisoner and the others that still had to be transported back to Fort Smith. Best he keep his mind focused on the task to be done.

Dell joined him as Melissa strode past both men as if they didn't exist, holding up her skirts and went on her way. Dell smiled sheepishly at Bass. "I do apologize for Melissa, Marshal. She tends to jump right to bein' mad quicker than you can spit. And she doesn't like lawmen much."

As the two men fell into step together, Bass asked, "What reason she got for not likin' lawmen?"

"Happened when she was a girl back east. Town she lived in had a white sheriff employed black and white deputies. Sicced the black deputies on the colored and the white deputies on the crackers when necessary. Melissa's pa got behind on the ranch mortgage and the sheriff sent three of his black deputies out to the place to collect or run 'em off. Well, things got outta hand. Melissa's ma come out with a shotgun and that was all she wrote. There was gunplay and when it was all over, Melissa's ma and sister lay on the ground dead with two of the deputies. The third one lit out back for town to fetch the sheriff. Melissa's pa got her and her brother into a wagon and they headed west. Didn't stop until they hit Oklahoma Territory. Her pa had been some kind of outlaw when he was younger and knowed they could hide out here. And that's why Melissa Brookins don't like lawmen."

"Can't say as how I blame her. That happened to me and mine I wouldn't be too partial to lawmen either."

"Here's the saloon," Dell indicated. It looked much the same as the other structures on the street, lacking the familiar batwing doors one usually expected to find serving as the business hours doors of a typical saloon. But no, this saloon had a regular door that Dell opened and gestured for Bass to go on in.

Once inside, Bass saw why the saloon had a regular door. This building did double duty as a general store. Barrels and crates were stacked neatly but still took up most of the floor space. There was still room for three tables. But most of the men were bellied up to the counter which also served as the bar. Both white and black men drank elbow to elbow. Along with one Chickasaw. Bass walked over to Tom Lucky and tapped him on the shoulder. "What you doing in here, Tom? Where be the prisoners?"

Tom downed whatever liver destroying liquid was in his shot glass before answering. "Wagon's parked in back of the store. Prisoners are all shackled securely hand and foot. But after what happened to Rowland, they ain't too keen on startin' trouble."

"Coulda sworn I give you orders to find someplace to secure the wagon and the prisoners."

"You did and I did. There's a roomin' house right next door and I got a room for us. Figure we can take shifts sleepin' in a decent bed while the other watches the wagon and the prisoners. Mr. Clyburn here says that we can keep the wagon out back until we're ready to go. He'll see to it that they're fed as well." Tom gestured for the bartender/owner to come on over to be introduced. And while the man ambled over, Tom couldn't help but add; "And I cain't help but notice you come on in here for a bit of liquid refreshment yourself, Marshal."

Bass smiled and nodded in acknowledge of the slight rebuke. Tom was a good posseman and had been one of the best lawmen in his day when he wore a badge. He knew his job. The incident that happened today was one that could have even happened to Bass.

The bartender wiped his hands dry on his apron and stuck out his hand. "Marshal Reeves. Mighty proud to have you visitin' our town. I'm Tee Clyburn and this here is my place. As I told your man, your money's no good here. Drink up and be welcome. You in need of any supplies, just let me know."

"I do thank you for and appreciate the hospitality. Still and all, we'll be settlin' up our bill before we take our leave of your community. You just tote up what we owe and Tom here will see that you're paid fair."

"What will you have to drink, Marshal?"

"Gimme whatever you're poisonin' Tom with. If'n it doesn't kill him I reckon it won't hurt me none."

Clyburn cackled at that with great good humor for a bit before asking Dell, "How about you, Joe?"

"Same as what these gentlemen are having, Tee."

"I notice he didn't call you parson," Bass said.

"Colored and white mingle together pretty well here in Lone Hollow, Marshal. For the most part we're all 'bout the same so we treat each the same. You see white men and colored men in here drinkin' together but they still prefer to do their churchin' separate."

"I'll be damned. Seems to me everybody be a lot better off if'n it was t'other way round."

Dell reached over to pick up his shot glass. "I agree. And agreein' is about all I'll do."

Bass laughed in perfect understand as he clinked his shot glass with Dell's and Tom's and all three men threw back their shots in unison. As Tom gestured for Clyburn to set them up again, he said casual like as if simply continuing their conversation, "Friends of yourn sittin' over yonder, parson?"

"Where?"

"Look over your right shoulder. The table next to them stacked barrels of flour."

Bass admired the way that Dell got his look at the men Tom pointed out. Using the pretext of waving to an acquaintance across the room and inquiring as to the health of wife and family, Dell gave them a looking over before turning around to reply to Tom; "Don't recollect their faces. They might have come in here before. Lone Hollow is a small town but we're not in the boondocks. We get saddle tramps and cowboys passing through."

"Them ain't no saddle tramps." Bass had himself given the men a look. "You eyeballed them mighty good, pastor. Sure you don't know them? They eyeballin' you pretty damn hard theyselves. They just ain't as good at it as you are."

Dell shrugged. Bass decided to leave that one alone. It could very well be as the pastor said it was. The three men continued drinking, talking about nothing of consequence and as they did so, the three men at the table finished their bottle of homemade washtub liquor and took their leave. They ambled away far enough from the saloon that they were sure they wouldn't be overheard. Still, they spoke in low voices.

Two of the men were white. Vernon Pryce's most distinguishing feature was his luxurious curly golden hair that he obviously took great pride in as it looked as if it had been freshly washed while the rest of him was still covered in that day's trail dust. The taller of the trio, he used his towering height to his advantage, intimidating the other two. Pryce swung on the black man at his elbow. "How about it, K.K.? That him or not?"

The black man who went only by K.K. scratched at the stubble of his cheeks, looking back at the saloon. "I dunno...I dunno. It could be him..."

"We ain't got time for you to be guessin' damn you! Now is it Baker or not?"

"And I tells you I ain't sure! I only got a glimpse of Baker when he grabbed up them money bags, slung 'em over his shoulder, got on his horse and rode outta New Bend like hell. I was behind a water trough, trying not to get my own head blown clean off."

The third man spoke. Davy Ford's voice was that of a man who possessed a dead soul. Five years of incarceration in Yuma tended to have that effect on most men. "But you said you got a look at his face when his mask come a'loose. Did you or did you not?"

"I did, dammit! But like I said, I was tryin' not to get shot. Bullets were flying everywhere...there was a lot of dust...men screamin' and dyin'..."

Ford ignored him and turned to Pryce. "What you think?"

"I think it's worth hangin' around another day or so. This here Joseph Dell does resemble the way them folks there said Joseph Baker looks."

Ford nodded. "I was thinking the same way. How 'bout you, K.K.?"

K.K. nodded. "Shoot, twenty-five thousand dollars is a lotta money. I'm still in."

Pryce was tall enough that he could give Ford a look over K.K.'s head without the shorter man noticing. That look was the confirmation of a bargain struck between those two men before the three of them set out on this manhunt.

"What about the Marshal?" Ford wanted to know.

Pryce frowned. "Marshal? What Marshal?"

"You don't know Bass Reeves?"

"Heard a'him. Never seen him."

"You peep the big man standin' next to Dell? The one with the bushy mustache, dressed kinda fancy?"

"Yeah. That be Reeves?"

Ford nodded. "That be Reeves. I saw him 'bout two years ago at Vicious Bluff. He come for the Blisslake gang."

"The Blisslake gang? A tough crowd, I hear."

"They were. When Reeves got done with them, two of them was dead, two give up and the rest hightailed it, never to be seen again in these parts. He's bad medicine. And he looked awful chummy drinking with that Joseph Dell. Almost like they were friends."

"You scared of Bass Reeves?"

"I ain't scared of no man what puts on his pants one laig at a time same as I do. But I'd also be worse than a fool not to respect the fact that there's a lotta men thought they could take Bass Reeves and he's still walkin' above the ground while they are layin' under it."

Pryce pondered that for a bit. "I ain't gonna lie and say you ain't got a point. And I ain't hankerin' to get into no gunfight with any Marshal. Not unless I have to. We're here to find that money. And I can't spend my share if'n I'm dead. Looky here, K.K., I got a job for you."

K.K. eyed the taller man with guarded suspicion. "And what would that be?"

"Dell and Reeves look like they're goin to be bendin' their elbows for a time in there. Ford and I are going to search that church and see if'n we can find that money there. You stay here and keep an eye on Reeves."

"Why can't I go with you and help search for the money?"

"And suppose Reeves and Dell take it into their heads to come on back to the church while we're in there?"

"An' let's say they do? How am I supposed to warn you they comin'?"

It was Ford who answered that. "They saw you drinkin' in the saloon. They come out, you just act like you drunk, whip out your gun and fire off a couple shots, singin' "Dixie". That'll convince 'em you're drunk for sure."

K.K. looked back and forth between the two men. "What if they shoot me?"

"Go across the street. See that bench over there? You can keep an' eye on the saloon from that bench. When they come out, just make like you is in a stupor and dreamin'. Once they see that you ain't aimin' at them, they won't shoot. Just fire two rounds. We'll hear 'em. Then let your arm drop and go back to making like you passed out drunk." Ford wisely kept it to himself that it wouldn't be such a bad thing for him and Pryce if Bass did take the random gunshots as an attack and retaliated.

"I still ain't sure about this. You boys sure you ain't got it cooked up betwixt the two of you to run off with that money?"

"We played fair with you so far, right?"

"Yeah, but you ain't got your hands on that money yet."

"Aw, don't go thinkin' crazy, now. Suppose we don't find no money? We still need you to get a real good look at Dell and see if you can say for sure if he's Joe Baker."

"You still need me, is that it?"

Ford sighed. "If that's the way you wanna put it, K.K. Far as I'm concerned, we're all partners in this. We treated you square so far, right?"

K.K. still looked slightly dubious but he had a plan of his own in mine just in case his "partners" decided to double-cross him. "Okay, I'll play along."

"Good. You go on over there and make like Pryce told you. C'mon, Pryce, let's get to that church and see what we can find."

"This has been a mighty pleasant evenin', pastor. But Tom and I best see to getting our prisoners fed and we need to get some sleep ourselves. Where be a good place to get our supper?" Bass gestured for Clyburn to fill up his shot glass one last time.

"There's a couple of eateries I can direct you to." Dell threw back his own glass. "Come on."

Tom Lucky reluctantly finished his own drink and the three men walked to the door, Dell acknowledging those fellow citizens of his who wished him a good night. They went out into the late afternoon sunlight. The day was still warm but with the sun disappearing behind the bald cypress trees covering the low hills west of Lone Hollow it wouldn't take long for the day's heat to evaporate and rapidly be replaced by the chill of the night. Bass intended to be well fed, the prisoners seen to and in a warm bed himself by the time that happened.

So quickly did Bass Reeves move that even as the sound of the first gunshot echoed away, he had one of his own revolvers out and cocked, dropping into a crouch. "What the hell?"

Next to him, Tom Lucky held a Mare's Leg Winchester he produced from under his buffalo hide coat. Joseph Dell also had his gun in his hand. All three men aimed at their target across the street but they held their fire.

Another two shots came from the gun held in the hand of a man slumping back and forth, rocking on a bench in front of the barber shop. "Dixie! Wheeee! Let's sing a song for good ol' Dixie, boys! Damn the Union and damn Abraham Lincoln! Hooray for Dixie! Hooray! Hooray!" And he fired off his gun one more time then fell over in an apparent drunken stupor.

The three men replaced their weapons. "Guess that old boy was dreamin' 'bout the good old days," Dell offered with a smile.

"Where's his two friends?" Bass wondered. "You think they would have put their pard to bed if'n he's that drunk."

Men came out of the barber shop. One of them took the revolver from the drunken man's hand and emptied it of the remaining shells. He gave it to the barber. "Give it back to him when he wakes up." The barber nodded and the men returned to their business inside.

Dell said to Bass. "C'mon. I thought you wanted to get something to eat."

"I'm comin'. Sure is a puzzlement to me why his friends would leave him there, though."

In the church, Pryce and Ford ceased their sloppy searching of Dell's private quarters in the rear upon hearing the shots. They looked at each other. "Dammit!" Pryce snarled. "We ain't hardly started! You reckon Dell and Reeves are really on their way back or K.K. just scared we gonna find the money and run off?"

"We can't take the chance. Dell and Reeves catch us here we ain't got no choice but to shoot it out with them. Best we leave and try again. I'm still hopin' that-"

"Mr. Joe? You in here?"

Pryce and Ford looked at each other in shocked surprise. The voice was that of a young girl. Pryce hissed in Ford's ears; "See if'n you can find a back way out of here!"

Footsteps approached. "Mr. Joe? You back there? Momma fried up some pork chops for dinner and sent me over with a plate for you."

"Shit!" Pryce snarled. He plunged through the blanket hanging over the doorway and seized hold of the girl. She dropped the plate and the cheap china smashed into bits, spraying Pryce's boots with the pork chops. The girl tried to scream and fight but a sharp blow to her chin ended her futile struggle. She slumped unconscious in Pryce's arms.

"What the hell you doing?" Ford demanded. "Have you gone loco?"

"She was coming on back anyway! It was either that or kill her! C'mon and help me with her! I got me an idea how we can use her to get Dell to give us that money."

Ford's face brightened with understanding. "Yeah! I think I got what you mean, boy! Yeah! It just might work!"

Ford helped get the girl over Pryce's shoulder and then he ran to the

Ford helped get the girl over Pryce's shoulder…

door of the church and peered outside. There were some people on the streets but they were further up, walking away from the church. Ford waggled the barrel of his gun, indicating that Pryce should come on. And soon they were on their horses and riding out of town for a camp they had set up in the hills about a mile outside of town.

Tom Lucky retrieved the plates from the prisoners in the wagon and walked them inside the saloon where he gave them over to a plump Chinese woman who lived in a room in the back along with two other women working for Clyburn. Tom returned to the wagon to give it one last check. He looked over at Bass rummaging through his saddlebags. "Whatcha up to there, Bass?"

Bass took out a thick folded sheaf of papers. He motioned for Tom to join him. "Take a set on that crate there." Bass did the same and handed Tom the papers. "You read me off them descriptions."

Tom nodded. He reached inside his buffalo hide coat, dug around for a bit before producing a well-used pair of round wire frame spectacles and put them on. He shuffled the papers for a bit. "Now, let's see here..."

"Just read 'em off, Tom." Bass pushed his hat back on his head and leaned forward, elbows on his knees, chin resting on his interlaced fingers.

Tom nodded and read. Not being able to read, Bass always had one of Judge Parker's clerks write down detailed descriptions of wanted men which Bass then carried around with him. Possessing an uncannily retentive memory, Bass recalled descriptions from past times when Tom had read them out to him but Bass always wanted to be sure of what he was doing before he did it. Successful as he had been so far, he knew full well that it would only take one time for him to bring in the wrong man to cast doubt on his proficiency.

Tom had no problem reading as two large lanterns hanging on either side of the door that led into the saloon cast extremely bright light. He continued reading. When he finished one paper, he would look an inquiry at Bass if he should continue on. Bass indicated that he should.

It was after he read the fifth description that Bass held up a hand. "Hold it. Read that one again."

Tom obliged, "William Kearney. Five foot eight. Dark-skinned Negro.

Known to be associated mainly with white outlaws."

"Don't that sound like it could be that character what fired off that gun in front of the barber shop? The one that was drinkin' with the two white men?"

Tom lowered the papers. Light sparkled on the metal frames of his spectacles as he replied, "Not uncommon for black and white outlaws to ride together in this part of the country, Bass. You know that better than most. And that description fits a lotta men. Hell, some of the men drinking in that saloon could fit."

"I know. But it bothers me that them two men left him there like that. If you've been drinkin' with a man and he gets too deep in his cups don't you think you got an obligation to see that he gets to a bed?"

"I do. But I long ago learnt the foolishness of holdin' folks to the same standards I got."

"Somethin' 'bout that just doesn't fit. I dunno what but it keeps on scratchin' at my brain."

"I'll tell you what really bothers me. When that fella started shootin' off his gun did you see how fast that there so-called pastor got his gun out?"

Bass nodded. "It was not lost on me. And considerin' that he had to reach around to the small of his back under his coat to get his gun out and he did so just as fast as we got to our guns is impressive to say the least."

"Whatever he claims to be now, Bass...he wasn't always so. There ain't many men who got that kind of speed. Could be that Dell isn't the name he was born with."

"Wouldn't be the first time a bad man changed his name and decided to go straight." Bass stood up, adjusting his hat. "Plenty of 'em here in the territory. You keep on reading through them description and see if you find any that seem like they could be Joseph Dell."

"Where you goin'?"

"See if'n I can find that drunkard and ask him a few questions. You stay with the wagon and the prisoners. You keep outta that saloon, y'hear me?"

Tom nodded. "Anything you say, Bass."

Bass grunted and strode away with his long-legged gait that ate up distance in no time. Once he was positive Bass was out of sight and earshot, Tom reached back into his buffalo hide coat and from somewhere in there produced a bottle of washtub hooch he'd had the foresight to procure from Clyburn earlier. Tom put down the papers, yanked out the cork and had himself a nice long drink before replacing the cork with a belch. Tom put the bottle down where he could get to it easy and replace in his coat quickly if he had to. He picked up the papers to resume his work.

The prisoners in the wagon stared at the bottle with expressions of utter mournfulness.

Bass made his first stop the barbershop. The bench was not occupied, as he expected. The barbershop itself was closed for business but the barber himself was still inside, smoking a cigar, reading a newspaper in his barbering chair. He obligingly opened the door when Bass knocked and answered his questions. No, he didn't know who the drunk fellow was. Didn't know him, hadn't seen him before that day. Got up five minutes after shooting off the gun, ran into the saloon. Probably to get another drink.

Bass thanked him for his time and made the saloon his next stop. Only two men were in there, sitting at a table, sharing a bottle and talking quietly. They nodded amicably at Bass as he came in and Bass returned the nod. Clyburn still was at his post behind the makeshift bar, wiping out shot glasses with a corner of his apron. "Evenin', Marshal? Come in for a nightcap?"

"No, thanks for askin'. I'm looking for the colored man that was sitting at that table there with two white men earlier on. They left a little bit after I come in with the pastor and my friend."

"He the one 'caused some ruckus earlier, I hear. Naw, I haven't seen him."

"Let me ask you something." Bass leaned on the counter, lowered his voice. "Any bartender worth his name keeps an eye on his patrons, 'specially ones he doesn't know to make sure they can handle their liquor and they ain't gonna start no ruckus in his place. You keep an eye on them boys?"

"You know I did."

"That colored man drink enough for him to start actin' silly the way he did?"

"He most certainly did not. None of 'em drank much, in fact. They were too busy eyeballin' the pastor."

"You noticed that, hey?"

Clyburn shrugged. "Like you said, Marshal...I keeps me a weather eye on them what drinks in here I don't know personal. Them boys wasn't lookin' to start no trouble but they weren't here for drinkin', either. They were too interested in Joe Dell, looked to me. Why, when they got up and left the bottle they was drinking from wasn't even half empty."

Bass nodded, stood up straight. He reached into a pocket of his double-breasted black satin vest and produced two silver dollars. He held them up in such a way that only Clyburn could see them. "One of these is for the information. The other is to be sure you keep your mouth shut about our conversation. We clear on this?"

Clyburn nodded and reached out to take the silver dollars. "Clear as mountain stream water, Marshal Reeves."

Bass touched the brim of his hat. "Then I'll be biddin' you a good evenin', barkeep. Much obliged for your time."

Back out on the street, Bass leaned up against a support post, hooking his thumbs into his gun belt. The more he thought about the actions of those three men the more he didn't like it. There was something not right about their actions and they had a decided interest in Joseph Dell. Bass hoped it wasn't what he thought it was. Dell seemed like a good, upstanding man. But as Bass said to Tom earlier, the Oklahoma Territory was full of owlhoots fleeing from the law in other parts of the country. It was easy for a man on the run to change his name and make a new life for himself here. A lot of lawmen wouldn't chase a badman into the Oklahoma Territory.

Bass consulted his watch. He sighed. He should be thinking about getting some sleep. Tom needed to get himself forty winks as well. Not that he would complain much. Bass would have confidently bet all the silver dollars he had on him that Tom had a bottle somewhere in that ratty old coat of his to keep him company.

Bass set his feet in the direction of Dell's church. He wouldn't take long. Just ask Dell a few questions to satisfy his mind. Otherwise he wouldn't be sleeping anyway.

There were few people on the streets now that it was full night. Large lamps, lit by young whippersnappers paid by the town merchants to see to such a chore hung on metal hooks in front of their places of business. Most were closed. Only a few such as Clyburn's place and the tailors were open. Bass walked by, saw the tailor and several women still hard at work, doing the sewing and mending for those who either couldn't do it or just didn't have the time.

That's why Bass was surprised to see the church all lit up. And as clear and still as the night was, he could hear excited voices coming from inside long before he arrived there. He didn't bother to knock, just opened the door slowly.

The door creaked loudly enough to get the attention of those inside, standing in front of the pulpit. Joseph Dell. Melissa Brookins. And a dozen men and women Bass recognized as being at the baptism earlier that same day. Some of them looking right jumpy seeing him standing there filling the doorway. Others looked suspicious. Melissa Brooking looked downright enraged. She stabbed a long finger in his direction. "You! You tell me where my little girl is 'fore I kill you!"

Bass blinked in total surprise. That was the last thing he'd expected to hear coming out of her mouth. "Beg pardon, ma'am?"

"My little girl is gone! One'a them men you got in that wagon got her! You tell me where she is!" Melissa started to charge Bass but Joseph Dell seized her by her upper arm and held her fast where she stood. Bass recollected that this morning it took three men to hold an enraged Melissa Brookins back. Joe Dell now accomplished the same task with one hand.

"Ma'am, I don't have the slightest idea what you're talking about or what's going on. But one thing I do know is that none of my prisoners has anything to do with it. I come from my wagon not long ago and every one of them men is inside and securely locked down for the night."

"Then that man Joe shot got her!"

"Ma'am, Rowland's got a hole in his chest big enough to stick an apple in. He ain't got the strength to go to the outhouse by himself much less take anybody's little girl."

"Nobody here in town got any reason to take my little girl! It must be one'a them men you got!"

"My prisoners ain't the only strangers you got in Lone Hollow, ma'am." As he said this, Bass kept his eyes on Joe Dell and saw in the pastor's eyes the expression he thought he would see there but he didn't like it. Because that expression said to Bass that the exactly same thought Bass had, Dell had as well. "There were three strangers drinkin' in Clyburn's the same time I was there with the pastor. Two white men and a colored man. Anybody seen them?"

That seemed to take some of the wind out of Melissa. "Them men ain't got no reason to take my little girl."

"They the only strangers in town besides me, my man and my prisoners, correct? And we don't have your daughter. Only makes sense we find them and ask them what they know. But first I'd 'preciate somebody tellin' me what's going on."

It was Dell who took it upon himself to answer that. "Melissa sent her daughter Sally here with some pork chops she fried up for me. After a while Melissa wondered what was taking her so long and come looking for her. She found her plate busted up and the pork chops all over the floor. My room in back is all tore up like somebody was searchin' for something."

Bass nodded. "You reckon whoever was tearin' up your room got interrupted by Miss Sally and they took her to stop her from tellin', is that it?"

Dell nodded back. "Sounds about right."

"What are these folks doing here?"

Melissa exploded once again, "I sent for 'em! We're gonna tear this damn town apart until I find my little girl!"

"No. You ain't. And these good folks are gonna disperse peaceable like. Go on back to your homes until I send for you."

"You! Who do you think you are?"

"I'm a U.S. Deputy Marshal. That's who I am. And in the absence of Lone Hollow having any official law enforcement officer, I hereby take on that responsibility. If there's a kidnappin' been done, I'll deal with it."

A tall, sober-faced man with a scholarly countenance about him spoke up; "Meaning no disrespect, sir. But I don't think you have any legal jurisdiction here in Lone Hollow."

In reply, Bass pushed back the lapel of his duster so that the light shone on his badge. "By the authority entrusted to me by the Honorable Judge Isaac Parker, my jurisdiction is wherever I stand. And by that authority I hereby direct you good people to go on home. Like I said, if'n I need your assistance I will summon you. But for right now the only ones I need to talk to is Mr. Dell and Miss Brookins here. Now, go on, y'all. Go home."

They grumbled and mumbled some but they did as they were bid. The men and women walked past Bass Reeves. Some dared to meet his eyes but seeing the righteous resolve those eyes contained they wisely decided to keep on moving.

Once they were out of the church, Bass turned his full attention back to Dell and Melissa. "There something you two want to tell me?"

"We got nothing to say!" Melissa snapped.

"Beg your pardon, ma'am, for I don't mean to call you a liar but I reckon what you say just ain't so. And I don't believe that you ever did think one'a my prisoners took your Sally. But you're scared and mad and when you saw me come in you had to let all that mad and scared come out some kinda way and so you took it out on me."

Melissa said nothing. She had no more mad left in her. All that was left was the scared.

"How about it, Joe? There something you want to tell me?"

"Only that if you're going after those men, I'd like to volunteer my services. I'm no lawman but I can handle myself."

"I just bet you can. Okay. Get yourself some sleep and I'll do the same. Come first light I'll come get you and we'll do us some searchin'."

"Ain't you gonna look for Sally?" Melissa wailed. "You gonna wait for sunup? She could be dead by then!"

"She could be dead now. Whoever took her had plenty of time to kill her. But I don't think so."

"How could you know that?"

"I got experience in this kinda thing, Miss Brookings. I don't think your little girl is dead. Like Joe said, somebody was searchin' his room back there and Miss Sally come in and they took her to keep from raisin' a fuss. They'll use her to bargain with. For whatever they think Joe got hid."

"But why can't we go look for her now?"

"If you raise a hue and cry now you may spook whoever has her bad enough that they may decide to kill her and run for it. We stay quiet for the rest of the night and set out early in the morning, we may get the drop on them." Bass lowered his voice slightly. "I know what I'm asking you ain't easy, ma'am. I got chirren of my own and if somebody took one of my little girls...well...I don't think I could be as calm as I am now or as calm as I'm asking you to be. And no, you don't have a reason in the world to trust me but I'm gonna ask that you do."

Melissa seemed to shrink into herself just a bit. She no longer had any energy left to yell. She looked in quiet despair at Dell. "I can't just go home and not know where my Sally is, Joe. I can't do it."

Dell wrapped a comforting arm around her shoulders. "I don't reckon we got much choice in this matter, Melissa. I think we best trust that Marshal Reeves knows what he's doing. He's law. He knows how to handle these things. And you got two other children you got to look after. They need their ma. You got to go home and see to their needs."

"You go on and take her home, Joe. And I'll meet you here at the church first thing in the morning."

"As you say, Marshal."

"Joe?"

"Yes, Marshal?"

"What them men think you got hid?"

Dell looked Bass squarely in the eye as he answered; "I don't rightly know, Bass. Why do bad men do the things they do? Maybe them men heard some crazy story and got it in their heads I got somethin' valuable."

"Where would they hear a story like that, Joe?"

"Like I said, Bass...why do bad men do the things they do?"

"Why indeed...why indeed...."

It wasn't more than a ten-minute walk to the cabin Melissa Brookings called home. Joe Dell walked beside her, arm around her shoulder, whispering in her ear. Words of comfort that didn't mean much but they were words Melissa needed to hear.

K.K. sat on a three-legged stool in front of the cabin, illuminated by a lantern between his feet. He grinned as Dell and Melissa came closer. "Been waitin' a while. Started to think that you folks might never show up."

"Who are you? Why you sittin' in front of my house?" Melissa started forward but once again Dell held her back.

"I'm a man what hates to see fambly separated. I got chirren of my own I ain't seen in two, three years. Hate to see you missin' your daughter, ma'am." K.K. heard a click and blinked. Dell now had a gun in his hand. A gun he'd produced so fast that K.K. hadn't even seen it. "Whew! You some kinda chained lightnin', ain't you, Joe Baker?"

"You got me mixed up with somebody else, mister. My name's Dell. Joseph Dell."

"No, it ain't. Your name is Joseph Baker. You and four other men robbed the bank of New Bend about a year ago. They all got kilt 'ceptin' for you. You rode outta town with twenty-five thousand dollars. I want that money and you're gonna give it to me."

"You're crazy. Say I am this Baker. Why wouldn't I take that twenty-five thousand and head east or to Mexico? Why hang around these parts?"

"I don't know and I don't care. But you look enough like Joseph Baker to satisfy me. So you're gonna give me that money and I'll tell you where that girl is."

"Who got her? Your partners?"

"Yeah, they got her. They think they're gonna double-cross me, take the money and leave me to get hung. Ain't gonna happen. I'm gonna come to the church first thing in the mornin'. You have the money waiting for me. I'll take it; tell you where my partners are camped with that girl. I ride on, you get back your little girl."

"And in the process your partners get killed, is that how it's s'posed to go?"

K.K. shrugged. "Onliest way you're gonna get back that girl is to kill 'em. The both of 'em ain't no more that no-good, low-bred white trash anyway so what's it to you? They'd kill you quicker than a rattler can bite. Hell, that ol' Bass Reeves might even give you some kind of ree-ward for killing two wanted outlaws."

Joe Dell took a step forward, the gun still pointed at K.K. "I could just lay this gun upside your head a couple times until you tell me where your partners have Sally."

"You could. But if'n you were to do that I'd scream and yell so loud that it couldn't help but bring the townsfolk to see what's goin' on. And then I'd be obligated to tell 'em, now wouldn't I?"

"Make him talk, Joe!" Melissa wailed. "Make him tell me where they got Sally! Make him tell me!"

Joe Dell plainly had no idea of what he should do next. But the decision was taken out of his hands by the big form of Bass Reeves emerging from around a corner of the cabin. He held one of his own guns in his hand and with one solid whack he laid the butt of that revolver against the side of K.K.'s head. He dropped with a burbling gasp and hit the ground out cold.

Dell and Melissa looked at Bass as if he were some kind of apparition from The Other Side. "How'd you get here?" Dell finally managed to croak out.

"Followed you, that's all. Thought maybe if'n I did I'd hear or see something interesting. 'Pears as if I was right." Bass bent down to take K.K.'s gun from his holster and stick it in his own gun belt. "Give me a hand with him, Joe."

"What you gonna do with him?" Melissa demanded.

"Gonna make him talk and tell us where your little girl is. Then me and Joe here are gonna go get her back. Step lively there, Joe. Lift him up by the laigs and get to movin'. Ma'am, you go on inside and see to your other chirren. Things go the way I hope they go; you'll have your Sally back by mornin'."

Hearing footsteps approaching, Tom Lucky stashed his bottle away in his coat. Not that he was alarmed. He recognized one of the footsteps as belonging to Bass Reeves. Tom could identify a man by his footsteps as well as he could by looking them in the face. He couldn't place the other set of footsteps but it sounded as if they were carrying something.

A few seconds later Bass and Dell stepped into the circle of illumination given off by the lanterns. The two men carried a third. Dell by the legs, Bass by the arms. They dropped the man at Tom's feet. "Who be this son of a bitch?"

"Remember the drunk man shooting off his gun earlier? Turns out he wasn't so drunk after all."

"What'd you tote him back here for?"

It took Bass two minutes to put Tom fully into the picture. Tom listened with a sort of bemused amusement. "So what you plannin' on doing? Getting the little girl back?"

"Yep. Wake him up, Tom. And back my play. Let's see if'n we can scare with we want to know out of him."

Tom nodded and hunkered down. He grabbed himself a piece of K.K.'s earlobe and gave it a good hard pinch. K.K. yowled and came to his senses as if a bucket of ice-cold water had been dashed on him.

Dell couldn't help but be impressed. "Never seen that trick before."

Bass nodded. "Never failed to see it work. Pinch a man's earlobe real hard and no matter how unconscious or drunk he is, he comes awake just like that," Bass snapped his fingers. "I learned how to do it when I lived with the Cherokee for a time. But I've seen Seminole, Creek and Chickasaw use it as well."

K.K. rubbed at his ear frantically, cursing something terrible. Bass stepped forward and silenced him with a firm slap. "You hush up, now. Don't be wakin' up my prisoners."

K.K. looked up and around the grim faces of Tom, Dell and Bass and he very quickly caught onto the fact that he was in some very serious trouble. "Now, just hold on a damn minute, Bass! I- "

Bass slapped him again. "You call me anything except Marshal Reeves and I'll break your scrawny neck. You ain't no friend of mine to be callin' me by my Christian name."

"Aw, c'mon, man! We's the same!"

"I ain't nothin' like you. You're a backwoods swamp rat who thinks that runnin' around with white outlaws makes you a better class of thief. It doesn't. Now, you're gonna tell me where your partners have Sally Brookings so me an' Pastor Dell can see about returnin' her to her ma."

K.K. brayed with laughter and slapped the ground. "Pastor! Why, he ain't no more a pastor than I'm Abraham Lincoln! And when I tell you

Tom grabbed himself a piece of K.K.'s earlobe ...

who he really is and what he's done it could just be that you'll let me go and arrest him, instead!"

"I'll deal with who and what he is later. Right now, we's concerned with you. And Sally Brookings. I'll say it just one more time: where your partners got her hid?"

"I ain't saying nothing until we get us a deal understood right here right now."

"No deal. You tell me what I want to know and you go into the wagon. I'll take you back to Fort Smith where The Honorable Judge Parker will have the say as to your fate."

"Then be damned to you."

Bass nodded. "Figgered that would be your attitude. Okay, Tom. He's all yours. Do whatever you like but he's got to be able to talk, y'hear me?"

"I hear you. I got to sharpen me up some sticks. Take 'bout ten minutes." Tom shambled away into the darkness.

K.K. tried to scramble to his feet but Dell shoved him back down to a prone position on the ground. "You stay right where you is. You ain't going nowhere."

"Where's that Injun goin'? What he said 'bout sharpening up some sticks?"

K.K.'s obvious terror would have been comical under other circumstances.

"Why you think I travel with that smelly old Chickasaw? 'Cause I like him? Hell, no. He comes in handy for situations such as this. You know when it comes to torturin' a man, there ain't no better at it than a Indian."

"Damn, Marshal...you can't let him dig at me with no sharp sticks!"

"You'll be getting off easy if diggin' in you is all he'll do with them sticks. Last man he worked over...well, it wasn't pretty, I'll tell you that. I seen a lot in my days but what Tom Lucky can do with a handful of sharp sticks...a man shouldn't go out that way."

From somewhere in the dark came the brittle sounds of wood being broken.

Dell looked indifferent.

Bass shrugged.

K.K. looked as if he were about to soil himself.

Tom came back into the light. In his right hand he held a number of long brown wooden sticks. "Gimme a few minutes to sharpen these up and I'll be ready, Marshal. Git them pants offa him."

K.K. lifted up his hands. "Wait! Wait! I'll tell! I'll tell!"

Tom looked disappointed. "Dammit, Marshal...I ain't had a chance to practice for a couple months now. Can't I have him for just an hour?"

"No! NO! Marshal Reeves, please! You can't let that crazy Injun at me! I'll tell."

Bass bent down, seized K.K. by the hair and yanked his head up so that he could look right straight into the eyes of Bass Reeves. "You tell me where your partners got that little girl and you tell me true. 'Cause if you lie it ain't gonna be that crazy Injun that will be dealin' with you. It'll be me."

Tom made sure the door of the wagon was securely locked and turned back around to Bass and Dell. "You sure you don't want me to come with you? Three guns is better than two." Tom jerked his head at the wagon and its cargo. "These boys ain't goin' nowhere."

Bass shook his head. "If this doesn't play out the way we want it to then it'll be up to you to organize these folks into a posse and come after us. I'm countin' on you, Tom."

Tom nodded. "Yeah, yeah...you always got to make sense, don't you?"

"And besides, K.K.'s partners will be getting nervous right soon if'n they ain't already. They may figure that he's already sold them out to me and if that's the case they may decide to kill that girl and make a run for it. Naw... me and the good pastor here have got to go after her now."

It wasn't lost on Dell the tone Bass put in his voice when he said the words, 'the good pastor.' Dell sighed. "Guess you an' me got some talkin' to do while we ride for that camp."

Bass nodded. "Reckon we do. There's a spare saddle on top of that wagon. Fetch it down and I'll help you strap it on one of these horses and we can be on our way."

Dell did as he was bid and with Bass providing assistance it wasn't long before they had the saddle on the back of one the wagon's horses. Bass swung up on the back of his white stallion Cisco. Tom handed Bass up one of the lanterns and whispered; "God be with you." And the two men departed on their errand.

Dell brought up the subject first. "Reckon you heard enough back at Melissa's cabin."

"I did. You gonna tell me the whole story? I like to think that I know the truth about a man I may have to trust with my life."

Dell went silent for about a minute or two. "Yeah...K.K. was right. I'm Joseph Baker. Me and four other men did rob the bank at New Bend. The others all got killed. I got away with the money and two bullets in me for my trouble."

"When this is over and we're still alive you know I'll have to take you and the money back with me to Fort Smith."

"Seems to me that you ought to see how this turns out, Bass. Could be that I'll get killed. Or maybe you will."

"Somehow you don't strike me as the bushwhackin' sort, Joe. If it comes down to a gunfight with those two men, I don't think I got to worry about you shooting me in the back."

"All I'm fixin' on is getting Sally back with her ma, Bass. Me and you can settle things up once that's done."

"Fair enough. I do got somethin' that's puzzling me, though."

"Why didn't I run off with that money somewheres safe?"

"Twenty-five thousand dollars is a lot of money. You act and talk like a smart man. My guess is you got some schoolin'. Man with your smarts and skills with all that money could have bought himself respectability anywhere. Why didn't you run off with that money, Joe?"

Dell went silent for a few minutes and Bass let him be. They rode for a bit, the lantern lighting the road and the soft clop-clop of the horse's hooves echoing in the night.

"It wasn't a clean robbery. It didn't go the way it was supposed to go. Me and the boys figured it would safe to rob the bank because nobody even was supposed to know all that money was in there. But one of the tellers told this whore he's sweet on. He's white and married but loves him some dark meat."

"So he talks big to impress this whore and she tells you?"

"Told Duncan. He's my...was my cousin. He rounded us up and said we could just walk in, take that money and ride out."

"So what happened?"

"The damn fool teller is what happened. I figure he got an attack of conscience and told the manager he talked. There were extra guns protecting that bank. Duncan and the rest all got killed. I got away with the money. Just barely. I managed to get to the next county over and stayed with a woman I knows there. She patched me up and hid me until I was fit enough to ride. I made my way here and just stayed on."

"Don't explain why you decided to take up preaching."

"My daddy was a pastor. Guess it's in my blood."

"Nah. That ain't it."

Dell fell silent again for a few minutes and when he again spoke; his throat was tight with emotion. "There were people on the street. Somebody...I dunno if it was one of us or one of them started shooting and that set it off. Next thing I know, everybody is shooting so fast and so furious it sounded like thunder. I saw two or three people go down. People who had nothing to do with the robbery or the men guarding the bank. Just regular folks out enjoyin' the day and minding their own business. One of them that got shot was a girl...mebbe a couple years younger than Sally Brookings. I saw her get shot in the forehead with my own eyes." Dell wiped at his eyes. "I still see that girl. See the brains comin' out the back of her head. See her hit the ground with a look on her face like she didn't understand what was happenin' or why." Dell sighed. "I guess I had some kind of idea in my head that I should try and give some of the money to her folks. Maybe make their life easier."

Bass shook his head. "Nothin' can make life easier when you've lost a child."

"That's what Melissa says."

"She knows who you really are? What you've done?"

"Yeah. I sure didn't plan on falling in love with her, Bass. I swear. I was just gonna lay low here for a time until I figured out what I was gonna do with the money. But I got to know her, got to know the people...next thing I know, I'm in love with her and folks is askin' me to be their pastor."

"I don't think you're a bad man, Joe. You made you a big mistake, sure. But by actions I seen you do with my own eyes I think I know what's in your heart. You got a powerful conflict going on in there. Sometimes people make a wrong decision and yeah, sometimes people end up dead. Usually the innocent ones. But I don't think you meant to see anybody get killed. Especially not that little girl." Bass reined in his horse. "We's close."

"How can you tell?"

"I smell their campfire."

Dell sniffed. He couldn't smell a thing but the usual night smells he was used to. And try as he might he could see a campfire either. Surely if they were close enough for Bass to smell it, they should be able to see it.

"I don't see a damned thing!"

"Keep your voice down and douse that lantern. They're over that way. Tie up these horses and follow me."

Dell did as he was told and followed Bass. With the lantern out, the darkness engulfed them totally. Dell prided himself on his night vision but it was a mystery to him how Bass was able to navigate so quietly through the brush and shrubbery. Once they'd gone about ten feet, Dell could indeed smell the campfire and another five feet past that, he saw the flickering orange flames of a campfire. Bass motioned Dell to hunker down.

The small clearing in front of them was occupied by two tents and a campfire. One man sat on a log near the campfire.

"There's supposed to be two of 'em," Dell whispered. "Where's the other one?"

"Hesh up," Bass ordered. They waited and watched. The man sitting by the campfire reached into his pockets for his makings and proceeded to roll himself a smoke. Bass and Dell saw the sides of one of the tents move as if someone stirred inside. Presently, another man climbed out of the tent. He stood up, yawning and stretching, adjusting his clothing.

Dell clutched Bass by his forearm. "Bass, you don't reckon he been at Sally, do you?"

Gently but firmly, Bass removed Dell's hand from his arm. "There's two tents, Joe. If'n that was on their mind they wouldn't go through the trouble of setting up a separate tent for her."

"You got a plan in mind?"

"I do. Could get you killed right quick, though."

"I'm here to get Sally back. Tell me what I got to do."

It didn't take Bass long to outline his plan. It was thin and sketchy, sure. But they didn't have time for much else. Dell nodded and stood up. He took out his gun from the small of his back and held it high above his head, letting it dangle by the trigger guard from his long forefinger. With no hesitation he walked toward the campfire.

Vernon Pryce dropped his cigarette, leaped to his feet and drew his gun, seemingly all in the same fluid motion. "Hold it right there, damn you!"

Davy Ford also had his gun out. "You heard him. And drop that gun."

Dell dropped it at his feet and kicked it a few feet away. But not so far that he couldn't make a dive and grab it.

Pryce said to Ford, "Go get the girl. Bring her out here." While Ford accomplished that task he said to Dell, "How'd you know where we were?"

Dell chuckled. "How do you think? Your partner K.K. sold you out. Said if I gave him five thousand dollars, he'd tell me where you were."

"Son of a bitch! Five thousand, huh? You give it to him?"

"Hell no. I made him tell me where you were then I killed him."

Pryce grunted. "Saved me the trouble, I guess. Where's the money?"

"Soon as you give me the girl, I'll tell you where the money is."

Ford joined his partner. Sally Brookings struggled in his firm grip. Her arms were tied and a rag stuffed in her mouth. Her eyes bulged in pleading terror.

"You think we're stupid?" Ford sneered. "You go git that money and put it right here at our feet. Then you'll get the girl."

"Now you're thinkin' I'm stupid. I give you the money and what guarantee I got you won't just kill the both of us?"

"You don't. In fact, you ain't got no choice but to do exactly as we say." Ford cocked his gun. "Go get our money."

"You go to hell. You kill her, I go for the hideout gun I got on me and I'm bound to get one of you before the other cuts me down. Whoever is left has three dead bodies to bury and no money."

"Sneaky bastard, ain't you?" Pryce said. He kept his eyes on Dell and said out of the corner of his mouth to Ford, "cut her loose."

"Like hell I will! She's the onliest leverage we got!"

"Dammit, Ford! We can't stand here all night palaverin' back and forth. You think he didn't tell the girl's mother where he was going? That he didn't tell her if he wasn't back with her little girl in a couple of hours to round up some men and come after him?"

Dell grinned. "Listen to your partner, man. He spins a good yarn, don't he?"

Ford ground his teeth in rage. "I still don't like it."

"Hey, man...look at it this way...you'll still have the satisfaction of killing me if I don't come through with the money, right?"

"I just may kill you anyway, nigger!"

Pryce yanked Sally away from Ford. "We don't have time for this!" He took out a knife from a sheath on his belt and with one swift stroke, cut her bonds. Sally half stumbled, half ran to Dell, pulling the rag out of her mouth.

"Mr. Joe! Mr. Joe! Oh, please take me home! Please take me home to my momma!" She threw herself into Dell's arms.

"Sally, go on home! I got business with these men!"

"Take me home! I wanna go home to momma!"

Pryce fired a shot into the air. "Send that child home and then get our money!"

The stern voice of Bass Reeves came from behind Pryce and Ford. "Drop them guns and put your hands up."

Ford screamed in rage and instead of turning to fire at Bass, he shot at Dell. But as soon as Bass emerged from the blackness of the woods and spoke, Dell threw Sally to the ground and dived for his discarded gun.

Pryce turned and fired twice at Bass who dropped to one knee and fired back. His shot took Pryce in the left thigh. Pryce cursed, toppled over; fired twice more.

Dell got to his gun and from his prone position shot Ford high up in his left shoulder. A fine mist of blood sprayed in the air, illuminated by the firelight. Dell shot him again, this time square in the chest, driving him back with the impact of the bullet. Ford stumbled backwards, fell right into the campfire. Embers cascaded upwards in a whirlwind of orange fire.

Bass walked over to where Pryce lay; his gun trembling. "Put it down. It ain't worth it."

"You'll take me back to Fort Smith to hang!"

"There is that possibility. Then again, you may not. But at least it's a chance worth taking. Because if you don't drop that gun right now I'm gonna kill you. And that is a certainty."

Pryce let the gun fall from his shaking hand. Bass kicked it away. "Now you just lay there while I fish your partner out of the fire."

Bass saw Dell comforting the wildly sobbing Sally. She hadn't been hit by all the bullets flying around, Thank God. Bass grabbed hold of Ford by an arm and dragged him out of the fire. Using a booted foot, Bass rolled him over until the fire burning his clothing was extinguished. He looked up at Dell and the girl. Bass supposed he could give them a few minutes more while he tied Pryce up and rounded up the horses.

Bass Reeves turned in the saddle to talk to Tom Lucky, driving the wagon. It was a little more crowded now with two new prisoners. Ford had been buried in an unmarked grave back Lone Hollow's graveyard in a spot reserved for men of his ilk. Behind the wagon Tibbett White drove a buckboard. Rowland lay in the back, unhappy as hell, true. But still alive.

"Y'all go on ahead and I'll catch up with you. I got me some business with Joe Dell."

Tom nodded, clucked to the horses and continued on down the road. Bass touched the brim of his hat in salute to White as he followed. Then Bass turned Cisco in the direction of the church where the man who called himself Joseph Dell lived and preached.

Dell obviously expected that Bass would come by the church as he stood out in front, Melissa at his side. In the middle of the road leading to the church were saddlebags. Bass stopped Cisco and climbed down. He walked over to the saddlebags, gave them a nudge. "That the money?"

"It is. Take it, Bass. I ain't spent none of it and I don't want it. They money ain't brought nothing but death and give me sleepless nights. It almost got Melissa's daughter killed. I don't want nothing to do with that money. Take it back."

"That just ain't good enough, Joe. You got to come back with me."

"I was afraid you'd say that." Dell pushed back his coat. He wore a gun belt. In the holster was a gun. "I got me a good life here, Bass. Got me good friends and a good woman. I don't want to give that up."

Bass stepped over the saddlebags, pushed back the lapels of his duster so that he could get at his own guns if he had to. "If it was up to me, Joe, I'd take that money and leave you be. But I just can't do that. You got to come back with me and answer for what you done. It's the only way you can square the mistakes you made."

"You leave him alone, damn you!" Melissa screamed. "You an' him got the same skin! Why you wanna take him back so bad? You love that white man you work for so much you wanna let him hang my Joe?"

"I want Joe to come back with me because he risked his life to save your little girl. There's another little girl who wasn't as fortunate as your Sally. She didn't get to go home. An' she's got a momma who deserves to know that her dead little girl got justice. Now, I can't speak for Judge Parker. But he's a just man. A fair man. I'll tell him what you done to help me and I'll tell him about the life you've made here. I don't know if that will be enough to swing the balance in your favor but you got my word, I'll do everything I can for you."

"But you can't promise I'll come back."

"No, I can't. But you got to come with me, Joe. Like I said to Miss Brookings before; if the law is gonna work for black and white alike then black and white alike got to respect the law."

"I like you, Bass. I'd hate to have to kill you."

"You're an honorable man, Joe. Don't make me kill *you*."

Melissa dropped to her knees, sobbing hysterically, beating the ground with her fists. Joe Dell took a few steps to his right so that she would be clear of any gunplay. "I'm giving you a last chance, Bass. Pick up them saddlebags and ride on."

"Not without you, Joe."

Joe Dell's hand sped to his gun, drew it from the holster and pointed it at Bass.

Bass hadn't even gone for his own guns. And Joe Dell didn't fire his.

Joe grinned a sheepishly wry grin. "Damn you, Bass Reeves. How did you know I wouldn't shoot you?"

"You do this work long enough and you get to size up the strength of a man's character real well. You got to if'n you want to stay alive. I figured you wouldn't shoot me but you were countin' on me shooting you. Wounding you or even killin' you. Either way the choice would be taken out of your hands. I wasn't gonna let you take the easy way out."

"Reckon you're a better judge of men than I am."

"Reckon I am."

"Give me time to say goodbye to Melissa?"

"You go on and take your time, Joe. When you're ready, I'm ready."

THE END

Behind "The Pastor of Lone Hollow"

I'm back. Didja miss me?

I say that because I had stories in the first two volumes of "Bass Reeves: Frontier Marshal" but missed the third. This caused some folks to email me asking why I didn't, thinking maybe health reasons or writer's block kept me from writing another Bass Reeves yarn for that third volume.

Such was not the case. I actually had two or three ideas for stories but was not satisfied with any of them. I look upon writing a new Bass Reeves story as an event and I have a horror of readers confusing my Bass Reeves stories. You hear the title of one of my stories and ideally, I would hope an image appears immediately in your mind as you clearly remember what the story was about and even more ideally, the themes and emotions of the story. And to my way of thinking the best way to distinguish my Bass Reeves stories are to be sure that each of them focuses on a different aspect of the man. And so, the first one showcased his celebrated talent for disguise and infiltration. The second one, an all-out action-based shoot-'em-up with Bass Reeves in full tilt boogie Badass Mode.

But with this one I wanted Bass to interact with other black people, something he doesn't do a lot of in my other two stories. Specifically, black people who don't see the law the same way he did and had no reason to trust white lawmen and even less reason to trust black lawmen. And after writing two stories where Bass has to do a certain amount of killing in the course of his duties, I was intrigued by the idea of him being in a situation where he would highly prefer to bring a lawbreaker back alive. One that he talks into coming back with him, compelled by the argument Bass puts forth in this story; that the law has to work for everybody. Otherwise it means nothing for anybody.

Which is only one of the reasons why I love writing Bass Reeves so much and I'm so grateful for the continuing opportunity to write stories about him. There's a lot of different kinds of Western stories Bass can effortlessly slide into and occupy. And in the course of the gunfights, slugfests and staring down the badmen, there's an awful lot that can be said about race relations, the American justice system and what it means to take on the responsibility of law enforcement. Which to me is an added bonus. Sure, my primary purpose in writing these stories is to entertain you, give you a little break from the Real World and give your brain a rest from dealing with the downright harsh and cruel reality we all find ourselves living in now. But if I can give you a little something extra to walk about with and think about...well, that's a bonus for all of us, isn't it?

As always, thank you for reading my story and hopefully you enjoyed reading it as much as I did writing it.

DERRICK FERGUSON - Best known as the creator of Dillon, Fortune McCall and Sebastian Red. He won the Pulp Factory Award for Best Short Story of 2016 for "Voodah of Thunder Mountain" which appeared in Legends of New Pulp Fiction and the Pulp Ark Award in 2012 for Best Collection: "Four Bullets For Dillon"

Ferguson Ink: https://fergusonink.com/

The Ferguson Theater: https://derricklferguson.com/

Dillon: https://my-dillon.com/

My Patreon: https://www.patreon.com/DerrickFerguson

A PRIVATE WAR

By Terry Alexander

Bass Reeves rode the gray gelding close to the jail wagon. He and Otto Redeagle, A Creek posse-man, were returning to Fort Smith, Arkansas with ten prisoners for Judge Parker. Bass reined the horse back and matched the speed of the wagon. "You see that smoke in the northeast?"

Otto nodded. "Yes, it's a big fire. Too big for a cook fire. Sometimes I catch the odor of roasting meat."

"I thought so myself. Must be a lot of meat for the smell to carry this far." Bass licked his lips. "I believe that's close to Simms Creek?"

Otto nodded. "If I'm figuring right, it's right next to the crossing." He removed his hat and sleeved the sweat from his brow. A red band held his shoulder length hair in place. "Best load that sixth bullet in that pistol. We may be heading into some trouble."

"Yeah, keep your rifle handy. I'm going to ride ahead and see what I can find. If you hear shooting, you'll know I'm in trouble." Bass touched his spurs to the gelding. The animal jumped forward, picking up speed with every step.

The trees and bushed thickened as he neared Simms Creek. Bass pulled back on the reins and slowed the animal's pace. He studied the path and found the prints of two unshod horses and one animal wearing horseshoes. *What is going on here?*

Bass removed the leather thong from the pistol's hammer and pulled the weapon free. He glanced at his surroundings, paying special attention to the dark shadows under the trees. The sickening smell of burned meat grew stronger.

"Blast." Bass moved his kerchief and covered his nose to filter out the stench. "Haven't smelled anything like that since the war." The smoke grew thicker, laying low to the ground. "It can't be him. It can't be."

He reined his horse to a stop. His eyes widened, the scene before him sent a shiver down his spine. Bass yanked the kerchief from his face and spit, to clear the bad taste from his mouth. "Lord have mercy."

The charred bodies of two people sagged against the ropes binding their hands to the small cottonwood trees around the creek. The flesh on the front side of the bodies were black and split. A clear fluid oozed from the cracks and dripped onto the bed of coals around the burned feet.

"Oh my God." Bass swung his leg over the saddle and stepped to the ground. He removed his canteen and swallowed a huge mouthful of water. Treading carefully, he circled the trees. A huge pile of dead tree limbs and other flammables had been piled around the feet. The back of the dead that were pressed against the tree were scarcely burned. Bits of clothing clung to the unmarked flesh.

He pulled one of the old shirts he used as a disguise from his saddle bags and approached the larger corpse. "That's a rough way to go." Bass cut the rawhide holding the man to the tree. The body pitched forward, scattering the coals. Bass circled the corpse and grabbed the shoulders, the flesh shifted as he pulled the body free.

"Damn Bass, what happened here?" Otto pulled back on the reins and brought the jail wagon to a stop.

"Terrible things, Otto." He glanced over to the posseman. "Get the prisoners out of the wagon and get the shovels. We need two graves." He walked over to the second body. It was smaller than the first. Bass knew it was a woman. He cut her bonds and dragged the body from the hot embers.

"Dig the graves right there." He pointed to a spot near the trees. "We can't move these bodies very far."

"I've seen things like this before, during the war." Otto stepped from the wagon. He unlocked the toolbox mounted on the side of the jail wagon and approached the barred door. "You men listen careful. I'm going to remove the center chain. I want each of you to grab a shovel from the box. I want two graves dug."

"What if I don't want to dig a grave." A thin man wearing dirty clothes with a ragged derby perched on his head folded his arms across his chest.

Bass approached the wagon. "I ain't got time for foolishness. Shoot the men that won't help with the graves."

Otto nodded. "You might want to rethink that position." He cocked the hammers on the double-barreled shotgun.

The thin man jumped to his feet as Bass unlocked the center chain and pulled it free. "When I unlock this door, come out slow and get a shovel, just like Otto said."

The prisoners nodded, a few of the more nervous ones glanced at the shotgun in Otto's hands and the pistols at Bass waist. The lock opened with a clack. Bass placed it on the step and opened the door. He stepped back and loosened the rawhide from the hammer. "Alright now, real slow." His hand rested easily on the pistol grip.

The men filed from the wagon, each one pulled a digging tool from the box and approached the spot marked for the grave. Otto eased over to Bass. "You've seen things like this in the war, didn't you?" he whispered.

"You remember a Comanche named Two Feathers during the war. He was a Comanche that had the run of the territory." Bass watched as the men set to work on the graves.

"Two Feathers." Otto's lip quivered. "He's back in the nations."

Bass nodded. "This looks like his work."

"I served with Stand Waite. I heard stories about the Tonkawa's." Otto ran a shaking hand over his face. "There were very few soldiers at the Wichita Agency. Most of them were white. I saw the remains of the buildings after; they were burned to the ground."

"Bass nodded. "They burned Fort Cobb and the Tonkawa ran toward Fort Arbuckle."

"All the tribes hated the Tonkawa, they worked with the Texas Rangers and they killed and ate their enemies."

"Is this deep enough?" One of the prisoners asked.

Bass approached the hold. It was nearly four feet deep. "That'll do. Put them in and cover them up. Then I want a good amount of brush piled on the graves. Hopefully it'll keep the coyotes away."

"Anything you want." The prisoner approached the dead man. He reached out and grabbed the burned flesh. A huge piece came free in his hands. "Oh God." He turned his head and retched.

"Use that shirt and the clothes he still has to work him into the grave." Bass instructed.

"I'm gonna get supper started." Otto mumbled.

Within minutes the prisoners had the bodies covered and a huge mound of brush piled on top of the graves. "Okay, get back to the wagon and put the tools up. Then all of you sit down next to the wagon. You know the routine."

The prisoners filed by and placed the digging tools in the box. Several of the men glared at Bass. "Ain't you fella's gonna feed us tonight. I mean we took care of that dirty job for you."

Bass nodded. "I'm gonna put you all back on the big chain and we'll have some supper. Hope you fella's like coffee and beans."

"Same as I liked it every other day." The derby man shook his head and spit on the ground as Bass approached with the chain. He dropped it on the ground next to the man on the end. "Run this through that big link in the leg irons." He did as instructed and passed the end of the chain to the next man. "Come on, fella's. Soon as we get this done, we'll start cooking supper."

"Hope you can keep the bugs out of the beans tonight. I'm not fond of bugs in my food."

"We'll do our best to please." Bass grinned.

Bass stared at the prisoners hours later. They all appeared to be sleeping peacefully, even the man with the big mouth. He rose from his place near the fire and approached Otto. "I'm pulling out in the morning. I'm going after Two Feathers."

"That's what he wants." Otto leaned forward and whispered. "That one wants to kill. He wants someone to come after him; he wants an enemy to fight."

"Yeah, I've thought of that. Means he's been watching the jail wagon. He knew I rode some with John Ross during the war." Bass licked his lips. "If I don't go after him, he'll kill more innocent people."

"He likes to kill, and he wants you to think about this." Otto pursed his lips for a moment. "He wants you looking behind every rock. He wants you to stay up at night waiting for him to come to you. He's challenged you to a fight to the death and he's setting himself up for the advantage."

"I know. I'm gonna have to play the game his way."

Bass spent an uneasy night. He heard every noise in the trees and along the creek. Each time sleep came a leering face of a large bloodthirsty savage invaded his dreams. He knew his mind provided the picture of starving wolf that was far from human, only a deranged monster could inflict a huge amount of pain and suffering on innocent people and enjoy the task.

Several people suffered in the war. His mind flashed back to the wounded men he'd found after the Battle of Honey Springs. The dead of both sides littered the field after the Confederate forces withdrew. Bass carried a message for the commanding officer; he rode a large circle around the encampment.

He found tracks and a copious amount of blood a half mile from the battleground. Three men were picking their way through the brush and trees around the springs. Bass followed the markings and soon came upon the body of a dead Creek Indian from the Second Battalion of Creek Calvary. He hesitated for a moment, his eyes scanning the trees and brush searching for a sniper. Most of the Indian soldiers had carried muskets and shotguns into battle. He reached down and unflapped the holster at his waist.

"I ain't interested in you two." He pulled the pistol free and cocked the hammer. "I don't want to kill you. Start moving down the trail."

"His name was John Cornsilk. He was a good man." A voice came from the tree cover. "He had a wife and two young ones. I'll have to tell his wife of his passing." The voice grew silent for a moment. "We can't take John with us. I will leave him in your care. Make sure he is deep. Don't let the carrion eaters find his body."

"I give you my word. He'll be buried with the rest of the Creek dead."

"What are you called?"

"I'm Bass Reeves. Who are you?"

"I have heard of you. You left your master in Texas and came to the nations. A rider comes." The voice went silent.

"Bass, what are you doing?" A Cherokee brave, wearing a blue shirt with sergeant stripes pulled a spotted horse to a halt. His eyes fell on the dead confederate. "Anymore?" He glanced over to Bass.

"No, this is the only one I've seen today." Bass nodded.

"We'll get him back to camp and take care of his body. You got a message for the Colonel?" The sergeant swung his leg over the saddle. "I'll help you get him on your horse, you can ride double with me."

He pulled a pouch from his shirt. "Message here for the Colonel." He passed the leather pouch to the sergeant. "No need for you to stick around. I saw a horse disappear in that brush. I'll find his animal. I'll get him loaded and be back to camp double quick."

"Alright, see that you are." The sergeant took the pouch, his spurs touched animal's sides. It moved forward at a brisk trot.

"You can come out now," Bass mumbled. "He's gone."

"Take care of our friend. We have to find our regiment." The Indian reappeared; he held the reins of a spotted gelding in his right hand. He quickly tied the reins to a low-hanging tree branch. "Perhaps we'll meet in another life, Bass Reeves." The Indian vanished.

Bass waited for a few seconds. He swung his leg over the saddle and stepped to the ground. He crossed the small clearing quickly and snatched the reins from the tree. The tired animal kept his head low to the ground as Bass led him to the body of John Cornsilk. The animal lowered his head to the body, the large nostrils sniffing the body.

Bass dropped the reins to the ground and stood on the leather straps. He bent down and caught the body under the shoulders and lifted it from the ground. The body of John Cornsilk proved to be much lighter than he expected. He managed to get the body off the ground and draped across the saddle in one motion. Bass found a short length of rope in his saddle bag and tied to body to the saddle. He slipped his boot into the stirrup and climbed into the saddle. His body settled into the aged leather. Holding the reins of the spotted horse in his left hand, he turned his mount toward the camp. He knew his regiment would take care of John Cornsilk. He never ran into the Creek Indian again after the war and often wondered if he survived. He looked to the eastern sky the darkness was growing lighter. He rose from the ground, his blanket draped over his shoulders. Bass walked silently to the graves of the two strangers and stared down at the mound of freshly turned earth. He didn't hear Otto approach from behind.

"You're going to have to keep your mind clear if you're going after Two Feathers. "

Bass nodded. "You surprised me."

"I know, your mind is on other things. You're looking at things that happened during the war. You need to focus on the here and now." Otto grew quiet. "Two Feathers will kill you if you're not prepared."

"I know." Bass turned his head catching Otto's eyes. "Did you know him during the war?"

Otto nodded. "He camped with the Shawnee during the war. He was a fearsome fighter, but never knew exactly who he was fighting. After the soldiers were killed at Fort Cobb and the buildings were burning. He screamed for vengeance against the Tonkawa."

"Did the Tonkawa really eat their enemies?" Bass asked.

"I don't know for certain." Otto shook his head. "Two Feathers knew that some young men from the Shawnee and Caddo were missing. He shouted that the Tonkawa had captured the boys and eaten them. The blood of the white soldiers inflamed the company and his words sent the company into action. The Tonkawa ran for their lives, but we caught them. A madness came over the men. Two Feathers screamed for revenge against the Tonkawa. We roasted them, just like those poor folks there." He patted the lawman on the back. "Take care and watch your back trail. Two Feathers is a very skilled tracker, maybe better than you."

"I know." Bass nodded.

Bass rode the gelding down a winding path through the trees. The tracks were deep and fresh. He'd found the trail easily. Two Feathers made no attempt to hide his tracks. The killer had kept watch on their campsite during the night. A movement to the right caught the lawman's eye.

He pulled back on the reins, the gelding stopped, something dangled from the limb of a massive elm. "What is that?" Bass reined the horse toward the strange object. A tattered blue dress dangled from a low hanging limb. Dark blood stains colored the material.

"What has he done now?" Bass eyed the ground around the tree; a mass of horse tracks circled the elm. He moved away from the tree and made a circle hundred feet away. He found a bent weed that bore the mark of a horse's hoof.

A sudden breeze sent a chill up his spine, the odor of wood smoke filled his nostrils. A vision of the two bodies he and Otto found at Simms Creek. His heels touched the gelding's sides, urging him forward. The tracks became easier to read. Two Feathers was leaving a plain trail, inviting him to follow.

A faint column of smoke rose from a small campfire. As he drew closer a wagon canvas came into view. Four old mules stood at a rope picket line under the shade of two ancient Cottonwood trees. Bass licked his lips. He wanted to shout, to call out to the camp and let the people know he was close. Something kept him quiet. He knew Two Feathers had left the campsite a short time ago and wondered how many dead he would find ahead.

He found a man tied to a wagon wheel. A sharp knife had taken his topknot, blood oozed from the wound and covered his face. He lifted his eyes and glanced at Bass as the marshal drew close.

"Check on Ruthie," he whispered.

Bass grabbed his canteen and swung his leg over the saddle, stepping to the ground. "Let me look at you first." He loosened the lid and held the canteen to the stranger's lips. "Just a sip or two now."

Bass poured a small amount of water down his throat. "Check on my wife. He dragged her over to the far side of the wagon, he came back later carrying her dress. I gotta know if she's okay."

"I'll check on her." Bass gave the injured man another sip of water and closed the lid on the canteen. He placed it next to the man's leg. He circled the wagon and spied the woman next to a pile of brush near the creek bank. Her undergarments ripped and torn. Blood seeped from a cut on her head and one on her shoulder.

"Miss, miss, can you hear me?" Bass drew closer. "Can you hear me?"

Her eyelids fluttered open. "Don't hurt me anymore. Please don't hurt me again."

"I'm Deputy Marshal Bass Reeves. I'm not gonna hurt you." Bass hurried to her side and scooped her up. "Gotta get you back over by the fire and warm you up some, then we'll see to them cuts."

She licked her dry cracked lips. "My husband, is he alive?"

"Yes, he is, but he's hurt bad." Bass circled the wagon and placed the woman gingerly on the ground near the mound of warm ashes. He brushed her blonde hair from her face and crossed over to her husband. He pulled his skinning knife and cut through the rawhide bonds holding the man to the wagon wheel. "Going to bandage you both and get a fire going. Gotta keep you warm tonight."

"Don't worry about me. You need to help Ruthie." The man whispered. "I'm done for."

"Ain't nobody done for. You'll see. Soon as I get you cleaned up and bandaged, you'll feel better."

The man didn't reply and closed his eyes. Bass threw some small sticks of wood on the ashes. A small curl of grey smoke rose toward the sky. He climbed into the wagon and rummaged through their belongings and found a box containing bandages. He scratched his whiskered jaw as he stepped from the prairie schooner. Nothing had been taken from the wagon, no food, no money, nothing had been touched.

Using a clean rag and the water from his canteen, Bass cleaned the woman as best he could. The wound on her chest was deep and needed stitches. He'd have to find the woman's sewing kit later and take care of her wound then.

Bass turned his attention to the man. Bass held his hand under his nose, a weak exhale touched his fingers. He noticed the left arm pressed against the side for the first time and pulled the arm away. He saw the bloody hole. Dark with crusted blood and nearly an inch in diameter.

"See you found my secret." The man wheezed.

"You should have told me. I could have fixed this up."

He shook his head. "Save Ruthie, she's the important one."

"Let me get you cleaned up. I'll wrap those ribs tight and stop the bleeding, then get you both by the fire. If I can get you both through the night, I can keep you alive."

The man attempted a grin. "Keeping me alive is gonna be tough." He looked toward Ruthie and swallowed. "The Indian caught me completely off guard. He was on me before I knew what happened. He had a strange looking sticker, never seen one quite like it. He nailed me with that thing and put me down, then he got his skinning knife and took my hair." A wheezing breath passed the man's lips.

"No need to talk now. You can tell me in the morning."

The right eye peeked open. "No need to lie to me. He's after you though. He knows you can't go far from this wagon as long as she's alive, and he wants you to know he's gonna make a wide circle and kill everyone he finds."

"Just rest now. I'll try to find something you can eat. Maybe I can boil some meat and give you the broth." He turned and glanced his way. The man's tongue hung from his open mouth, his eyes were locked and still. "Damn." Bass mumbled.

"Kevin, how is Kevin?" Ruthie asked, her voice barely above a whisper.

"He's sleeping now," Bass lied. "Best thing he can do is sleep and rest until he's healed up." He rose to his feet. "I'll rustle up some grub.

"We had some side meat, wrapped up in a newspaper under the seat on the wagon. It needs to be cooked up." Ruthie stopped to take a breath. "Hang it over a spit and let it smoke and then cut off a big chunk and put it in a pot to boil for the broth."

"I reckon I can make a meal out of that." He brushed the dirt from his pants and made his way to the wagon. He climbed topside and spied the bundle of newspaper. He also spotted the ten-gauge coach-gun wedged under the seat. Bass tugged the weapon free and checked the loads. It looked to be loaded with double ought buckshot. "I wonder if Two Feathers knew about this gun?" Bass lifted the scattergun from the hiding spot and carried it near the fire. He placed it behind some rocks and stepped back to see if it was visible.

"You'd never see it unless you were looking for it."

"What did you say?" Ruthie whispered.

"Nothin', getting ready to start cooking. Then check on the horses."

"Bless you, Bass Reeves. Thank you for helping us."

The fire had burned down to embers. Bass glanced at the shotgun butt, he sensed Two Feathers out in the woods, watching and made no move to reach for the weapon. He lifted a battered tin cup to his lips and sipped at the lukewarm liquid. *Come on, come and get me.*

The forest gradually grew quiet. Bass shifted position. The feeling of being watched slowly subsided. He placed the tin cup on the ring stones and climbed to his feet. He crept slowly to the wagon and removed the shovel from the lashings that held it to the outside of the bed.

"Best deal with Kevin while she's sleeping." He swung the tool over his shoulder and walked out into the woods. He spied a flat piece of ground between two trees. "What in the world?" He stopped and gazed into the darkness.

A shiver of fear ran the length of Bass' spine. Someone had stuck a spear into the ground, the bloody head of a fox decorated the butt of the shaft. Crimson streams had dried on the handle. Bass approached the spear, he reached out and touched the hardwood shaft.

"He's telling me, he can get me anytime he wants." Bass yanked the spear from the ground and tossed it aside. "Guess we'll have to see if he's right." He drove the shovel blade into the soft earth.

Bass rode a wide circle around the wagon. He had cleaned Ruthie's wounds again this morning and helped her eat breakfast. After the woman fell asleep, he saddled his gelding and rode out in search of the Comanche. He found the tracks on the far side of the campsite. The Indian had tied up his mount there and crept around to the spot where he left the spear.

The unmistakable sounds of a horse and rider came to his ears. He pulled the gelding to a halt. His hand crept to the butt of his .45 and loosed the rawhide from the hammer. A flash of blue showed through a gap in the brush cover.

Joe Staghorn emerged from the timber and rode up to Bass. "Figured I'd find you nearby. I ran into your Posse-man yesterday. He should make it back to Fort Smith late this evening." The tired pinto stopped, head to the ground.

"What are you doing here, Joe?"

A half grin touched the Indian lawman's face. "Same thing you are. Looking for Two Feathers. He killed a family of Cherokee's near the Arkansas River about ten days ago. I've been trying to get a line on him for over a week."

"Good thing you ran into Otto then." Bass nodded.

"Unless I miss my guess, he's close by. I've spotted more of his sign today than I have in a week." Joe removed his hat and sleeved the sweat from his brow.

"What in the world?"

"He wants you here for some reason."

Joe scratched at a spot beside his nose. "That's the way I figured it. Can't figure him out."

"Two Feathers likes to kill people. Whether they're Indians, white folks or people like me, doesn't make a difference to him. I saw some of his handiwork during the war." Bass turned his gelding toward the wagon. "Come on, we best get back to camp. I've got an injured woman to check on."

"What happened to her?"

"Two Feathers came on the wagon. He stabbed the man and then had his way with the woman." Bass shook his head. "Gave her a terrible beating. Think she's got some broken ribs. I wrapped them the best I could."

"He's a bad one, that's for sure." Joe grew quiet for a few seconds, allowing his pinto to match the pace set by Bass' gelding. "Two Feathers rode with the Union forces that attacked the Wichita Agency and destroyed Fort Cobb. General Stand Waite sent me to scout about three weeks after the massacre. I was looking for union positions. I'll never forget what I saw. They burned most of the Tonkawa alive and feasted on the remains."

Bass nodded. "I was there with General Ross, about ten days after the massacre. It was one of the worse things I've ever seen. We tried to bury the dead, but we didn't want to get caught out in the open by the confederate army, we didn't do a good job." His hands rested lightly on his saddle horn. "We searched for Two Feather's and some of the others, but he'd already slipped back over into Texas." He nodded toward the wagon.

A small tendril of smoke rose from a small fire. A hunched over figure with a bloody head bandage eased around the camp.

"Looks like your patient is getting up and around." Joe said.

"Sure does." Bass swung his mount to the picket line and swung his leg over the saddle line and stepped down. He looped the reins around the stout rope. "What are you doing up, Ruthie?"

She turned and stared at the marshal. Her gaze shifted over to Joe Staghorn. "Is he a lawman also?"

"Joe Staghorn, Cherokee Light-horseman." He stepped to the ground, and brushed dust from his shirt.

"What are you doing up?" Bass repeated.

"Some one was wandering around the camp. I thought it was you. I opened my eyes and was getting ready to speak when I saw him. The Indian that killed my husband. He was rummaging in the wagon like he was looking for something." She stared at Bass' face. "You didn't fool me none. I know you buried Kevin last night after you thought I was asleep."

"He's taking a might big chance. No way he could know when you'd come this way." Joe shook his head.

"He might have been looking for the coach gun." Bass patted the ten-gauge strapped to his saddle. "Where did he go after he left the wagon?"

"I couldn't see him real good, didn't have my eyes open very much. Afraid he's spot me looking." Ruthie sat on a large stone and let a deep breath escape her lips. "Near as I can tell he went out to the west. He stayed out there a few minutes and came back to the wagon and went up to the seat. Then he came down and took off."

"I'll check up in the wagon, see if he left anything behind." Joe turned to the wagon.

"I'm gonna look in the woods." Bass took an uncertain step. "Ruthie, why don't you sit down. You'll wear yourself out."

"I want to pull out of here tomorrow." She leaned against the wagon and wiped sweat from her brow. "I'd like to bury Kevin proper, but I guess this will have to do."

"I'll find some wildflowers for his grave and plant them, before we pull out." He scratched his head. "Where are you wanting to go? I'm not going toward Fort Smith."

"There's a farm-house about ten miles from here. Bud and Sara Connors place. I can stay with them for a few weeks." She sat on the log and held her head in her hands. "I don't want him sneaking into camp and having his way with me again." Tears flowed down her cheeks. "I've never been scared much in my life, but this fellah has me scared."

"Me too." Bass nodded. "We'll be pulling out in the morning, if you're fit to travel."

"I'll be ready." She wiped the tears from her face. "I think your friend wants you over there." She pointed to Joe.

"Be back in a few minutes." Bass glanced at Joe Staghorn, the lawman loitered around the wagon tongue, one arm behind his back. Bass sensed the tension in the man's face. "What did you find?"

Joe pulled a man's heart into the light. "Found this on the wagon seat. Figure Two Feathers meant for her to find this. Where did you bury her man at?"

"Come on." Bass walked to the flat space between the two Cottonwood trees. A half-naked body lay on the disturbed earth. The Comanche had desecrated Kevin's body. The eyes, ears and nose were missing, replaced by red gaping holes and the lips and cheeks cut away. "Damn, he's sending a message." He looked over to Joe.

The Cherokee nodded. "I figure he wants to do that to me."

"We could take turns searching the woods for him. We might get lucky and take him." Joe suggested.

"That would get one of us killed for certain, maybe all of us." Bass shook his head. "He's better than we are out there. That's his natural environment. You may be good in the woods, Joe, but he's better. We'd best stay with the wagon and make sure he stays out there."

"I'll take first watch." Joe licked his lips. "Relieve me about three."

"That's fine. He nodded toward the fire. "Get some supper going. I'm gonna get enough wood to keep a fire going all night."

"Okay. I saw some squirrels back down the trail a ways. Couple of young ones would be mighty tasty." Joe pulled the rifle from the scabbard.

"Sounds good." Bass nodded. "Remember, just hit the tree limbs near their heads."

"Naturally. I'm an Indian."

Bass caught himself staring at the same spot in a small stand of Red-oak trees. Something seemed off, he couldn't put his finger on it, but something was strange. He scanned the other trees, but his eyes kept returning to the clump of Red Oak trees.

"You're out there." Bass removed his pistol belt earlier and placed it on his saddle. He pulled the weapon free and positioned it next to the coach gun he'd taken from the wagon. If Two Feathers attacked, he wanted to be ready.

He heard the sound behind him and felt the prick of sharp metal at the back of his neck. "Don't move or I'll kill you."

"I'm not moving." Bass licked his lips and resisted the temptation to turn his head for a look at the elusive Indian.

"Take the woman and the Cherokee north tomorrow. Leave her at the log house. Then ride west to the water you whites call the Caney River."

"I'm not white."

"You are not of the people. You were a slave before the war of the white men. You fought for the white men. Now you work for the white man." Two Feather's grew silent. "You are a white man."

"I'm surprised you were able to sneak up on me this easily." Bass whispered.

"I tied a rabbit out in those trees. You were looking at the movements and thinking I was hiding there." The knife pressure eased from Bass' throat. "I will be waiting in the low hills."

"That's a lot of country out there. I may not find you."

"You will see my sign." Two Feathers jabbed him with the knife again. "Remember leave here tomorrow. If you are still here tomorrow night, I will kill all of you."

"We'll leave in the morning."

"Leave the tame one at the log house with the woman."

"What if Joe doesn't want to stay out of this fight?"

"Then I'll kill him." The pressure eased from his neck a second time. He felt wind on the back of his ear and knew Two Feathers was no longer behind him. He reached forward and grabbed his pistol, hoping for a quick shot at the retreating figure. The Comanche vanished like a ghost.

Bass grabbed his pistol and thumb cocked the hammer. The clack of metal boosted his confidence. He knew Two Feathers was toying with him, trying to unnerve him. Problem was, it was working.

A sigh of relief passed his lips when the sun broke over the eastern horizon and drove the shadows away. He threw small sticks on the embers and waited for them to catch before he slid the coffee pot close to the flames. Bass gained his feet, brushed dirt from his clothes and walked over to Joe Staghorn. He tapped the bottom of the lawman's moccasins with the toe of his boot. The man's eyes popped open.

"He came into camp last night. Outsmarted me, and made it look easy." Bass whispered.

"Why would he come back?"

"Wanted to make sure we were pulling out today." Bass rubbed at the nick on his neck. "He wants you to stay at the log house when we drop her off."

"What do you mean stay? I don't like that at all." Joe sat up and rubbed his upper lip. "You're gonna need me on this."

"I know." Bass nodded. "We've got to handle this right. He'll be watching the house after we drop Ruthie off. He can't stay long. He promised to leave me a sign near the Caney River."

"You might run into some of the Osage." Joe climbed to his feet. "How are we gonna time this?"

"Give me three days. He can't stay longer than two days and even hope to get in front of me. He'll have to have two mounts and push them hard to beat me to the river." Bass stroked his chin. "I figure you can pull out on the third morning and come after me."

"What if I can't find your tracks?"

"A full blood Cherokee lawman should be able to find an albino squirrel in a snowstorm."

"You're funny, Reeves." Joe grinned.

"What are you two going on about over there?" Ruthie demanded. "I'd like to have some breakfast and coffee before we pull out."

Joe popped the reins over the draft mules. "Come on, get up there." He took a moment and glanced at Ruthie resting on a quilt in the back of the wagon.

Bass aimed his gelding at the wagon seat. "She wore herself out, didn't she?"

"She did. She's a tough woman though, most females that endured what she went through, would be sitting around crying." Joe glanced at the trees to his right. "You figure he's watching?"

"You can bet on that." Bass nodded. "He taught me a lesson last night, things ain't always what you think."

"You know, it takes a lot to catch a live rabbit and tie its legs so every move it makes will shake and move the grass." Joe patted his vest. "Sure, would like a smoke."

"Later after we get to the cabin. Figure I can get a good night's rest and move out early in the morning." Bass removed his hat and sleeved the sweat from his forehead. "After I leave, go outside and make yourself busy, move around a lot, let him see you."

"Make him work to keep up with me?" Joe cocked an eye at Bass.

"Don't make him work too hard, Two Feathers might think it'd be easier to kill all of you and then come after me."

"Sure, don't want him thinking along that line." Ruthie's voice came from the wagon bed.

"I'm sorry, Ruthie. We didn't mean to wake you." Joe turned his head as the woman climbed into the wagon seat.

"Can't nobody sleep with you two going on like two old gossips." She looked over to Joe. "Give me those reins and roll a smoke." She took the reins from Joe and looked over to Bass. "Can't say I'm fond of your plan."

"I ain't either, but it's the only plan I've got." Bass nodded.

"We're close to Bud and Sarah's cabin. Another mile or two and we'll be there." Ruthie turned her attention to the trail. "Wish I could get a bead on that devil."

"He's not going to be stupid." Joe rolled the cigarette and poked it between his lips. He popped a match against the wooden seat and puffed it to life. "He might be out there watching us right now." He inhaled deeply and released a column of smoke. "Or he could be keeping an eye on the cabin waiting for us to get there." He glanced over to Bass. "That's the way I'd do it."

"Maybe." Bass nodded. "We can't be sure where he is, so we're going to play this straight and go right to the cabin. If he thinks we're playing him false, he'll kill your friends and be waiting for us."

"Get up there, Boss." She popped the reins over the horses.

"Don't push the animals like that." Joe took the reins from her hands. "They're doing fine, no need to rush them. You may need them later."

"I smell wood smoke." Bass glanced up the trail. "Sure, hope they don't mind some company tonight."

"Sarah and Bud are good people. I guarantee you two will get a good meal." She looked over to Bass. "I want you to kill Two Feathers. I don't want him to get a trial. I want him dead."

"I know how you feel, but I need to catch him if I can, and take him to Parker." Bass grinned. "Sure, hope these friends of yours can make some decent coffee."

"Sarah's a great cook, and her coffee's smooth." Ruthie nodded.

"I've drank a lot of coffee and I've never tasted any that was smooth." Joe rounded a curve in the trail; the cabin slowly came into view. "I didn't think ladies were supposed to lie."

"Maybe just a little white lie."

Bass spied a movement to his left, a brief glimpse of Two Feathers. A fleeting image that evaporated from sight. He turned his attention to the cabin. He saw a man out front with an armload of firewood. "Looks like we made it in time for supper."

"Ruthie, what are you doing back this way?" Bud cautiously approached the wagon. "Where's Kevin?" He glanced up at Joe Staghorn on the wagon and Bass mounted on the grey gelding. "Reckon I know you two. You're one of the lawmen from Tahlequah, and you're Bass Reeves. I seen you on my last trip to Fort Smith." He glanced back to Ruthie. "Sara, get out here. We got company."

A frail woman came to the door. Her bare feet kicked up dust. "Ruthie, what happened to you?" She looked from her husband to the two lawmen. "Put that wood in the house, Bud. Then help these fellah's get her inside." She ran to the wagon and grabbed the woman's hand. "We'll have you in the house in two shakes. I've got some squirrel stew on and we'll have fresh biscuits."

"Got any coffee?" Ruthie asked.

"Not much, we're nearly out." Bud answered.

"Don't you worry about it. I've got plenty of Arbuckle. I'd be proud to share." Bass grinned.

"Let me get this wood in the house, and we'll tend to Ruthie." Bud hurried through the door.

Joe rolled a cigarette three hours later. He looked out into the western sky at the dying sun. "That's a great view. Reminds me of the one I've got back in Tahlequah."

Bud held a rifle in his lap, his head constantly moved back and forth as his eyes scanned the far woods. "You think he's out there right now?"

"If he ain't, he's close by." Bass sipped a cup of strong coffee. "He won't attack tonight. He wants to get me out there."

"Wonder how many people he's killed since you found Ruthie?" Bud glanced over to the marshal.

"I don't know. I hope his focus is on me." Bass blew the steam away from the beverage. "He's keeping track of my activities."

"If you think he's going to keep an eye on Joe for a couple of days, why don't you ride in a big circle and wait for him to show himself." Bud offered.

"What if he doesn't do that? He might stay around and watch the house for two or three hours and then come after me." Bass drained the remainder of the coffee. "Or he might follow me out, make sure I'm going the right way and come back here after three or four hours."

Joe nodded. "Two Feathers is smart. You can't take him lightly. He's killed a lot of men."

Bud shook his head. "I imagine he's raped several women also." He cast a glance toward the house. "He's nothing but an animal." His eyes went to Bass. "Kevin Frazier was a good man and a good friend. I hope you kill this heathen."

"You can call him whatever you want. His ways are different from ours. His people controlled most of Texas and a good portion of this territory during their time." Bass placed the empty cup on the ground. "They didn't ask for any quarter and they never showed any mercy to their enemies."

"Why is he after you?" Bud licked his lips.

"It goes back to the Tonkawa Massacre." Bass gazed out into the woods, knowing that somewhere out there Two Feathers was staring back at him. "The Tonkawa were life-long enemies of the Comanche. "

"That's true, they scouted for the Texas Rangers and led them to several villages." Joe nodded. "The Comanche's hated them almost as much as they hated the Rangers themselves."

"I don't know if it's true, but most of the Texas tribes said the Tonkawa were cannibals. Bass glanced over to Bud. The man's face was flushed. "They supposedly killed and devoured a Caddo boy shortly before the massacre. When the Indian troops attacked and killed the confederate troops at Wichita Agency and Fort Cobb, they went after the Tonkawa."

"The Tonkawa ran south, trying to get to Fort Arbuckle." Joe nodded. "They didn't make it. They were caught on the trail and over a hundred were killed." His shoulders shivered. "They burned the Tonkawa alive. I've heard that the Comanche's in the group ate them."

"Two Feathers was at the massacre. He had a long-standing grudge against the Tonkawa. Not sure why" Bass gained his feet. "Think I'll turn in, get some sleep." He glanced at Joe. "Wake me in four hours."

"Is that necessary?" Bud asked. "Thought you said he'd back off and watch the house for a day or so."

"He might change his mind." Joe said. "Comanche's have a different way of thinking than most Indians, and Two Feathers is a very different Comanche. He's liable to do anything." He slowly climbed to his feet. "I'll be over by the wagon. Let me use that coach gun. If he does show up, I'm bound to get him with that spread."

"If he's such a danger, why did you bring him to my door?" Bud's face reddened.

"I don't think he'll do anything." Bass stretched. "Still it's better to play it safe and not take any unnecessary chances." He glanced at Bud. "You best get in the house with the women and bar the doors."

Bass wrapped the drawstring on a cloth bag, filled with dried beef around his saddle horn. "Remember, move around a lot. Make him work, but don't venture too far away."

"You figure he's watching?" Joe asked.

"Not really. I figure he's down on the trail waiting on me to ride by."

"Why is he after you?"

Bass slid his boot into the stirrup and swung up into the saddle.

"Bass Reeves, you hang on fer a minute. I've got something to say." Ruthie walked from the house. A patchwork quilt wrapped around her body. Her hand wrapped around the bridle rein. "You be careful out there. This fellah is dangerous, and he hates you."

"I'll be careful, Ruthie." Bass grinned. "I'm taking the coach gun, like Joe said, if I get a shot, I'm sure to hit something with that spread."

"Take this too." She released the rein and pulled a small .30 caliber colt from under the quilt. "This was Kevin's hideout gun. It might come in handy."

'You're right. Could come in handy." Bass jammed the weapon under his pistol belt. He tugged on the reins and applied pressure with his legs. "Let's go, Buster." The horse moved forward slowly. "Keep a good eye on things and be careful." He touched his heels to the animal's side the horse broke into a canter.

Bass kept his eyes focused on the trail. He didn't want to be gazing from side to side. He knew that would only give Two Feathers confidence. After an hour he reached for the cloth bag free. The hammer on the Colt jammed into his belly. He pulled the hideout gun from his waist and dropped it in bag. He pulled a length of dried meat free and bit into the tip. He twisted the meat and succeeded in tearing a chunk off. He worked the meat between his teeth, softening it up.

"Could've used a little salt." He mumbled. Bass caught a glimpse of a man on horseback on a low hill half a mile away. He swallowed the chunk of meat and tore another off another piece. "Guess you'll stick with me for a little while then check on Joe." Bass took his canteen and sipped at the tepid water. "Let's see what your animal can do." He hung the canteen on his saddle horn and spurred the gelding.

The animal jumped into a gallop. Bass gave the animal its head. It raced under a small stand of trees, which hid the hillside from view. A well trampled trail branched off to the left. He gave the reins a slight tug and the horse took the narrow path. Bass let the animal run for a few minutes then gradually slowed its pace to a walk.

"If I'm right, he'll be expecting us on the main trail." Bass patted the animal on the shoulder. "When we don't come out on the other side of the trees, he's bound to come looking for us." He glanced at the close packed growth around him. "We'll follow this for a ways, then double back to the main trail."

"You make a habit out of talking to yourself?" A woman wearing a patched shirt and pants with gaping holes in the knees stepped from behind a tree. She held a single shot smoothbore in her hands. The muzzle pointed at Bass. "Or was you talking to that animal?"

Bass drew back on the reins. "Guess I'm in the habit of talking to this old hoss like he's a human being. Expect he'll answer me back one of these days." His hands settled on the saddle horn.

"Who're you hunting?" The shotgun barrel shifted a bit. "You're out of your normal stomping grounds."

"What makes you think I'm hunting someone?"

"I know who you are. You're one of them marshals from Fort Smith." She paused for a moment. "You're after someone, else you wouldn't be here. If you're looking for Bobby Morse, you're on a cold trail. He struck out of this country last week. Said he was going to Kansas."

"I ain't hunting Bobby Morse." Reese shrugged. "I'm getting tired of keeping my hands on this saddle-horn. Can I move my arms?"

She tilted the barrel to the sky and eased the hammer down. "Sure, go ahead and move." She pulled a corncob pipe from her pants and stuffed the bowl with tobacco, scratching a match on the stock she puffed the pipe to life. "Bobby, ain't much count, but he is kin."

Bass lifted his canteen and tilted it to his lips. "What's your name?"

She cast him a hard look. "Shirley, Shirley Brown. My family come into these parts from Missouri when the war started."

Bass wiped water drops from his lips. "Tell me Shirley, how many Indians have you seen in this country?"

"Several, the Osage and the Cherokees are always sniping at each other here. Nothing really serious, only been one or two killed." She shrugged. "I stay out of their business. I don't want them stealing from me."

"Man, I'm talking about is a Comanche. He's a dangerous man."

"Two Feathers is back in these parts." The color drained from Shirley's face. "Last time he came through he killed three Cherokee and two Osage."

"What can you tell me about him? Where does he camp when he's in this country?"

She shook her head. "Two Osage boys tried to steal his horse. They were anxious to be men. They never saw another birthday." Shirley ignored his question. "The Cherokees rode up on him and took him for an Osage and wanted to play games. He killed them fast and made it look easy. Why is he here?"

"He's after me. Now tell me where he likes to camp?"

"I hate to tell you this lawman, but he's liable to kill you too." She pulled the pipe from her mouth and popped it against her moccasins, knocking the ash free. "We need to get out of here. He'll kill anyone who comes against him. Men, women, kids, it don't matter to him. He just likes to kill."

"Yeah, I know. I saw his handiwork before." He stared at the woman. "Now, can you tell me where he camps?"

There's some low hills west of the Caney River, close to an Osage village. He has a place on the top that gives him a great view of anyone coming toward him." She licked her lips nervously. "When did you see him last?"

"He's the reason I took this trail. He was on a hillside staring down at me. Thought I'd make him work at finding me."

Shirley wiped sweat from her brow. "You idiot. You brought Two Feathers into my back yard. He'll kill me for sure."

"Get your stuff and start riding. You'll get away. It's me he's after."

"You don't understand. He'll see my trail and figure I helped you. He'll follow me and kill me when I'm sleeping." She glanced warily at Bass' trail. "Give me a few minutes. I'm gonna ride with you for a few miles. If I can get with Bobby, I should be okay. That red devil ain't after Bobby."

"Are you sure about that? Seems like the smart thing is to ride hard in the opposite direction." Bass shook his head. "Beside's, thought you said Bobby rode out of here last week."

"So, I lied, ain't anyone ever lied to you before?" She disappeared into some brush. "I'd have to stop and rest sometime, then he'd walk into my camp when I'm sleeping and slit my throat." She disappeared into some thick brush. "I figure I'd have a better chance if I can get with Bobby."

"Suit yourself, but I don't understand your reasoning." Bass glanced at his back-trail. "Best get a move on. I expect he's getting anxious, might come in here looking for me."

"I'm ready." Shirley led a pinto into the clearing. The saddle was patched and needed oil. She slipped her foot into the stirrup and swung her leg over the top. "See you're packing a coach gun." Shirley nodded. "What kind of kick does it have?"

"Never fired it. Woman back down the trail gave it to me after Two Feathers killed her husband."

"Hope you get to use it on him." Her heels drummed on the pinto's sides. "Come on we need to get moving."

Bass fell into line behind the woman. The trail narrowed ahead, tree limbs and leaves slapped at his face and tugged at his clothes. The pair kept a steady pace; the sun appeared in irregular patches through the thick cover. The trail widened after nearly an hour.

Shirley glanced over her shoulder. "The trail splits on the far side. You take the right Fork, I'm going left. With any luck I'll catch up with Bobby by sundown."

"I figured as much. We've got to cross that clearing." He patted his gelding on the shoulder. "I'll go first, draw his fire."

"Like hell." She drummed her heels on the pinto. The horse broke into a spirited run. "First one across has the best chance."

Bass spurred his mount. The gelding jumped forward, his long legs eating up the distance separating him from the pinto. Bass expected to hear the echo of a heavy rifle. The forest was strangely quiet. He glanced ahead and saw that Shirley had pulled her horse up short of the trail she planned to take. Within a second Bass saw the reason why.

A severed head hung from a low-hanging tree limb. His long hair looped around the rough bark and tied in a knot. Bass knew he was staring at Bobby Morse.

Shirley palmed tears from her eyes. "Damn it, Bobby. You had a lead. Why did you slow down?" Her hands covered her face, her shoulders shook for a few moments.

"You need to get riding. I hope Two Feathers follows me." Bass glanced over to Shirley. "I'll try to lead him on a crooked trail, keep him looking for me. That should give you enough time to get out of this country."

"You ain't gonna fool this Indian." She dropped her hands and lifted her face. "I can't go out on my own, he'll kill me sure. We've got to go with you. It's the only chance we've have to keep living."

"You're talking nonsense." Bass straightened in the saddle. "I told you he wants to kill me."

"You rode off the main trail and brought him straight to me and mine." Tears stained her face even while it turned a dark crimson. "It's your fault Bobby got killed. If you had stayed on the main trail, Two Feathers might have passed us by."

"I didn't have any idea you two were hiding out down that trail, and if you hadn't stopped me and let Bobby get a lead Two Feathers might have stayed on that hillside, waiting for me to come out."

"Doesn't matter one way or another. We're going with you." Her voice took on a husky quality. "Less you shoot me down right now, and from what I've heard about Bass Reeves, I doubt you'll shoot me."

"Two feathers might save me the inconvenience and kill you before he gets me."

"Maybe so." She turned her horse onto the wider trail going to the right.

"There's a water hole about two miles ahead. We need to give these horses a rest when we get there. It's a good place to camp."

"Lead on. I'll follow." Bass settled the gelding in behind her animal. "I've got some dried beef in my saddle bag. I'd like to find a couple of rabbits though. We might need to stretch that dried meat out as much as possible."

"I'll scout around when we get to the water hole and see what I can find." Shirley mumbled. "I'm sure I can come up with something."

"What's that?" Bass drew back on the reins. "I saw something up ahead."

"Ain't nothing there. You're just seeing things." Shirley kept her horse moving. "Come on, I want to get to that waterhole."

"I knows something moved ahead." Bass followed reluctantly.

A teenaged boy, holding a toddler, led a thin blue roan filly from the trees. "He moved the child from his right hip to his left. "Bout time you got back." The boy said. His eyes fell on Bass. "Who's this? Where's Bobby?"

"Bobby's dead, Two Feathers killed him." Shirley answered. "We ain't got much time, we need to get moving. Did we get anything in the traps?"

"Not a thing." The boy's eyes settled on Bass. His left hand circled a derringer at his waist. "What's this fella doing here? He smells like a lawman."

"He's one of Parkers marshals from Fort Smith." She glanced back to Bass. "That's Georgie and Pearly. Bobby and I found them at a deserted shanty about a month ago. Not sure whether their folks run out on them or died."

"Tell Georgie to get his hand away from that hideout gun." Bass said. "I don't want to kill a boy."

"Georgie." Shirley's voice turned shrill. "Listen to me, we've got to get to the water hole, and we need something to eat."

A half grin touched his face. "I caught two black snakes today. One of 'em's big, close to five feet long." He nodded toward the roan. "Got 'em in that bag."

"Get on that horse. We've got to get traveling." Bass glanced from Georgie to Shirley. "Why didn't you tell me about them two?"

"You balked at taking me." She nodded to the youngsters. "I knew you'd dig in your heels on these two."

"Damn it woman." Bass shook his head. "I've got a Comanche Indian after me. He's killed men and women. It doesn't make any difference to him. You saw his handiwork a few miles back. He's wanting to add my scalp to his collection." He glanced over to Georgie and the child. "If I can get to the far side of the Caney River ahead of Two Feathers, I'll delay him long enough for you three to get to safety."

"Mount up, Georgie." Shirley ordered. "We need to get moving."

"We might push on for a few more miles after supper." Bass mumbled. "If the children can handle the hard riding."

"They can handle anything." Shirley yanked on the pinto's reins urging it down the trail.

George cast a hard look at Bass and followed Shirley. Bass shook his head. "Sure, hope that mare don't come into season. I don't need any more problems."

"She'll be fine." Georgie drummed his heels against her sided.

Nearly an hour later, Bass led the gelding to the water hole. The horse bent his head to the still water. "Don't let your horses drink too much. Cool 'em off slow."

"We know how to handle horses." George snapped. "My daddy had two nice plow horses, I watered those animals every day, I know about horses." He turned to Shirley. "Wonder if Cicero got away?"

"Who's Cicero?" Bass pulled the horse away from the water and led him to a patch of grass.

"That's the horse Bobby was riding." Shirley slapped her pinto on the shoulder, backing it away from the waterhole.

"I expect Two Feathers killed it and cut some meat from the shoulder or hindquarter." Bass stripped the saddle away and removed the bridle. He looped the rope around the animal's head and made a loop to go over the nose and staked the horse out on the grass. "We'll let these animals rest and eat for four hours, then we'll head out."

"These horses are tuckered out." Georgie handed Pearly to Shirley and stepped from the filly. "Old Polly is near done in. She needs rest and good grass."

"We can rest for six hours then pull out." Shirley balanced the child on her hip and stepped to the ground. "That should give these animals enough time to recover."

"Alright, six hours it is." Bass conceded. "See to the horses and make sure they don't wander off."

"I'm not an idiot." Georgie pulled a cloth bag from the roan's saddle and passed the reins to Shirley. "I'll be back in a bit with supper. Might see if you can scare up some fire-wood while I'm gone."

"Where's he going?" Bass frowned.

"He's gonna skin them snakes out, get 'em ready to cook." Shirley led the horses to the water. Both animals drank greedily. She pulled them away and Bass helped her strip the saddles.

"How many times have you patched this cinch strap?" He pulled the saddle from the filly.

"More than I can count. Poor folks have poor ways." Shirley placed the saddle to the ground and led the animals to the grass. "We learn how to make do out."

"I'm sorry we didn't have time to find bobby's body and give it a proper burial."

Shirley shook her head. "I knowed you wasn't after him. Tried to tell him that. He was convinced you wanted to take him back to face Judge Parker. Hell, he never stole anything worth more than fifty dollars at one time in his life. He was strictly small time." She grew silent for a moment. "Sure, filled him with pride when he thought they sent you all the way up here to catch him. He let on how he wanted to tangle with you, but he was more concerned with riding off."

Bass nodded. "Hate he met his end the way he did. I know he didn't deserve to suffer like that."

Shirley closed her eyes for a moment, a tear coursed down her cheek. "Reckon I'd better get some firewood. Georgie will be back with them snakes before you know it. He'll be expecting me to have a fire ready."

Bass removed his canteen and rummaged through his saddlebags for the frying pan and the coffee pot. He placed the items on the ground and went stood at the water's edge. He stared off into the trees, looking for movement. He glanced over to Shirley gathering wood for the fire.

"Gotta admit, those snakes were mighty tasty." He leaned toward the small fire and poured his tin cup with coffee. "I'm surprised that Pearly ate them as well as she did."

"She's learned to eat what we have or go hungry." Shirley nodded.

"Still, I've got to give you and Georgie credit. That was a real tasty meal." He rattled the coffee pot. "Sounds like there's another cup here. You want it?"

She leaned forward and passed the lawman her cup. "Thanks, it's been a long time since I've had a real cup of coffee."

"You still wanting to leave about midnight?" Georgie asked.

Bass nodded. "We need to stay ahead of Two Feathers. If we get to the

Caney River ahead of him, I'll send you north to Kansas."

"Pearlys tuckered out, she's sleeping already." Georgie smiled.

"You need some sleep too." Bass climbed to his feet and brushed the back of his pants. "I'll clean up this mess, I'll have the horses ready when I wake you."

"No need to do that." Georgie stood. "I can saddle my own horse."

Bass shook his head and grinned. "Get some sleep. Night traveling ain't easy." He pulled the shotgun free and stared out into the darkness. He glanced toward the fire several minutes later. Shirley and Georgie curled up in their ragged blankets next to the small blaze. He knew they'd be asleep soon.

"Time to wake up." Bass shook Shirley's shoulder. "I figure it's about one, maybe one-thirty."

Shirley wiped sleep from her eyes. "You gave us some extra time."

"Figured Pearly needed extra rest." He moved over to George. "Didn't want to start a fire, in case anyone is watching us, we can munch on dried beef when we get hungry. I've got enough for all us."

Georgie yawned and stretched. He glanced over to the roan. "I figured she'd fight a stranger."

Bass grinned. "I've dealt with stubborn horses before. Make sure Pearly is ready to ride. I want to travel some miles before we stop to rest."

Georgie scratched his belly and climbed to his feet. "I'll be ready in a couple minutes."

"Come on, Pearly." Shirley and the young girl vanished into the bushes.

Georgie disappeared to the other side of the camp.

Within five minutes everyone was saddled and riding away from the pool. "Keep these horses as quiet. If he's out there, I hope he's sleeping right now."

Cedar needles scratched at their faces, briars and thorns tore at their clothes as they traveled through the darkness. The appearance of the sun lifted their spirits till noon, then the heat and their growling belly's drove away any good feelings they possessed.

Shirley lifted her canteen to her lips and took a long pull of the contents. "It's gonna be a scorcher this afternoon. Bass, you might think about resting these horses for an hour or two. We've been pushing them awful hard."

"I know. If memory serves me right, there's a water hole about three miles ahead."

"I'm hungry. That snake supper has wore out." Georgie said. He shifted Pearly to a different position. "We're gonna have to stop soon. Pearly needs some rest."

"Eat some of this beef. Soon as we get to water, we'll rest." He glanced along his back-trail. *Sure, hope Two Feathers is keeping an eye on Joe right now.* His lifted the cloth bag from his saddle horn and rummaged inside for a slab of dried meat. His hand encountered the .30 caliber colt pistol Ruthie had given him. He released the gun and grabbed some beef. "Here Georgie, this should hold you till we get to the water hole."

"My horse is near tuckered out. She's gotta have some rest." Georgie leaned forward and patted the animal's shoulder.

"We all need rest." Shirley nodded in agreement. "I've been in this saddle so long my butts numb."

"We'll rest for three hours, eat, then push on." Bass turned in the saddle studying their back-trail. "I'm hoping we're getting a good lead on him."

"If he's a good judge of horse flesh, He didn't kill Cicero." Georgie mumbled. "That animal was fast, he could go all day like it was nothing."

"If the animal was that good, I hope he killed it." A tingle ran the length of Bass' spine.

They arrived at the waterhole thirty minutes later. Bass dismounted and led the gelding to the water. Georgie jumped from the roan and bellied down at the waters edge. He and Pearly gulping the liquid. "See to your horse. Don't let him drink too much." Bass yanked the mare away from the water. "You can fill your belly later."

"Here, let me have the mare. I'll take care of them." Shirley held the reins and let the horses drink. "Put Pearly under the shade yonder, then see if you can scare up a squirrel or a rabbit." She led the animals away from the water to a fair-sized spot of grass.

Bass stripped the saddle from his horse and staked him out. He pulled the coffee pot from the saddlebag and lifted the can. "Ain't a lot left. Enough for two, maybe three days." He shook the tin near his ear.

"My Granny used to make something close to coffee out of dried sweet potatoes." Shirley yanked the battered hat from her head. "It tasted really good if I remember right." A crooked smile crossed her face. "Sure, miss my Granny."

"We all have people we miss." Bass grabbed the sack of dried beef. "If he doesn't find anything, we can boil some of this and make broth for Pearly."

Shirley turned toward the tree. The girl played in the loose dirt under the leafy canopy. "She'll like that. That girl loves soup, doesn't matter what kind. She'll slurp it down all day if I'd let her."

"Her having a good appetite is a good thing." Bass grew still. "Don't move real fast. We've got company watching us from the hill to our left."

"Is it Two Feathers?"

"No, they're Osage." Bass gathered a handful of sticks from the ground and arranged them in a pile. "See if you can find some rocks to put around those sticks. Try to catch a glimpse of Georgie while you're at it."

"Shirley, There's Indians movin' through the woods." Georgie hurried into camp. He held a dead rabbit by the hind legs. "You think they're after the horses?"

"Never can tell about the Osage." Bass moved the rawhide lace from the hammer of his pistol. He lifted the weapon slightly and let it slide back into the holster. "I hope they ain't in a fighting mood." Bass glanced over to Georgie. "Get my rifle."

"I can use my own gun." George moved toward his saddle.

"Get my rifle. It's a lever action and fully loaded. Ease over and pull it free, do it real slow. Shirley, get Pearly over by those saddles, take the rabbit with you and make like you're cleaning it." Bass removed his hat and wiped sweat from his brow. "Anything happens, you get that child behind the saddle and stay there."

"When do you want to start shooting?" George's voice cracked.

"I don't want to start shooting if we don't have to. When you get that rifle free, turn around and watch the back door. I figure they'll hold up when they spot you with that rifle." Bass jammed his hat on his head and stepped out into the sun. "If you hear shooting, you cut loose with that thing. Make sure you hit something with that first shot."

"They're taking their time." Shirley took the rabbit and walked calmly over to Pearly and lifted the child to her hip. She walked over to the saddle and flopped down. She pulled a short-bladed knife from her clothes and attacked the rabbit.

"They're coming in now. Three of them. How many are you looking at Georgie?"

"Two."

Bass lifted his hand in greeting and took two steps forward. "Hello there, fellahs. What can I do for you men today?"

The lead rider turned to the others and spoke. Bass continued to smile. "I can't understand a word your saying. I don't speak Osage."

"We can boil some of this and make broth for Pearly."

The leader wore patched and tattered britches and a torn shirt. A simple red band circled his head. "Speak English. We need food. Very Hungry."

"Sorry, all we have is one stringy rabbit." Bass' hand drifted to his pistol grip. "I don't think we can stretch it that far."

The leader paused for a moment. "You work for the graybeard, why are you here?"

"I'm minding my own business. I think you should do the same and move out."

"We're hungry, we want food." The leader glanced over to Shirley and the child. "We could take your food."

"You could try, but some of you will die." Bass let his hand circle the pistol grip.

"Some of you will die as well."

"That's true. We might kill each other. The survivor will eat the rabbit. If they're able." Bass nodded. "Tell you what I'll do. I'll let you have the rabbit. We might be able to get another one before sundown."

The warrior looked at the men behind him and nodded. "Bring us the rabbit."

"Shirley, bring that rabbit over here." Bass kept his eyes on the leader.

Shirley climbed to her feet, gripping the rabbit's hind feet she advanced on the Indians and stopped on the lawman's left side. "Here you go. I didn't have time to finish cleaning it."

The leader passed the rabbit to the man on a thin black horse. "Why are you here? Why are you on Osage land?"

"This is Cherokee land." Bass answered.

"There are no Cherokee here. Only Osage." The leader fastened his dark eyes on Bass. "Why are you here? What man are you after?" He pointed at Shirley. "We found this one's man. Someone cut his head from his body."

"Two Feathers," Bass said. "Two Feathers killed him. We buried his head yesterday."

The leader's eyes widened. "Two Feathers is in Osage land?"

"He wants to kill me. He's got a special place picked out. Some low hills near the Caney River." Bass waved Shirley away.

"We know this place. Go north half a day and turn toward the sitting sun. The hills he favors are half a day beyond the river." The spokesman gripped the reins of his mount tightly. "We return to our village. We will watch for Two Feathers." His heels drummed along the animal's sides. "Aya, Aya," he screamed. The other Indian's followed him as he galloped away. The two behind Bass circled the camp and chased after the others.

"What did they act like that?" Shirley asked.

"They've had a run in with Two Feathers before." He grabbed the cloth bag and pulled some dried beef from it. "We'll have to make do with this and some coffee."

"How much is left?" Georgie asked.

"Enough for another day or two. Get some firewood, we need to get this coffee brewing. I'd like to move out in four hours."

"The Osage might start thinking about the horses and creep in here and steal them." Shirley mumbled.

A series of gunshots echoed in the distance.

Shirley turned her wide eyes on Bass. "You think that's him? Do you think that's Two Feathers?"

"I don't know. Ain't no reason for the Osage to start shooting like that." Bass shook his head. "Fill your canteens and get your horses saddled, you're riding north."

Georgie hurried to the roan mare and led her to the waiting saddle. More shots echoed in the distance. He froze in place gazing at the tree line. "That's two different guns, maybe three."

"You're right." Bass agreed. "The Osage ran into an enemy." He glanced at Shirley. "Get on those horses and get out of here. I'll hold him here as long as I can. I might get lucky and kill him this time."

The shooting died abruptly.

"Damn." Shirley mumbled. "It sure got quiet." She licked her lips. "Put that saddle down, Georgie. We ain't going anywhere. If that's Two Feathers out there, he might circle this camp just to kill us, so he can hang our heads in the trees."

"He'll come after me. I know he will." Bass glanced from her face to the trees. "You need to get moving."

"I think we'll stay here and take our chances." Shirley's voice turned to a squeal. "I don't favor riding through these woods; it'll be too easy for him to come up behind us."

"You'll be away from the woods in an hour," Bass argued.

"We should to stay here." George countered. "We can gather enough wood and have a big fire going all night."

"He's after me, you two mount up and ride out of here. I'll buy you enough time to get well clear." Bass pointed at their horses. "Get those animals ready and get moving."

"He was after you when he killed Bobby." Shirley glanced around the small clearing. "If we're gonna die, this is as good a place as any." She met his eyes. "I reckon we'll stay with you."

Realizing Shirley wasn't about to change her mind, Bass Reeves took charge.

"Georgie, gather all the wood you can find. I want that fire burning high and hot." He turned his attention to Shirley. "See if you can find something to dig with. I want you to dig a hole close to those saddles for Pearly. Don't want her stopping a stray bullet."

He followed Georgie off into the woods. "I've got an idea." He pulled his knife free. "I may have a surprise for Two Feathers." He walked over to a small stand of sassafras trees, each one an inch to inch and a half in diameter and began cutting them down.

"That green wood won't burn very good." George bent and picked up a handful of dead wood from the ground. "It'll smoke a lot."

"You're right." Bass nodded. "Get as much dead wood as you can for the fire."

"I spotted a huge deadfall back in the trees. Enough for a week if you want."

"Good. Gather all you can, enough to keep a good fire going tonight." Bass attacked the small trees with renewed vigor. After several minutes he carried a huge armload of the small trees and dropped them on the ground around the growing pile of wood.

"I got the hole dug. Pearly's getting hungry." Shirley wiped the sweat from her brow with a grimy hand. "Need to boil some more of that dried meat."

Bass removed the bag from his saddle and pulled a handful of meat. He passed her the coffee pot. "Boil it really slow."

"I've been around the corner a time or two." She took the coffee pot and the meat from his hands. She glanced down at the small trees. "What are you going to do with these?"

"After you feed Pearly, I want you to work these trees into the ground, make a circle around us if you can. Put them about a pistol barrel apart."

"This won't fool Two Feathers. He'll see it ain't real right off." She threw several dried sticks into the rock circle and added some dead leaves and a bird nest. Touching a match to the nest. She had a fire going within seconds.

"I'm counting on that." Bass dug into the ground and stuck the small Sassafras tree into the hole. "I want enough little trees surrounding us that he'll have a hard time locating the horses or picking us out."

George dumped an armful of dead wood by the fire. "I'm gonna bring up three or four more loads, that'll be more than enough to keep the fire going."

"That's good. I want this fire blazing tonight."

"I agree we need a big fire, but those trees don't make a lot of sense to me." Shirley shook her head.

"I'm going to get some more. I want to make him really work to see what's going on in here."

"I hope this idea works." Shirley stirred the dried meat, and kept it swirling in the coffee pot.

"Me too." Bass replied. "Me too."

It was nearly dusk when Bass finished working. He had a circle of Sassafras trees around the perimeter of the camp and had taken strands of thorns and wove them through the trees. "Now, I don't want anyone but me going near the barrier." He brushed the dirt from his hands. "Now we wait."

"You want some of the broth from this meat?" Shirley asked. "Everyone else has had some and I figure the rest is yours. It made a passable soup. It filled Pearly up, she's already asleep." She filled a tin cup and passed it to him.

Bass took the cup from her hands and sipped the liquid. "Not bad, needs a little pepper."

"That's what I said." George chuckled. He took his single shot smoothbore and walked over to his saddle. He leaned against it and placed the weapon within easy reach. "You figure Two Feathers will try to kill us tonight?"

Bass shrugged. "Maybe, maybe not. Hard to tell with a man like him. He might see this fence and decide to leave us alone tonight and come after us tomorrow." He paused for a moment. "Then again he might decide to kill us all."

Shirley stood and brushed dust from her pants. She walked over to Pearly and joined the girl behind the saddles. "I'm going to keep this with me, if you don't mind." She tugged the coach gun free and broke it open, examining the loads.

"That thing kicks like a mule." Bass warned her. "You might be better off with a short gun or a rifle."

"This will do." She knelt behind the saddles.

"I want everyone to stay low, don't stand up. Get around on your knees if you have to."

"What if one of us has to find a privy?" Shirley asked.

"Then you'll have to get over your shyness. Now try to get some sleep. I'll keep watch." Bass threw more wood on the fire sparks broke away from the blaze and floated in the air.

Shirley nodded and curled up on the ground next to Pearly.

Bass crawled over to gap he left in the small fence. It gave him an unrestricted view of the woods to the west side. He knew Two Feathers was a crafty fighter, who always sought any advantage he could find. While the gunshots and the sounds of battle had come from the south earlier, he figured Two Feathers to come at them from the west. That side offered the best cover. A movement caught his eyes.

What in the world is that? Bass licked his lips. Surely that ain't Two Feathers. He remembered the rabbit, how Two Feathers kept his attention on the rabbit and circled into their camp from another direction.

He wouldn't try to pull the same trick again. He knows I'd be looking for it. A frown crossed his face. *He might figure I'd think that way and do it anyway, just to cause confusion.*

Bass crawled away from the fence and approached the fire. He added more sticks on the flames. *I hope he's confused by the fence and the fire.* He crawled back to his saddle and pulled the bag containing the dried meat free. He belly-crawled to his hiding place.

A faint rustling came to his ears. It grew progressively louder only to fade away to nothing. Bass tugged a piece of meat from the bag and bit off a chunk. He moved his rifle to a more accessible position. *I know that's you out there. What are you going to do?*

A shadow flitted between the tree trunks. Bass saw it for an instant as it melted away into the darkness. Reaching down he loosened the rawhide lace from the hammer of his pistol. His eyes slowly scanned the dark woods, looking for movement. A possum darted from the forest and ran toward the fence.

Bass moved the rifle to his shoulder. *Come on. Come on out.* A bullet struck the sassafras just above his head, snapping the small tree. Bass triggered a quick shot at the shooter.

"Damn. It's Two Feathers." Shirley screamed. Pearly immediately started crying.

"Where is he?" Georgie demanded. He knelt and lifted the single shot to his shoulder. "Where is he?"

"Shirley, you and Georgie hush." Bass shouted. "And quiet that child down."

The horses snorted in panic and pulled against the ropes holding them to the trees.

A rifle thundered. A muzzle flash briefly split the darkness. "Damn it,

I'm hit." Georgie screamed. "He hit me." Panic colored the young man's voice. "Shirley, he hit me."

"Hang on Georgie. I'm coming." A shuffling came from her position as she moved Pearly to her hip. The child continued to cry and snivel.

"Shirley don't move. Stay where you are." Bass yelled.

"Damn it, Georgie needs help."

"Georgie, crawl back to cover. Use your shirt to wrap the wound." Silence returned to the small clearing. "Georgie, did you hear me?"

"Yeah, I'm behind the saddles. The bullet went through the meat, didn't hit any bones, hurts like hell."

"Tear one of the sleeves from your shirt and wrap the wound tight to stop the bleeding."

"Okay, I'll do it."

"Now I want everyone to be as quiet as a mouse."

Bass scanned the darkness, searching for movement, wondering where the next attack would come from. A second possum scampered across the clearing, coming straight toward the fence. He focused on the animal and nearly missed the movement to his right. He shifted the rifle over and tried to sight down the barrel. His finger tightened on the trigger. The dark shape dropped away to the ground.

"Bass, did you get him?" Georgie whispered.

"Shut up!" Bass snapped. He risked a quick glance to Shirley. She crouched behind the saddle holding Pearly. The child stared at the fire with wild eyes.

He saw the Indian behind her, outside the makeshift fence. He tried to bring the rifle to bear but couldn't move it in time. Two Feathers jumped the fence and grabbed Shirley by the hair. A dark stain colored his shoulder, ran down his arm, and dripped from his fingers. He held a knife to Shirley's throat.

"Put the rifle down." He whispered. "The pistol too, very slow." He glanced over to Georgie. "Tell the boy to put the shotgun down. I'll kill her and shoot him before he can lift that weapon."

"Do what he said, Georgie." Bass slowly placed the rifle on the ground, he pulled the pistol from the holster placed the colt beside it. He lifted his hands in the air.

"I have to give you credit, no one has ever put a bullet in me before." Two Feathers glared at Bass. "You should be proud."

"I'd be a lot prouder if I'd killed you. You speak our language very good, where did you learn?"

"I learned well," Two Feathers smiled. "These tricks of yours puzzled me. I couldn't spot anyone inside the circle as long as they kept down." He glanced over to George. "The boy got too high and gave me a good shot."

"What are you planning to do now?"

"I'll kill these people first and save you for last. I want to take all your power." The point of his knife pricked Shirley's neck starting a small string of crimson running down her throat. "I'm taking you to my sacred place in the hills beyond the river. I can make your death last for three maybe even four days."

"If it's all the same to you." Bass lowered his arms. "I'm going to sit down and eat a bite. I haven't had a decent meal since I started on this trip." He flopped down on the ground, near the cloth bag. "How is Joe Staghorn?"

"The Cherokee is well. He is on his way here. I'll kill him as well when I'm done with you."

"You're planning on doing a lot of killing." Bass glanced toward Georgie. "Hey boy, how's the wing?"

"Hurts like hell." George answered.

"Think, you could throw a big piece of wood on the fire. I want a big piece of dried beef, don't want to grab a piece of that snake by accident." Bass glanced at Two Feathers. "You don't have a problem with that, I hope."

"Throw wood on the fire." Two Feathers told the boy.

Bass locked eyes with Shirley for an instant. He reached over and grabbed the bag. "There's a nice piece right there. Big slab of beef."

"You're going to eat?" Shirley's eye's bulged. "This heathen is gonna kill me and you're going to eat."

"I'm hungry, I haven't had a good meal since I ran into you three." He pulled the big piece free and bit into the slab. "Damn, that's tasty." His eyes settled on Shirley. "It hasn't been easy taking care of you two and that squalling kid. None of you listen, I wanted to stick to the main trails, but you and Georgie convinced me to follow this goat trail to this duck pond." Bass carefully emphasized the word duck.

Shirley's eyes held a grim awareness. She brought her elbow up sharply and struck Two Feathers in the thigh. The movement confused the warrior for a moment. He sliced her across the shoulder. The sharp blade cut through her clothes to the flesh beneath.

Bass grabbed the cloth sack, his hand closed on the pistol grip. He pointed the weapon and squeezed the trigger in one motion. The .30 caliber Colt bucked in his hand. Two Feathers stumbled back a step a pained look crossed his face. He released Shirley's hair and fumbled with his rifle, trying to bring it to bear on Bass.

The lawman cocked the hammer and squeezed the trigger a second time. Two Feathers lined the rifle on Bass, the bullet slammed his chest before he could pull the trigger. The barrel dipped toward the ground. The third bullet struck him in the throat before he could lift the rifle.

Two Feathers dropped to his knees. He clamped a hand over his throat. Each breath sent fresh blood spurting between his fingers. In a final act of defiance, the Comanche grabbed the discarded knife and threw it at Bass. Two Feathers collapsed on his face his final breaths came in ragged gurgles. The knife thudded to the ground three feet from his outstretched fingers.

"Shirley, are you okay?" Bass jumped to his feet and ran to the woman and child.

"He got me good with that knife, but I'll heal up."

"Gotta get you and Georgie by the fire. Get you patched up and we'll start for Fort Smith in the morning."

"Boil some more of that beef." Georgie awkwardly gained his feet and stumbled to the fire. "I really liked that stuff."

Bass led the way through the close packed trees on the trail, Pearly balanced on the saddle in front of him. Shirley followed directly behind riding Cicero. Bass had found the horse earlier that morning. Georgie followed along behind Shirley on her pinto. The blue roan followed behind him.

"How long will it take to get to Fort Smith?" Shirley asked.

"A week, maybe ten days. Depends on how hard we push these animals." He drew the gelding to a stop. "We're gonna have company."

Joe Staghorn appeared on the trail before them. He reined the horse to a stop. "I was worried that Two Feathers had killed you. I was all ready to get revenge for your death. Now I see you've found a child and her family."

Bass grinned. "He nearly killed me. I'll tell you about it. Help me get these three to Fort Smith. I'm gonna try to get them some reward money for Two Feathers."

"Think you can do that?" Joe frowned.

"Maybe, two of the territory's finest lawmen will swear they have it coming." Bass' heeled the gelding's side. It moved forward, carrying him toward Arkansas.

THE END

The Osage and Cherokee battles and The Tonkawa Massacre

In my Bass Reeves story, I mentioned two historic facts, the bitter feelings between the Osage and the Cherokee and the Tonkawa Massacre. Prior to the forced removal of the Cherokees to Indian Territory the Osage Indians controlled a major section of southern Kansas, and Missouri, northern Arkansas and northeastern Indian Territory (primarily the area where the four states currently border). The Osage and The Cherokees clashed in Arkansas Territory several times during the early 1800's. The Lovely Purchase of Osage lands created a buffer zone between the two. When the Cherokees were forced to come to Indian Territory, they found the land occupied by their old enemy. Clashes between the two tribes over land and resources became common. Additional troops were sent to Fort Gibson to deal with the battles between the two tribes. In 1839 the federal government took the Osage lands in Indian Territory and relocated the tribe to Kansas to eliminate the fighting. In 1871 The Osage returned to Indian Territory. The Osage were forced to sell their land in Kansas to the United States Government for 1 dollar and 25 cents an acre.

On October 23rd, several tribes that professed loyalty to the Union forces attacked the Wichita Agency, near Fort Cobb in Indian Territory, which was in the hands of the confederacy. The Caddo, Osage, Shawnee, Kiowa, Wichita, Seminole, and even some Comanche's combined into a large force. The Union forces riddled the agency with bullets and set the buildings on fire, they then attacked Fort Cobb again all the confederate troops were killed and the buildings torched. The Tonkawa Indians who previously established a campsite along the Washita river fled south hoping to reach the safety of Fort Arbuckle. The Tonkawa were hated by the southern plains tribes, part of this hatred can be traced to the tribe working for the Texas Rangers prior to their relocation to Indian Territory in 1859. They led the rangers to several Comanche campsites, and even actively fought against them. The Tonkawa were also rumored to be cannibals. Prior to the attack on the Wichita Agency, they were suspected to have killed two Shawnee warriors and a Caddo boy.

The Union tribes caught the fleeing Tonkawa on the 24th of October. The Tonkawa were tortured and bound to stakes and small trees and burned alive. It was claimed that the Comanche's feasted on the Tonkawa.

Of the 300 tribe members, 137 men, women and children of the Tonkawa were killed. The survivors of the group made it to Fort Arbuckle and from there were relocated to Fort Belknap in Texas. After the war The Tonkawa were relocated to Fort Griffin and later to Fort Oakland where they lived near the Nez Perce.

TERRY ALEXANDER - and his wife Phyllis live on a small farm near Porum, Oklahoma. They have three children and ten grandchildren. Terry is a member of the Oklahoma Writers Federation, Ozark Writers League, The Tahlequah Writers and The Fictioneers. He has been published in various anthologies from Airship 27, Pro Se Press, Metahuman Press, Pulp Modern, Hazardous Press, May December Press, to name a few.

THEM BONES

By Mel Odom

The fat carnival barker in the bright green suit mistook United States Deputy Marshal Bass Reeves's interest in the colorful painting hanging on the side of the tent for real curiosity. It was, but not the way he thought.

The canvas image showed a young, slim woman with long red hair who wore an emerald dress tight enough to hint at feminine wiles. The woman's clothing was scandalous by conventional standards.

The fan the woman in the painting held in one hand hid most of her bright red beard, but not all of it. The beard was enough to make anyone who saw it stop and gawk, and probably have a lot of questions. It was the perfect bait for a traveling circus that offered "death-defying feats" and "oddities" like a rubber man, giant rats, a strong man, a two-headed calf, and…a bearded lady.

Still, the barker held up a minute before he came over to Bass to unload his spiel.

Bass figured the man's hesitation was on account of he'd been riding hard through wild country in Indian Territory the last few days and looked like a rough man not wanting to truck with any foolishness. He stuck out like a curly-haired wolf wearing his two Colt Model P .44 revolvers and most folks fought shy of him.

Behind him, his horse stamped her feet and blew an annoyed breath. She shook her head and her bridle rattled. He held the reins with his right hand to keep her in check and turned slightly to stroke her neck reassuringly.

"You just hang in there, girl," Bass crooned. "You'll be eating good tonight. Ain't gonna be no prairie grass for you. Gonna be sweet feed soon's we check into the hotel."

He should have been at the hotel already, maybe tucked into a good steak and enjoying conversation with Alfred Tubby, his posseman. He'd been looking forward to sleeping in a bed instead of around a campfire as he'd been doing for the last week.

Instead, he stood there in the middle of the curious gawkers that had showed up to have a look at Bishop and O'Malley's Traveling Circus of Amazing Enchantments.

Things would have been different if he'd seen the painting tomorrow morning when he was set to meet Miss Augustine O'Malley and talk about her dead father. That was the work he was sent here to do by Judge Isaac Parker.

But nope. Drawn like a kid by all the color and noise and tents, despite the fatigue from road travel that piled on him as surely as the trail dust, he'd had to come to the circus.

He sighed. He was afraid he was going to miss his supper because he had marshal work to do.

He never put that work off.

"Hello there, mister," the barker said and stopped in front of Bass.

The man removed his derby, faded from being too long in the sun along the route the circus traveled when it was on tour, and probably from standing out in front of the tents in all manner of weather and trying to strike up a crowd. He stuck out a hand and smiled broadly.

Bass took the man's soft, wet hand, squeezed it, and quickly released it. He knew he needed to chat up the barker to see what he knew, and he couldn't be a marshal when he did that. Not yet. Circus folks didn't like talking to the law unless they had troubles they couldn't handle.

That was the kind of trouble Miss O'Malley had.

Right now Bass needed to be somebody who wasn't threatening and was easy to talk to. Hiram Bell was just that kind of character, and the alter ego was a favorite of Bass's. He slipped easily into the man's ways, relaxed his features just a little, and spoke softly. "Hello."

"I'm Oliver Worthy," the barker said. "I'm a host here at the circus."

Bass nodded.

Worthy glanced back at the painting. "I guess maybe you haven't seen a bearded lady before."

"Actually," Bass replied, "I have."

Worthy blinked in surprise. "You have?"

"My daddy's momma," Bass said, "bless her soul on account of you couldn't have met a more lovin' woman, had her some side whiskers that she was a mite embarrassed about. I'm talkin' whiskers that would have made a billy goat envious of chin fringe."

He held his big hand up an inch or so from his face to show how long they were.

"Wasn't nothin' she could do about it," Bass went on, "on account of her bein' old an' all, and folks just naturally tend to fall apart in their final years. My daddy said she was a fine lookin' woman in her day, though. Fine-boned and trim. Told me it was likely my granddaddy had him a private graveyard hid back somewhere in the swamps along Muddy Boggy

Creek that was full of would-be courters from back when my daddy's momma was young because Granddaddy was a jealous man and Granny liked men's attention."

The barker blinked again and looked a little confused. He hadn't been able to immediately launch into his spiel because Bass had gotten there first with a story.

"Well, that's interesting," the barker said.

Bass was sure the man was lying because he'd just made up the whole story right there on the spot, but it had thrown the barker out of his rhythm, which was what he'd hoped it would do.

"What you see right there," the barker turned to wave at the painting of the bearded lady and raised his voice to possibly draw in more of the passersby, "is a fine specimen of a woman. She's lean and pretty and just about every man's dream—if he could get around her having a healthier beard than himself."

Alfred, Bass's posseman, stepped over and joined the conversation. He held the reins to his own horse. Alfred was in his early seventies, twenty years older than Bass. He was lean where Bass was broad and muscular, but the old man still moved quick and fought like a wildcat.

Alfred was more tidy than Bass even though they'd been riding the same trails. Alfred was like that, always looking out after himself, making sure he was squared away. His suit appeared fairly well dusted and his long, salt and pepper hair was tied in braids that hung well past his shoulders. His copper-colored skin advertised his Cherokee ancestry just as surely as the paintings on the carnival tents advertised the presence of oddities.

"Now why would you be so interested in a bearded lady when we got supper to get to?" Alfred mused.

"Don't *she* look familiar?" Bass asked.

Alfred squinted up at the painting wafting gently in the dry breeze that wound through the Woodward streets.

"Of course she looks familiar," Worthy said in an attempt to take control of the conversation. "Mademoiselle Vivienne DuMont has trod stages in France and Spain before royal audiences in her time. Despite her *unfortunate* hirsute appearance, she has a beautiful singing voice. She's been known to sing operas and bring kings and queens to tears even during times of joyous occasion. We here at Bishop and O'Malley's Traveling Circus of Amazing Enchantments are fortunate to have her. Mr. Bishop and Mr. O'Malley both had to negotiate Mademoiselle Vivienne's contract from a Parisian baron."

"I thought Napoleon Bonaparte and the French Republic put an end to royal titles," Alfred said. "They had a big war and everything over there to put a stop to them."

Worthy's face colored a little and he looked off-balance. "I'm sure not every baron was deposed."

Bass smiled a little. "Probably not. I reckon it's hard to get them all."

"It is," Worthy said.

"She sings?" Alfred asked.

"Indeed, she does," the barker said.

"Well, isn't that something?" the posseman asked. He sounded like he was in awe.

Bass kept a smile at bay with effort. Alfred was having fun at the barker's expense. Worthy just didn't know it. The true entertainment was that Alfred still hadn't seen what Bass had seen. It wasn't often he got ahead of his posseman because Alfred was almost as good with remembering faces as Bass was.

"Her performance *is* something," Worthy said. "You should all come and hear Mademoiselle Vivienne sing tonight. She does a beautiful rendition of 'Green Grow the Lilacs.' I swear, that story about the American soldier's love for pretty little Mexican senorita will bring anyone to tears."

"When is Mademoiselle Vivienne gonna sing?" Bass asked.

Worthy straightened his jacket, took out his pocket watch, and checked the time. "In a little less than two hours, gentlemen." He snapped the watch closed, looked around the crowd, smiled, and tipped his derby. "And ladies."

"You reckon we might be able to meet her before the show?" Bass asked.

Suspicion tightened Worthy's eyes and he studied Bass more closely. Some of his polish and wordplay drained away. "Why would you want to do that?"

"Because the man I work for," Bass jerked a thumb over his shoulder in Alfred's direction, "is Mr. Alfred Tannenbaum. He's a circuit newspaper reporter. Writes stories on all manner of things for papers in Indian Territory, Texas, Kansas, and Colorado. Some of them stories get out as far as San Francisco and New York."

Alfred stood a little straighter and added a subtle layer of dignity. He and Bass had worked together so long the posseman just naturally followed any tune the marshal called up.

Worthy studied the posseman more closely and Bass guessed the fib had a fifty-fifty chance of working because circus folk were suspicious by nature, but they were also more than a little nosy.

"I figure Mademoiselle Vivienne is likely someone Mr. Tannenbaum would write about," Bass went on. "Might help you fill more seats as you wander through the Territories. Mr. Tannenbaum's a good writer. And news stories travel along telegraph wires faster than you can go in your wagons."

"Do you want to tell me what you're doing?" Alfred asked in Cherokee.

"I'll show you in a bit," Bass replied in the same language.

Worthy frowned. "What did he just say? I know he speaks English. I heard him."

"I was just chastising my lackey," Alfred said in an even more cultured accent, though the change was subtle, "and I did not want to embarrass you with my agitation. I was prepared to put an end to my evening when he insisted we come look at the circus. It's not seemly for him to press you for a story. You've probably already got someone doing a story on her." He shot Bass an annoyed look. "Sometimes I swear he doesn't have any more gumption than a child, and is about as attentive."

Worthy blinked and looked like he was doing some fast reconsidering. "A reporter, you say."

"Not a reporter," Alfred said, "I am a wandering correspondent. I go see the world and bring it back to newspaper readers wherever they are."

It was a good line and Bass appreciated it. He figured Alfred had picked it up from something he'd read in the papers. Alfred was always reading.

"I'd hate to bother Mademoiselle Vivienne," Worth said.

"And I'd hate to miss my supper," Alfred replied. He switched his attention to Bass. "Let's go."

Bass took a step toward Alfred, away from the circus paintings.

"Wait," Worthy said. "Let me get someone to take my place and I'll take you to see Mademoiselle Vivienne."

"All right."

Worthy darted away.

"What are you doing?" Alfred asked in Cherokee.

"You still don't see it?" Bass jerked a thumb at the painting.

Alfred studied the painting again for a moment, then shook his head.

"You will," Bass promised.

A few minutes later, Bass stood in front of the door to room 2F in the Köhler Hotel. The hallway held groups of men and women, families and drovers, all going about their business.

The crowd discomfited Bass and he frowned.

"Is it always this busy?" he asked.

Worthy looked around. "I wouldn't know for sure. We've only been in town three days. I do know folks have traveled to Woodward from a few towns over."

Bass wondered if there were any rooms left to let.

"Ain't you been over here to get Mademoiselle Vivienne now and again?" he asked.

Worthy shook his head. "No. Usually one of the young trapeze artists comes for Mademoiselle Vivienne when it's showtime and escorts her over to the circus."

"A trapeze artist?" Bass scratched his jaw. "A woman?"

"One of Mr. Cuoco's daughters. They travel with the circus and do the trapeze acts." Worthy glanced at Alfred. "Mr. Cuoco comes from Naples. That's in Italy. His family has been in circuses all around the world. You might want to talk to him too."

"Let's get Mademoiselle Vivienne chatted up first," Alfred said.

Worthy nodded and turned to address the door. He rapped politely.

A scurrying noise came from the other side of the barrier. A feminine voice said, "Just a minute, please."

"It's Mr. Worthy," the barker said. "I've brought a couple of visitors."

"I can't entertain right now, Mr. Worthy. Could you come back at a more opportune time?"

The scurrying noise quieted a little, and Bass was certain he heard a young woman's voice inside the room as well.

"One of the gentlemen is a news correspondent," Worthy said. "He'd like to do a story about you. It would help the circus. After Mr. O'Malley's recent passing, I thought some good news would be in order."

Worthy smiled at Alfred and Bass.

"The circus owner," the barker explained. "He passed away unexpectedly three days ago."

A bullet through the heart is about as unexpected as it gets, Bass thought, but he didn't let anything show on his face.

"Just a moment," Mademoiselle Vivienne said. "Isabella and I were just finishing up adjusting one of my outfits."

"Yes, ma'am," Worthy replied.

A moment later, the door unlatched and opened.

Mademoiselle Vivienne stood there in all *her* glory. The painting portrayed her as more feminine. She wore a blue dress and had her hair pulled back. Her beard looked fierce. Behind her, a young woman adjusted her clothing. To the side, the bed was in disarray.

"Hello, Mr. Worthy." Mademoiselle Vivienne glistened with sweat. She looked at Bass only briefly, then moved on to Alfred. "You're the news correspondent?"

She offered her hand.

Alfred took it, hesitated a moment, then smiled broadly. He kept hold of the hand and glanced at Bass.

"You could see that from that painting?" the posseman asked.

"It was a good painting," Bass answered.

"Indeed, it was," Worthy said. "It was done by Mr. Russell Hull. All those paintings were. He studied in Paris before he joined the circus."

Mademoiselle Vivienne tried to free her hand from Alfred, couldn't, and frowned in frustration. "Sir, perhaps you'd return my hand to me."

"This hand?" Alfred made a point of studying it. "I have to say, there are a lot more calluses on your hand than I'd expect to find on an opera singer's hand."

Mademoiselle Vivienne pulled her hand again, but she still couldn't free it. "Sir."

Worthy's eyes rounded in surprise. "What's going on here?" he asked.

"The opera singing is new," Bass said. "First I've heard of it. So is the dressing up like a woman. But that there is Edward Hough, a known thief who specializes in hotel robberies. He's wanted throughout the Territories, in Texas, and in Arkansas. If we talk to the folks running the hotel, I'll bet they've had some folks who had some valuables go missing. And if he ain't stole from here, there'll be other places he's took from. Probably as far back as when he first joined the circus."

The barker looked at the "bearded lady." "Mademoiselle Vivienne?"

Edward Hough cursed, shoved his free hand into the top of his dress, and came out with a dulled gray Remington Derringer that fit inside even his small hand.

Alfred hauled on the slim-built man, yanked him out into the hallway, and tripped him. Hough fell into an upended sprawl that smacked him into the opposite wall. Still, Hough came up with the derringer pointed at Alfred.

Folks up and down the hallway scattered like a covey of quail.

By that time, Bass and Alfred had their own guns out and pointed at Hough.

"You go ahead on with that popgun," Bass warned the thief. "Me and

Alfred will put enough lead in you that you can be used as a boat anchor."

"Okay, okay!" Hough tossed the small pistol away and held up his hands. "Don't shoot. I surrender."

"You've certainly had an auspicious beginning, Marshal Reeves," Augustine O'Malley said. "I certainly expected nothing like this."

"I didn't either," Bass admitted.

Augustine was small and pretty, a young woman in her early twenties. Her dark hair and brows gave her pinched face a severe look, but that might have been her recent loss taking its toll. From Judge Parker's accounts, she and her father had been close ever since her mother had died when she was a child. Conall O'Malley's death had hit her hard.

She wore a simple off-white dress trimmed in blue. It looked efficient and comfortable, and she wore it well.

They sat at a breakfast table in the Red Rooster Diner that was next door to the Köhler Hotel. Most of the early morning crowd were businessmen getting set for their day.

Alfred sat on the other side of the room so he could watch over Bass and Miss O'Malley. Someone had murdered her father, and there was no reason not to think that that person or persons might murder again.

Bass had worked his way through a full breakfast of sausages, eggs, wheat cakes, and grits.

Augustine had had tea and toast.

"I had no idea Mademoiselle Vivienne wasn't a woman," Augustine said. "And there was certainly no indication she—*he*—was a thief."

"Hough fooled a lot of people," Bass pointed out. "There's no reason to feel badly about it, Miss O'Malley."

"I'll try not to, but I'm afraid I'll be the butt of jokes for a while."

"You're bringing shows to people who don't get to see much," Bass said. "They'll remember the performers and the trapeze artists, not a bearded lady who wasn't exactly that."

She tapped nervously on the checked tablecloth. "I do hope so. Truthfully, the circus wasn't doing well before all of this. My father—" Her voice broke and it took her a moment to get control of her emotions. "I'm sorry."

"There's no reason to be. You just take the time you need."

She nodded, took a handkerchief from her small handbag, and dabbed at her eyes. "I'm stronger than this. Truly I am."

"I can see that."

"It's just a lot," she said. "My father. Keeping the circus together. All those people depending on me to do that."

Sympathy for the young woman filled Bass, but he knew he couldn't do anything about the circus troubles. He wouldn't know where to start, but bringing in murderers and thieves, that was something he knew how to do.

"I was the one handling the books," she said. "I have been for so long. My father, God rest him, did what he could, but he had no real head for the business side of things. That was my mother. She taught me everything she knew. After she passed, I took over. My father wanted this circus for one reason only."

"What would that be?" Bass still didn't know much about the particulars of Conall O'Malley's murder.

"He wanted to see the West, Marshal Reeves. As much of it as he could. He was a scientist. Did you know that?"

"No, ma'am, I did not."

Across the way, Alfred was reading a paper, but he remained watchful and Bass knew the man was listening to their conversation.

"Well," Augustine said, "he was. He collected things, interesting things, that he chanced upon out here in the West. The circus gave him a vehicle from which to explore all the lands out there."

"There's a lot to see."

"I know. My father collected many things, Indian weapons, pottery, pieces of meteorites various tribes used in their religious ceremonies, animal skins, insects. Anything that was different."

Bass nodded and sipped his coffee.

"My grandfather was a scientist too," Augustine said. "He knew President Thomas Jefferson, and he traveled with the Corps of Discovery when they went to map the Louisiana Purchase."

"Yes, ma'am."

"All of this is too little to explain my father," Augustine said, "and I certainly don't know why he was killed."

"Can you tell me about that?" Bass asked quietly.

She shook her head. Tears gleamed in her eyes, but she held them back.

"Sadly, there's not much to tell. Four days ago, sometime in the evening, someone sneaked into the wagon that carries all the artifacts my father had rounded up this trip, caught him working there, and killed him. My father never carried a gun. He was unarmed." Her voice turned ragged at the end.

Bass gave her a moment to pull herself together.

"Was anything missing from that wagon?" he asked.

She shook her head. "No. I don't think so."

"You don't think so?"

Augustine lowered her voice till it was barely above a whisper. Bass had to lean in to hear her.

"There might have been a bone," she said.

"Might have been?"

"My father and Russell Hull talked about a bone that he expected to get. My father was working on a deal to acquire it."

"What kind of bone?"

"A dinosaur bone."

The word was still relatively new to Reeves. Dinosaurs were supposed to be animals that lived a long time ago. Some of the churches were up in arms over them, saying that the devil had put them in the ground to fool people into believing Charles Darwin's nonsense that man had descended from apes. Bass didn't truck with any of that, but Alfred had an interest.

"Do you know anything about this dinosaur bone?" Bass asked. "What it was? Who your pa may have been getting it from?"

Augustine sighed. "I tried to keep up with my father's work, but he was always exploring and trading and picking up things. There were just too many."

That was frustrating news. Digging into a crime was easier when the criminals were known and why the crimes were committed. Judge Parker was a friend of the family. He'd told Bass in no uncertain terms to find Conall O'Malley's murderer because Parker intended to hang whoever did it.

"Marshal Reeves," she said, "do you think that man, Hough, killed my father?"

Bass only thought about the likelihood for a moment. "No, Miss O'Malley, I don't. Edward Hough is a thief, but he's no murderer."

"I heard he pulled a weapon on you and your friend in the hotel."

Bass nodded. "He did, but that was in the heat of the moment. A man suddenly trapped is likely to do anything at all to get away. I suspect, when push came to shove, Hough wouldn't have shot me or Alfred."

"Where is he?"

"In jail. Once I find whoever killed your father, I'll be taking Hough on back to Ft. Smith."

"What are you going to do next?"

"Find out more about that bone, if I can. Who could I talk to about that?"

"A dinosaur bone?" Alfred asked.

"That's what she said," Bass replied.

They walked down the rutted street toward the area where the circus tents were set up just outside of town. Horses and wagons moved constantly up and down the thoroughfare. A lot of them were headed toward the circus.

"What kind of dinosaur?" Alfred asked.

That question puzzled Bass for a moment. "There's more than one kind?"

Alfred snorted. "Is there more than one kind of cow? More than one kind of horse? More than one kind of chicken?"

Bass held up his hands in surrender. "She didn't know."

"Did you ask?"

"No. How could I ask? I didn't know there was more than one kind of dinosaur. She didn't mention any special kind of dinosaur. Why would you even need more than one kind?"

"Because some of the big ones ate the little ones. You have to have little ones to feed the big ones. Or maybe you don't. We eat bears and some of them are bigger than us."

Bass could tell Alfred's mind was busy with the new information and he left him alone. Trying to talk to the old man now would only spur on conversations about matters—in this case, dinosaurs—that Bass would rather not think about. He had a murder to solve.

"We'll talk to this fellah we're going to see," Bass said. "See if Russell Hull can narrow things down."

According to Augustine O'Malley, Russell Hull, the circus's marketing artist, makeup specialist, and fire-eater, was working in the tent Conall O'Malley had set up to organize his collection. Augustine said there was always cataloguing to do, and her father constantly produced small scientific

"A dinosaur bone?" Alfred asked.

monographs about his findings for various science-oriented journals.

If anyone knew about the existence of a dinosaur bone, she assured him, it would be Hull.

The paulin tent was much smaller than the main tent and was located next to the corral set up to contain the circus animals, mostly oxen to pull the wagons and show horses, but there were a few goats and chickens and even a tawny-colored mountain lion in an iron-barred cage.

"Do you suppose that big cat is trained?" Bass asked. "What do you think it's been trained to do?"

"As long as it's trained to stay on that side of those bars," Alfred said, "I'm perfectly entertained."

Bass grinned. He studied the big tent and the smaller ones that held the sideshows and other equipment. The circus people were moving around slow this morning after putting in a late evening and even later night entertaining folks. Miss O'Malley had promised Russell Hull would be up and around.

Bass was almost within reaching distance of the tent flap. Before he could reach for it, the extra paulin was flung back and someone inside shouted, "Stop, you scoundrel!"

A thin young man in a white shirt, a suitcoat, and dungarees exploded through the tent's doorway and continued running. Desperation gleamed in the young man's wide, blue eyes.

"Stop, thief!"

Alfred stepped to the side, out of the fleeing man's way. The man was only a couple inches over five feet tall and might have weighed a hundred and twenty pounds.

Bass shot out a hard, right arm and slammed it into the man's chest just above his stomach. The man's momentum and the torque Bass put into his hips at the point of contact caused the man's feet to leave the ground. He almost turned a complete flip, but he landed on his head and shoulders.

Dazed, the man groaned in pain and rolled onto his hands and knees. He tried to suck in a full breath but failed at that.

Bass lifted a foot and put it into the middle of the man's back between his shoulder blades. He leaned on his leg just enough to pin the man to the ground.

Alfred leaned down and ran his hands through the fallen man's pockets. He took removed a pocketknife, slid it into his own pocket, looked up at Bass, and said, "That's all there is."

A man in his thirties with sallow features, ginger hair, and mutton-chop whiskers ran out of the tent next. He stopped immediately when he spotted Bass and Alfred.

"Good," the new arrival said. "You got him."

"I do," Bass said. "Who is he?"

"I don't know. He's a thief."

"I ain't no thief," the young man managed to gasp.

"He's a thief," the older man said. "I am Russell Hull. I work with this circus. I walked into the tent and found him going through everything. He took something."

"I didn't take anything!"

"Yes, you did." Hull knelt beside the young thief and pried his right fist open.

A long, wedge-shaped bone lay in the thief's hand.

"I walked in with that," the thief said.

"No, you didn't." Hull plucked the bone from the thief's hand. "This is the tooth from a *Carcharias megalodon*, and we have it—*had* it—in our collection."

He turned it over to show to Bass a symbol rendered in black ink. Bass had never learned to read, so he didn't know what the mark was, a letter or just some kind of pictograph.

"This is my mark," Hull insisted. "Mine and Dr. O'Malley's. Proof that we took custody of this tooth."

"That don't prove nothing," the thief said.

"It's proof enough for me," Bass said.

"I was just looking at it," the thief said. "Then he came outta nowhere and scared me. I took off runnin' is all. Just reflex." He eyeballed Bass. "And who are you to come up and ambush a man?"

Bass pulled back his jacket and tapped his forefinger against the marshal's star pinned to his shirt. "I'm the law."

The thief paled and looked like he was going to be sick.

"Me and you," Bass said, "we're going to have us a talk."

He removed his foot, reached down to grab the back of the thief's shirt with one big hand, and effortlessly hauled the young man to his feet. He looked at Hull.

"You got someplace we could have that conversation?"

Abner Pettigrew, the thief, sat on a storage crate in the open space within the tent. Bass had used a piggin string to bind the young man's wrists and Pettigrew sat there looking like a recalcitrant child.

There wasn't much extra space to go around because nearly every inch of the tent's interior was filled with all manner of things. Some of them Bass recognized as Indian things, clothing, weapons, and everyday items like pots and bowls. Boxes of bones, from several different animals, all thrown in together shared space with rolls of Indian blankets from at least a half dozen tribes that Bass could identify. Chunks of lightning-blasted trees, rocks that included quartz and obsidian and agate, filled more boxes.

"What's all this?" Bass asked.

"Garbage," Pettigrew said sourly. "Nearly all of it. They were supposed to have been dinosaur bones."

"It's not garbage," Hull objected. "There are several collectors who will pay top dollar for these rare items. Dr. O'Malley and I donate several of them to fine education institutions. We are—*were*—not mercenaries like you."

Pettigrew folded his arms over his thin chest. "Y'all are sellin' goods, just like me."

"Not like you." Hull leaned over the younger man and cowed him down. "We're—we *were*—selling goods we found on our own. We didn't take them from other people."

Pettigrew opened his mouth to speak, but Bass leaned in too.

"You come in here after a dinosaur bone?" he asked.

"Yeah," Pettigrew said sullenly. "I heard they had some you could see. Only they didn't have a big one. I only found that tooth…that I took by mistake."

"We did have a big one," Hull corrected. "It was stolen the night Dr. O'Malley was killed."

Bass shifted his attention to Hull. "How many people knew you folks had a dinosaur bone?"

Hull shook his head. "No one. It was a recent acquisition. Dr. O'Malley wanted to make a big to-do out of it, so we were keeping it under wraps."

"That dinosaur bone was a big thing?"

Hull brushed his unruly ginger-colored hair back with a hand. "Dinosaurs are mighty popular right now, Marshal. Lots of folks are interested in them."

"Why would someone want to steal one?"

"Because they're worth money is why," Pettigrew said.

"You were stealing that tooth to sell?" Bass said to Pettigrew. "To who?"

"I can tell you who," Hull said. "Dinosaur collectors. Probably to buyers working for either Edward Drinker Cope or Othniel Charles Marsh. Those two men are digging the West up looking for dinosaur bones. The papers have claimed they're conducting 'Bone Wars' to get the biggest and best and most dinosaur bones. Their competition is highly contentious."

"Has their competition ever gotten anybody killed?" Bass asked.

"I've never heard of that, but with the way those two men are throwing money around, I wouldn't be surprised to find out someone had been killed over a discovery."

"If a man can get the right bone," Pettigrew said, "he can get himself set up right fine."

"Is that something you've done?" Alfred asked. He sat on a box next to a stack of circus flyers.

"Not me," Pettigrew, then caught himself. "I only heard tell of such things. Because I'm no thief. Like I said, I only ran out of here with that tooth on account of him surprising me and me forgettin' I was holdin' onto it."

"Then how do you know about dinosaur bones?"

"On account of I try to learn things," Pettigrew said. "The world is a fierce place for a man who's got no education."

Bass wondered briefly who had told the young thief that, then he dismissed his curiosity. There were other things that made him curious. He shifted his attention to Hull.

"What about you? Did you and Dr. O'Malley have the right bone to set yourselves up?"

Hull glared at Pettigrew. "Not in front of the thief."

"Hey!" Pettigrew complained.

"I'll be right back." Bass grabbed the piggin string securing Pettigrew's wrists, pulled him to his feet, and walked him outside to the corral.

"What are you doin'?" Pettigrew demanded.

Using another piggin string, Bass lashed the young thief's wrists to a post.

"Putting you where I can keep an eye on you," Bass answered.

Three of the goats ambled over to Pettigrew and nuzzled his clothing in their search for treats. One of them licked Pettigrew's cheek.

"Marshal," Pettigrew whined. He tried to escape the goats' attention but couldn't get out of their reach. "You can't do this!"

Bass grinned at the man and walked back into the tent to find out what Hull and O'Malley had been concocting together with the missing dinosaur bone.

"Based on what we were able to put together about the bone," Hull said, "we believe the dinosaur it came from was an allosaurus."

Bass stared at the painting of one of the strangest creatures he'd ever encountered. The dinosaur looked a little like a Gila monster in its thick-bodied build, only with the chest and stomach made bigger, more powerful, the forearms shortened, and it was dark green. It stood on two back feet, and in that it reminded Bass of a mountain boomer. The colorful collared lizard ran on its back feet when startled.

In the painting, the allosaurus stood on a mountain ridge, looked like maybe the Arbuckle Mountains, but Bass thought maybe he was just seeing those mountains because they were what he knew. The dinosaur looked like it was challenging the Almighty and anyone else who wanted a piece of it.

"Big sucker, ain't he?" Bass asked.

Hull nodded. "My best guess is that the one the bone belonged to was probably thirty feet long from head to tail, and stood at least ten feet at the crown. In the flesh, it probably weighed more than two tons."

Bass didn't bother to hide his skepticism. "You can tell that from just one bone?"

"I can," Hull said. "Because Dr. O'Malley and I do—did—considerable research on these creatures. We have photographs of assembled skeletons for comparison. Marshall Felch, a noted finder of dinosaurs, recovered what looks to be a complete allosaurus skeleton in 1883 in an area known as Garden Park in Colorado. Have you heard of that area?"

Bass shook his head.

"I have," Alfred said. "They're still digging up dinosaurs out there."

Hull nodded. "They are. The nearby town, Cañon City, was built during the Pike's Peak Gold Rush in 1859. Dinosaurs were discovered during that same time."

"But only bits and pieces of them?" Bass asked.

"Yes," Hull said. "That changed a few years ago."

"The first nearly complete dinosaur skeleton was found in New Jersey in 1858," Alfred said.

"You were there?" Bass asked just to aggravate the old man.

Alfred shot him an irritated glance. "No. But I read, and dinosaurs are interesting. My people never found them."

"Seems like they've been there a good long while," Bass said. "Surprised Indians didn't find them."

"Indians don't go around digging up the ground," Alfred said. "We were taught not to disturb the Earth Mother. Only the weak among us followed the greedy ways of the white man."

"Mr. Tubby is correct," Hull said. "About the Indians, and about the first complete dinosaur discovery. The Hadrosaurus, they called it. Until that time, even the British paleontologists had only found dribs and drabs of dinosaurs. The discovery in Haddonfield started the whole dinosaur fever that has swept this country, especially after it was put on display at the 1876 Centennial Exhibition in Philadelphia. That event hosted ten million people from all over the world. The torch that is now held aloft by the Statue of Liberty was also showcased there. That discovery of the Hadrosaurus, and its attendant fame, set Cope and Marsh into the collecting war with one another."

Bass rubbed his jaw. "How much is the dinosaur leg bone worth?"

Hull shrugged. "To the average person? Virtually nothing. To a museum? Only as much as they can afford, and I can guarantee you that wouldn't be much. But to Cope and Marshall, who continue their war with each other?" He shrugged. "I don't know. I can, however, tell you this: a complete dinosaur skeleton would be worth a fortune to them. Therefore, it would be worth a fortune to the man who has it."

"This is just a piece," Bass said. "One bone."

For a moment, Hull remained silent, then he said, "What I tell you, Marshal Reeves, stays between us. I have your word on that?"

Bass nodded and wondered what he was getting himself into.

"Dr. O'Malley shared with me, in the strictest confidence, that he believes that somewhere, not far from here, lies the rest of that dinosaur's skeleton just awaiting its birthing from the earth. He was certain the bone he had had only just been removed from other bones."

Put like that, Bass thought the whole thing sounded eerie.

"Why would O'Malley think that?" Bass asked.

"He was told that by the man who sold him the bone," Hull said. "Dr. O'Malley told me only hours before he was shot dead."

"Are you planning on filling my small jail while you're in town, Bass?" Cherokee Lighthorseman Everett Big Turtle grinned at Bass to let the marshal know he was kidding.

Bass shoved Pettigrew into the small cell at the back of the jail. "With the railroad running through here, I'm surprised you got any room left. Figured you'd be up to your ears in lawbreakers with the way this town is growing."

"Friday and Saturday night," Big Turtle admitted, "it can be busy. Middle of the week like it is, you caught me at a lull."

Tall and broad chested, Big Turtle matched his name. He was young enough to be Bass's son and wore his hair pulled back in a queue under his Stetson. A Colt revolver hung at his hip and his badge was pinned to his fringed shirt.

The jail still smelled new, though traces of body odor, alcohol, and vomit were creeping in. All four cells in the back were now occupied.

Edward Hough, still wearing his blue dress, which looked worse for the wear, sat in one of the back cells with his knees crossed. He smoked a hand-rolled cigarette. The blue-gray smoke drifted out through the bars set in the back window. He stared at Bass.

"You got something to tell me?" Bass asked.

Hough held his silence for a moment, then shrugged. "You know I didn't kill O'Malley."

Bass walked over to stand in front of Hough's cell. "I suspect I do."

"All you got on me is some warrants for suspected hotel thievery. A good lawyer will get me off most of those charges. Those incidents will be hard to prove."

"Maybe, maybe not," Bass said. "I know Judge Parker ain't gonna hang you for what you did…or didn't do. But there are those warrants, and now I got you drawing down on two peace officers in the pursuit of their duties."

"I never fired a shot." Hough took a nonchalant drag off his smoke. "I got a good lawyer coming, Marshal. He'll get me off that charge too. Your posseman yanked me out of my room without so much as a by-your-leave. For all I knew at the time, you two were there to rob me."

Bass smiled. "Better have a really good lawyer."

"I do."

"He's also going to have to prove you innocent of stealing that bone that's gone missing." Bass thought he'd throw that into the mix just to see what happened. Hough was a thief, but he wasn't overly bright.

Hough squinted. "That dinosaur bone's missing?"

"It is." Bass studied the man and thought the reaction was a true one, that Hough was surprised by the theft. He also knew about the dinosaur bone, which was mighty interesting.

"I didn't steal that bone, Marshal," Hough stated. "I was the one who sold it to O'Malley. You keep digging around, you're going to find that out."

"Well," Bass said, "I guess we'll see about that."

"You ever known Edward Hough to put back money?" Bass asked.

"You've had more dealings with him than I have," Alfred said.

They were having lunch at the Red Rooster Diner because breakfast had been so good Bass figured they should give the mid-day menu a try. He and Alfred dug into steaks and baked potatoes, and they washed it down with tea. Bass was saving a spot for a piece of the peach pie he'd seen behind the glass at the counter.

"Signing onto the circus disguised as a bearded lady who sings opera is about the most forward-thinking thing I've ever seen Hough do," Bass admitted. "Hough's a habitual criminal, always in trouble somewhere."

"But he's no killer?"

"Not yet, but a man can't run the owlhoot trail forever without getting his hands bloody at some point."

Alfred nodded. "True. A smart man gets out quick. A smarter one never gets started." He chewed thoughtfully for a moment. "You changing your mind about Hough killing O'Malley?"

Bass chewed, swallowed, and sipped tea. "No."

"What about his claim that he was the one who sold O'Malley the dinosaur bone?"

"I've been giving that some thought. I'm thinking that is possible. But Hough's not gonna go dig up a dinosaur all on his own. Too much work involved in that."

"So he stole it from somebody."

"That's what I'm thinking."

"Maybe that leg-bone was just a taste of what was to come. Maybe whoever Hough took that bone from knows where the rest of the dinosaur skeleton is."

Bass cut another piece of stake and enjoyed looked at the marbled meat, so tender it almost melted in his mouth.

"We don't even know there are any more bones," Bass said.

"You know what I'm thinking?" Alfred asked.

Bass sighed because he *did* know. "That one dinosaur leg-bone ain't enough to kill a man over."

Alfred pointed his fork at Bass. "That's what I'm thinking. The good thing is, that maybe means we still have time to catch whoever did this."

"Unless he's already ridden off."

"Maybe he has. But if there's still a dinosaur skeleton, or at least more of it, lying out there, chances are good that man might still be around hoping to sell more of it. Do you think a man could murder another man and slip out of town with a dinosaur leg-bone under his arm?"

"From Hull's description, that thing was several feet long, and a bone that size would draw attention. I wouldn't think so, no."

"Still, he could have," Bass said. "Might have got a wagon and hid it there. But let's suppose he didn't. Let's suppose he couldn't."

"On account there are more bones out there waiting to be gathered up."

"Yeah."

"Because otherwise we're chasing the wind."

"O'Malley and Hull kept the dinosaur bone secret," Bass said. "It's likely O'Malley was killed because the thief got caught in the middle of things, killed O'Malley, and had to get away quick. A man couldn't hardly go lugging it around the circus after he killed somebody."

"No," Alfred agreed. "Not if it happened like that."

"Let's say it did, for now. Means the killer needed somewhere quick to stash the bone."

"You believe it's still somewhere at the circus?"

"I think that avenue bears investigation," Bass said. "We'll get to it after we finish up our meal."

Alfred cocked an eyebrow. "And I suppose you're counting a piece of that peach pie I saw you eyeing earlier as part of the meal?"

"I am."

Hours later, irritated at his lack of success in finding a dinosaur bone that might or might not still be in town, and aggravated because he didn't have any other leads to follow, Bass wandered back to the big top to watch the trapeze artists work the high wire. He wanted something to take his mind off his frustration for a minute. Sometimes a man did his best thinking when he wasn't thinking at all.

And part of him wanted to see the circus.

Oliver Worthy waved him on in free of charge. Bass sat with the crowd on the hardwood benches that had been set up around the small ring at the center of the tent.

Overhead, the Flying Cuocos performed gracefully and fearlessly in skintight red uniforms. Several times Bass caught himself holding his breath when they swung through the air and did handstands and other things on the bars, then he felt foolish because they were professionals. Part of their job was to make everything look more dangerous than it was.

Alfred excused himself down the line of spectators. He spoke softly and carried a small bag of pecans. He sat next to Bass and offered the bag.

"Get tired of looking?" the posseman asked.

Bass took two pecans and cracked them in one big hand.

"I did," he admitted. "I'm thinking finding this bone isn't going to be an easy thing."

"Likely not," Alfred agreed.

"Whoever took it is going to want to sell it," Bass said.

"There's a train coming in tomorrow afternoon."

"We'll have a word with the Pinkertons riding aboard it; make sure no one loads a dinosaur bone in baggage without somebody noticing."

"We could send a telegram down the tracks," Alfred suggested. "Let them know ahead of time."

Embarrassment touched Bass for a moment. He hadn't thought about that, and the reason primarily was because he didn't read.

"You take care of that," Bass said.

"I'll send out a notice tonight."

Overhead, one of the Cuocos leaped gracefully from one trapeze bar and the crowd held its collective breath. The airborne Cuoco was caught by another Cuoco hanging upside down from another bar. The crowd "oohed" in appreciation and clapped thunderously.

By the time everyone was settling back down, Everett Big Turtle strode down the row of benches and waved to Bass and Alfred. The Lighthorseman walked back to the end of the row and waited.

Bass and Alfred excused themselves and joined the tribal peace officer.

"Got some bad news," Big Turtle said. His face was serious. "Somebody killed your thief."

Bass tried to make sense of the announcement.

"Which one?" Alfred asked.

Edward Hough lay on his back in the small cell, almost filling it up while prone on the floor. One of his hands had passed through the bars out into the space between the cell and the wall. His head lay almost touching the bars.

The man stared sightlessly at the ceiling and blood flecked his face and bright red beard.

A bullet had punched a hole almost in the center of his forehead and made a mess of the back of his skull. A pool of blood surrounded Hough's head and shoulders.

Outside the barred window, shadows filled the alley behind the jail. Day had turned into night only an hour or so ago, and the air carried a slight chill.

Breathing out in disgust, Bass looked around at the other prisoners. He was more exasperated now than ever. Hough hadn't killed Conall O'Malley, Bass was convinced of that, but Hough had known something somebody hadn't wanted him to tell. His murder proved that.

And now whatever Hough had known was lost.

Bass glowered at the other prisoners. All of them stood watching.

"Y'all all in here, and none of y'all saw nothing?" Bass asked in a louder voice than he'd intended.

The two other prisoners in lockup cowered back.

"I saw something," Pettigrew said.

Bass walked down to join the young man. "What did you see?"

"That bearded fellah got called over to the window there." Pettigrew pointed like he had to, like it wasn't the only window in the cells.

"Did you see who called him over?"

Pettigrew shook his head. "I was curious, thinking about having a look, but then I saw the barrel of the Colt that got stuck through that window. I cut clean shy of being curious and got myself as out of the way as best as I could."

"Hough just stood there and looked at that gun?"

"I think he was surprised. I know I was. Maybe he got scared just before it went off and backed up, but I can't swear to that. After that gun come through the window like it did, it all happened pretty quick."

"Hough knew the man?"

Pettigrew shrugged. "He was talkin' to him for a minute. Didn't call him by name or nothin'. They talked quiet-like, I suppose so nobody'd know, but that pistol shot was loud."

"You're sure it was a man."

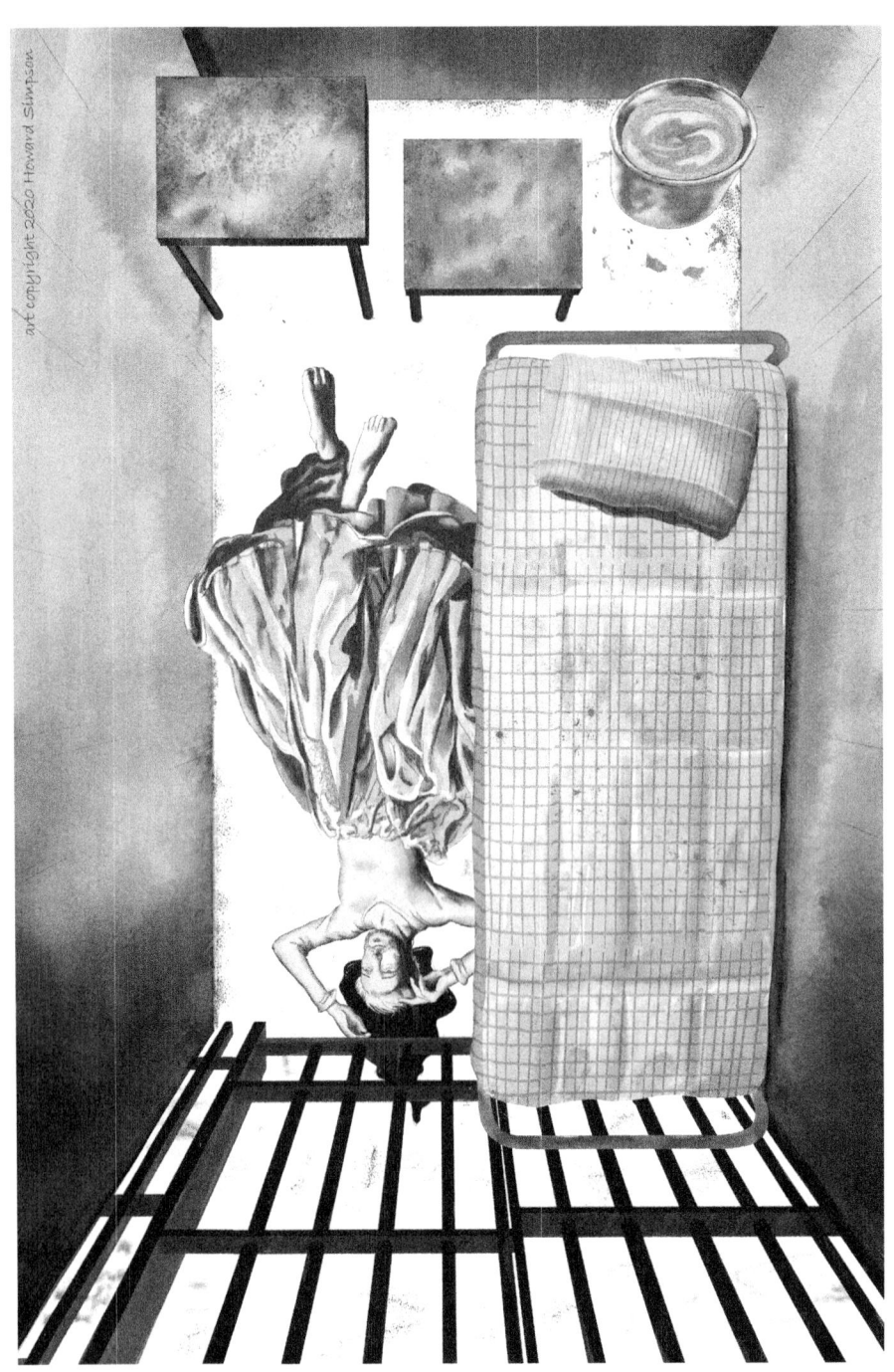

The man stared sightlessly at the ceiling...

"Sounded like a man." Pettigrew looked at Hough lying dead in a blue dress. "But things tonight ain't always looked like what they ought to."

Bass looked back at the dead man, then turned on his heel.

"Let's go have a look out in the alley," he said to Alfred and Big Turtle.

Pistol in hand, Bass walked cautiously through the darkness behind the jail. It stood to reason that the murderer had already fled, but criminals weren't always logical. Killing Hough could have just as easily been a way to get Bass out into the alley for an ambush by somebody who'd heard he was in town and held a grudge.

Alfred came from the other end of the alley. The posseman held his .44 in one hand close to his side. Big Turtle, carrying a Greener shotgun, flanked Alfred.

Bass looked at Alfred. "Well?"

The posseman shook his head. "We didn't see anything."

"Me neither." Bass returned his Colt to his holster and peered at the window at the back of the jail.

The window was high enough that a man passing by would have to stand on something to peer into the cell.

"A man would have to have a ladder or a stepstool to get up to that window," Alfred said.

Bass nodded, but another thought struck him. *Or he was riding a horse.*

Bass waved to Alfred and Big Turtle. "You two step back."

"You figure it was somebody on a horse?" Alfred asked. The old man was quick too.

"I do." Bass waved to the ground. "These hoofprints look fresh, like they just been turned."

"You think somebody on a horse rode up, stuck a gun through that window, and shot your prisoner?" Big Turtle's words carried disbelief.

"Can you think of another way it happened?"

The Lighthorseman shook his head.

"Everett," Bass said, "you got a lantern in that jail of yours?"

"I do," Big Turtle replied. "I'll fetch it."

The Lighthorseman walked back the way he had come.

In the scant moonlight and the glow from the lantern in the back of the jail coming through the window, the fresh hoofprints showed almost clearly in the loose dirt.

Big Turtle returned with the lantern a moment later. Even with the added light, though, Bass couldn't make out any distinguishing features among the prints. They looked uniform, and there were plenty of them, like the horse had stutter-stepped while standing there, or maybe balked when the shot was fired.

Bass looked at Alfred. "Do you see anything I'm missing?"

"Nope." Alfred shook his head. "Man who did this takes care of his horse. Looks like it was wearing new shoes. I don't see anything we can use to track the shooter."

Horseshoes got worn in places and nicked in others. Over time, they could become as uniquely identifiable as fingerprints.

Bass stood up to rest his aching back. It was another reminder he wasn't as young as he once was.

"Your back?" Alfred asked.

"It'll be fine," Bass said.

"Maybe that missing dinosaur bone isn't the only fossil in town."

"Speak for yourself, old man."

Alfred smiled because they were equally aggravated and his needling of Bass was at least a nod toward everything being okay despite the setback caused by Hough's death.

"If you're right," Big Turtle said, "and I think you are, whoever killed your thief rode his horse up here, called your prisoner over, and shot him through the head. Takes a pretty cold man to do that."

"It does," Bass agreed. "It also means the killer has something to lose. Hough knew something he hadn't told us yet."

He moved the lantern so the light played over the ground at different angles. On his second pass he spotted a wet blob wedged into the small space where the jail's wall met the ground. He leaned down to look closer.

Alfred hunkered down as well. "What's that?"

"I don't know. As dry as it's been, this can't have been here long."

"Could be blood," Big Turtle said. "Maybe some sailed out when your thief was shot. I've seen it happen."

Bass reached into his coat pocket and took out a handkerchief. Slowly, he dipped it into the wet blob, then hauled it up to have another look.

The brownish smear stood out against the white cloth of the handkerchief. Small, fine flakes mixed in with the gleaming wetness.

"Looks like tobacco," Alfred said.

"That's 'cause it is tobacco," Bass said.

He waved it under his nose and inhaled. The strong scent of the leaves filled his nostrils, but there was something else too.

"Do you think you're going to track the scent of tobacco spit?" Big Turtle asked. Doubt rang in his voice.

Bass ignored the Lighthorseman, stood, and extended the handkerchief to Alfred. "Tell me what you smell."

Alfred inhaled, held his breath a moment, then let it out. He smiled knowingly. "Lime."

Bass grinned and nodded. "Me too."

"What does smelling lime in tobacco spit have to do with anything?" Big Turtle asked. "There are lots of brands of chewing tobacco, and lots of men who chew it. I favor Mail Pouch myself."

The younger peace officer pulled a pouch from his back pocket to show them.

"He's a young pup," Alfred commented and stood. "He still has a lot to learn about manhunting. Even about tobacco."

Big Turtle glared at the old man. "What do you mean by that?"

"Stick your nose in your pouch," Bass directed. "Tell me what you smell."

"I'll smell tobacco," Big Turtle said. "That's as plain as…"

"The nose on my face?" Bass asked.

He smiled because he thought he had a thread he could pull, provided Hough's murder had anything to do with O'Malley's murder. That wasn't a sure thing yet.

"Smell your tobacco," Alfred suggested.

Big Turtle stuck his nose near the pouch, eyed Bass and Alfred suspiciously for a moment, then inhaled.

"I smell tobacco," the Lighthorseman announced.

"What else?" Alfred prompted.

"Molasses. Smoke."

"The makers add molasses to cut the harshness of the tobacco," Alfred said. "And they smoke the tobacco leaves in barns to add that flavor."

Big Turtle returned the pouch to his pants pocket. "I knew that."

"Know what you don't smell?" Bass asked.

The Lighthorseman thought for only a second. "Lime."

"That's right."

"What does that have to do with anything? Growers flavor tobacco leaves with all manner of things these days. Peaches, berries, and the like. I never heard of lime, but maybe they use that too."

"Using lime is part of the old Indian ways," Alfred said. "They used to put mineral lime into the leaves to help bring out the nicotine. That's what your pa probably did, and if not him, then at least your grandpa."

"I don't see how that's going to help you."

"That killer rode up here," Bass said, "to put a bullet through Hough's head and he was chewing tobacco while he did it. That means he's got a serious habit of chewing."

"And he favors the old ways," Alfred said. "The old taste. That sets him apart. A man alone, Bass and I can find. That's what we do."

Bass looked at his posseman. "There are four stables in town. I'll take the east end."

Alfred nodded. "I'll take Richmond's to the north and the one on the west side of town."

"Watch your back, old man," Bass said. "Whoever did this doesn't hesitate when it comes to pulling the trigger."

Alfred nodded and they parted ways.

"You're looking for tobacco spit," Marvin Portis said. "Well, I never heard of such a thing."

The old hostler was short and lean to the point of emaciation. Dressed in overalls and a flannel shirt, he resembled an unkempt scarecrow. He scratched the back of his neck with one hand, held a lantern aloft with his other, and watched Bass. He stood between Bass and the big black bay who stood eating out of a feedbag.

Squatted down in the paddock, Bass dragged another corner of his handkerchief through a blob of spit.

Thankfully there hadn't been many of those. This was the third blob he'd located. Spit spattered the straw lining the paddock floor and the bottom rails. Whoever the chewer was, he had a serious tobacco habit.

"You can tell a lot about a man from the things he leaves behind," Bass said. He breathed in the spit scent and detected the hint of lime he was hoping for. Excitement thrilled through him. There was nothing like cutting the trail of a man he was hunting.

Bass stood and folded his handkerchief.

"That spit tell you something?" the hostler asked.

"It does," Bass said. "Tells me this is probably the man I'm looking for." He ran a hand over the bay horse and felt the animal's muscles twitch restlessly. "The quality of this horse tells me the man likes his horses."

"That hoss is a good'un," Portis allowed.

Bass looked at the horse's flank and noted the brand. The letter B was bold and underscored by a curved arc.

"Do you know this brand?"

Portis leaned closer with the lantern and squinted. "The Rocking B? Can't say as I do. Got a lot of folks out here who mark their livestock on account of rustlers over in Texas who steal from Indians in the Territories."

"Did the rider leave his saddle?" Bass asked.

"Took it with him."

"He's a careful man, somebody who takes care of his things."

"Saddle was high-dollar," Portis said. "I'd have taken it with me too. Not that there's anything wrong with my business. I never had no horses go missing. It can be hard to keep up with tack at times."

"If he's got an expensive saddle—"

"It was that. Looked Mexican. Good leather. Had silver worked in."

"Then he's a man accustomed to making and spending money." Bass mulled that over. "What did he look like?"

"Big man," Portis answered. "Probably as tall as you, not quite as big. He was something of a dandy, all polished up, but the way his face was scarred, you knew he wasn't afraid of mixing it up when it come to that."

"Did he carry a gun?"

Portis nodded. "Rifle and pistol. He was quiet, steady. A man not to be trifled with."

"Did he leave a name?"

Portis led the way out of the paddock to a small desk. He set the lantern on the desk and opened a ledger. He trailed his finger slowly down the list of names.

"That horse is in number twelve. That would make his owner Kellen Falkirk." Portis looked up at Bass. "That who you're looking for?"

The name didn't mean anything to Bass, and he had a good memory for people whose paths he'd crossed. That meant the man hadn't committed any crimes in the Indian Territories that Bass was aware of.

"Maybe," Bass said. "Do he say where he was staying?"

"Over to the Cranmer Hotel," Portis said.

"Thanks," Bass said.

"Is that man in some kind of trouble, Marshal? Because I don't harbor no criminals. Ain't good for business."

"Right now I just want to talk to him."

Bass was seated in the lobby of the Cranmer Hotel when Alfred arrived. He'd left word for the posseman at the desk of the Köhler Hotel about where he'd be.

The hotel lobby was well-to-do, carpeted and laid out with nice furniture. This time of evening, the lobby was mostly deserted but it was lit with small lamps that had colored glass to mute the brightness. A young clerk behind the counter looked anxious to serve and remained watchful.

Alfred sat beside Bass in another chair against the wall.

"Did you find who we're looking for?" the posseman asked.

"I think so," Bass said. "Man named Kellen Falkirk. Mean anything to you?"

Alfred thought for a moment, then shook his head.

"What about a Rocking B brand?" Bass asked.

"Nope."

"Me neither."

"Falkirk's probably not from around here," Alfred said. "Makes you wonder what he's doing in town."

"You mean, besides killing Hough for some unknown reason?"

"I do. I reckon we'll have to ask. Is he up in his room?"

Bass pointed at the dining hall connected to the hotel. "Actually, he's sitting down to a late supper."

"That's a cold man," Alfred said, "if he can ride over to the jail, blow out a man's candle, then mosey back to his hotel to tuck into a meal."

"I was thinking the same thing. We'll want to go slow and careful."

"We'll do that."

Bass got to his feet and led the way.

The dining hall was every bit as elegant as the hotel lobby. Only a handful of people sat at the tables.

Kellen Falkirk sat in the far corner near the dining hall's exit to the street with his back to the wall so he could watch all the entrances. He wore an expensive suit with his tie neatly knotted. His cheeks showed slight bluing from whiskers already growing back from a recent close shave. His carefully manicured mustache snaked across his upper lip and down a short distance past the corners of his mouth. His hair was neatly oiled and combed.

His startling blue eyes locked on Bass as soon as the big lawman entered the room.

Knowing he had Falkirk's full attention, Bass didn't try to hide his objective. He strode across the room and stood at the table.

Behind him, Alfred came in the door from the street and sat at a table a short distance away. Falkirk's gaze cut to the posseman for an instant, then flicked back to Bass. Falkirk waited as though he had all the time in the world.

"Mr. Falkirk?" Bass said.

If he was surprised at the use of his name, Falkirk showed no sign of it. He picked up a napkin from his lap with his left hand, blotted his lips, and laid the napkin on the table. His right hand stayed out of sight. Bass figured it was holding a pistol under the table.

"I don't know you," Falkirk said. His voice was low and polite, and it didn't carry far.

Moving carefully, Bass hooked the fingers of his left hand to his jacket lapel and pulled it aside to reveal the star. "United States Deputy Marshal Bass Reeves, Mr. Falkirk."

Falkirk smiled. "You go around introducing yourself to everybody, Marshal? If that's so, it's going to make for some mighty long days."

Bass grinned back. "I'd like to ask you some questions, Mr. Falkirk."

"You can."

"How long have you been in town?"

Falkirk made a show of thinking about that. "Four days. Something like that."

Bass was sure that was the truth because it could be easily checked at the hotel. He hesitated for a moment, trying to figure out how brassy to be about everything. With as cool as Falkirk was, he decided to jump in whole hog and see if he could shake the man up.

"About the time Conall O'Malley got himself killed," Bass said.

Falkirk sipped his coffee. "I don't know who that is, though I did hear there was a murder a few days ago. One of the circus people, I believe. Other than that, I wouldn't know."

"You mind telling me where you were about an hour ago?"

Falkirk regarded Bass coolly. "As a matter of fact, Marshal, I do. I'm a private man, and I treasure my privacy."

"I'm afraid I'm going to have to insist," Bass said with a little more authority. "I've got reason to believe you killed a man named Edward Hough an hour ago."

"You've got reason to believe?" Falkirk cocked a mocking eyebrow.

Knowing he was being baited, Bass didn't say anything.

"Evidently you have no proof of any such nefarious dealings as murder," Falkirk said.

"I'm working on that," Bass countered.

A smile twisted Falkirk's lips. Using his left hand, he dipped the first two fingers of his left hand into his jacket pocket and withdrew a small business card.

"You'll have to work without me, I'm afraid," Falkirk said. "And if you should desire to interfere with me without any true legal cause in the future, I suggest you take it up with my attorney. He'd be happy to oblige you. I will not."

Even though he didn't want to, Bass took the card. He couldn't read it, but he made a show of looking at the name written there, then he pocketed it.

"I'll bid you a good evening, Marshal," Falkirk said.

"For now," Bass said.

Angry, certain he'd found Hough's murderer but frustrated because he couldn't do anything about it now, he turned and headed out the door to the street. Alfred followed him.

A block away from the diner, Bass handed the posseman the card.

Alfred read the name on the card aloud. "Charles Ward, attorney at law. His office address is here in Woodward."

"I've never heard of him," Bass said.

"He's probably new. When the Southern Kansas Railway came through, it brought a lot of business with it. Lawyers too. Once they get dug in, we'll probably never get rid of them." Alfred looked back toward the dining hall. "What do you want to do about Falkirk?"

"We'll sit on him, see where he goes. He's involved with everything going on here. I'm certain of that."

"All right. Want me to take first watch?"

"No," Bass said. "I've got it. I'll catch a few winks over at the stable. I suspect Falkirk won't go anywhere without that horse of his."

"It would be a long walk if he does," Alfred said.

Freshly bathed and dressed in his second suit, Bass finished shaving around his big mustache and patted his face dry with a towel. He'd been tempted to go to the barber to have it done, but he just didn't feel comfortable paying for something he could do himself.

Cleaning his other set of clothes was another thing. He'd left those downstairs for the people in the bath to take care of.

Someone knocked at the door.

Bass tossed the towel aside, slipped one of his .44s from his gun belt because the meeting with Falkirk had made an unwelcome impression on him, and went to answer the door. He braced his left foot a few inches behind the door, then opened it.

Oliver Worthy stood in the hallway and looked anxious.

"Marshal Reeves," the barker said, "Miss O'Malley would like you to join her. Something's come up."

"What?"

The man shook his head. "She didn't tell me."

"She's okay?"

"Yes. A couple of the men are staying with her. We draw kind of close to our own when we need to, Marshal." Worthy frowned. "Ever since the killing in the jail last night, we've been concerned. I'm going to be happy to get shut of this town."

Bass nodded. "Let me get my hat."

Augustine O'Malley stood awaiting Bass under the flapping folds of the Big Top. She held her hands clasped and looked nervous. The morning sun was bright, and it didn't sit well with Bass after a night spent semi-sleepless in the stable.

"Good morning, Marshal," Augustine greeted.

"Good morning, Miss O'Malley. Is there a problem?"

"I don't know." She bit her lower lip. "An oddity I don't much care for more than anything, perhaps."

"What might that be?"

She handed him a letter. "This was delivered to me this morning."

Bass took the letter and looked it over, but he couldn't make heads or tails of it. He looked up at her and felt lacking.

"I apologize, Miss O'Malley, but I can't read."

"Oh." Augustine looked surprised, then flustered. "I'm sorry. I didn't know. I didn't mean to offend you."

"No offense." Bass smiled. "Mrs. Reeves darns my socks and sews up busted seams on my shirts because I lack those skills as well. There are things I know and don't know. Mostly, I know the things I need to know."

She nodded.

"Maybe you could tell me about the letter."

"It's an offer for the dinosaur bone," she said. "If I can produce it, I can be paid quite handsomely for it."

"Who's making the offer?"

"An attorney here in town. Mr. Charles Ward."

Bass couldn't darn, though he could sew a little, and he couldn't read, but he knew when a convergence of circumstances got suspicious.

"Maybe we should go see Mr. Ward," he suggested.

Augustine looked troubled. "I don't have the dinosaur bone, Marshal. I don't know where it is."

"Yes, ma'am. I know that. I thought maybe we could talk to Mr. Ward and find out what he knows. Especially since he wasn't supposed to know about the dinosaur bone. I find that mighty interesting."

"The offer doesn't come from me, Miss O'Malley," Charles Ward said. He steepled his hands behind his big desk and leaned back in his leather chair to gaze at her sitting opposite him in the expensive office. The space still smelled of new paint. "I merely represent a buyer who is interested in obtaining that artifact."

Augustine glanced at Bass and let him take the lead.

"Who's the interested party?" Bass asked.

Ward, blond and suave and thirty pounds overweight in his fifties, fixed Bass with his gray eyes.

"And who are you?"

"A man asking a question," Bass said.

Ward shook his head. "A question I'm disinclined to answer, sir, if you'll permit me my boldness in the interests of brevity."

Bass shifted his coat and revealed the star. "Let me rephrase that, counselor. I'm a *United States Deputy Marshal* asking that question."

Ward smiled gently. "I'm afraid that doesn't make any difference,

"It's an offer for the dinosaur bone."

Marshal, and you know that. I'm still disinclined to name my client, especially since that would go against his wishes."

Bass wasn't surprised, but the lawyer's stonewalling effort made him mad. He gazed around the big law office and took in the wall of books, the pricy décor, and the large windows overlooking Main Street.

Ward turned his attention to Augustine. "Back to the matter at hand, Miss O'Malley. Would you like to sell that dinosaur bone my client wants? I'm prepared to draft a check right now."

"Why does your client want the bone?" Bass asked.

"I haven't asked." Ward shrugged. "That's out of my purview, and I don't question tasks I'm given. I merely try to achieve results."

"I'm thinking maybe Cope or Marsh might pay better for it," Bass said. "They seem to be the men with all the money for dinosaur bones. We haven't even talked to them yet."

Ward frowned and looked like a man who'd had a sudden attack of indigestion. "I, and my client, would prefer you not deal with those gentlemen. I also promise you this: whatever offer either of those men might tender you, should you pursue that course of action, we can do better."

Bass wondered how the lawyer could say that. The market for dinosaur bones was small, and Cope and Marsh were at the top of it. Only their interest in the bones made them worth anything.

Who was the other person willing to bid against the two bone hunters?

It was curious. And evidently whoever was hiring Ward was in a hurry to get the bone.

Bass stood. "Miss O'Malley, I think we should go."

Augustine stood.

"Wait," Ward said. He looked surprised and disgruntled. "What about my offer?"

"We're going to think it over," Bass said. "Then we'll get back in touch with you."

He followed Augustine to the door, let her out, and went through. He looked at the big black horse tied to the hitching post in front of the law office. It was a fine-looking horse.

And it wore a rocking B brand.

"Miss O'Malley." Ward stood in the open door of the law office.

Augustine turned to him. "Yes."

"I must tell you, ma'am, that my client's generous offer will not exist in perpetuity. There will come a time when he's no longer interested."

"That would seem strange," Bass said. "A man going to all this trouble, then just walking away. I think we've got some time before that happens."

Ward scowled and turned away.

"One more question, Mr. Ward," Bass said.

The lawyer looked at Bass but didn't say anything.

"Where'd you get your horse?"

"Why?"

"That's a mighty fine horse. Might want one like it."

"I got that one from a satisfied client," Ward said. "That's how I get everything."

He disappeared into the law office and closed the door.

Bass strode off and the young woman fell into stride with him.

"Did you discover something, Marshal?" Augustine asked. "Because there for just an instant you looked happy about something."

Bass hoped Ward didn't see that. "I am happy. I think we just got closer to knowing who's behind your father's murder."

"The Rocking B brand?" Big Turtle gazed down the street where a gentle wind pushed a small dust cloud along. He sat out in front of the jail in a wooden chair. The boardwalk was covered in slivers from a piece of wood he'd been whittling. "Walter Bilodeau owns that brand."

"I've never heard of him," Bass said.

"He's got a spread up in the Cimarron Territory and runs cattle on it."

The Cimarron Territory was up in the northwest corner of the Indian Territories and butted up against Kansas and Colorado. It was all part of what was currently called the Unassigned Lands, an area the Creek and Seminole nations had to cede back to the United States after fighting on the side of the Confederacy during the Civil War.

"Bilodeau sounds like a white name."

Big Turtle nodded. "It is. Bilodeau's people originally came from England. You can't get any whiter than that."

"Last I heard, whites can't own land in Cimarron Territory."

"They're not supposed to," Big Turtle agreed. "All those are disputed areas. There's some who say nobody owns it because the white government hasn't figured out what they're going to do with it. But there's owning something through a piece of paper, and there's owning something because nobody else is strong enough to take it away from you."

"He's a squatter?" Bass knew several white people had moved into those lands from Kansas, Colorado, and Texas.

"He is. And he's got a lot of guns to back his play."

Bass considered that and tried to make all the parts of the murders and the theft of the dinosaur bone fit. He still couldn't get a firm grip on everything, or why O'Malley and Hough were killed.

"You ever had any dealings with Bilodeau?" Bass asked.

"I arrested his son on a drunk and disorderly charge about a week ago," Big Turtle said. "He came through town raising hell and carrying on. He got into a fight with Oliver Worthy, the circus barker, over Vivienne DuMont, who, as we know, wasn't Vivienne DuMont."

"What's the son's name?"

"Jacob Martin."

"Not Bilodeau?"

"Jacob Martin is Bilodeau's stepson. He's raised that boy most of his life, but they got bad blood between them from what I saw. Bilodeau didn't care that his stepson got arrested other than it would make him look bad. So he got him out of jail. I tried to charge Martin for bringing liquor into the Territories because he brought a load in. I couldn't make that charge stick. He had a pretty slick lawyer who's new to town and the lawyer put it on two other men who were helping Martin."

Bass remembered the fresh paint smell in the lawyer's office. "Any chance the lawyer was a man named Ward?"

Big Turtle nodded, surprised. "That's the one." He looked at Bass. "You know Ward?"

"Just met him a short while ago," Bass said. "He got referred to me by Kellen Falkirk."

"Is that the man you think killed Hough?"

"It is."

"Alfred told me he believed you two had turned him up." Big Turtle folded his knife and shoved it into his pocket. "I don't much care for Ward."

"Me neither." Bass folded his arms across his chest and thought some more.

"You haven't brought Falkirk in."

"I haven't arrested him. I can't make the murder charge work yet. Judge Parker is mighty particular about getting everything done by the book."

"So you're going to let Falkirk go?"

"No," Bass said. "I'm going to give Falkirk some rope, follow him around, and see if he hangs himself." Bass smiled humorlessly. "It's a funny thing, him having the same lawyer Bilodeau has."

"That's pretty convenient."

Bass nodded. "Until it's not. That lawyer ties all of them together. Martin, Falkirk, and Bilodeau. Ward even puts a bow on the missing dinosaur bone because he's chasing it too. I just have to prove what they're up to. Those men are all out of convenience. They just don't know it yet."

Bass was glad the circus was in town because it drew a crowd. After a change into some clothing he purchased at one of the general stores in town and a secondhand hat he bought from a trailhand, he looked like another person. He walked differently and even appeared shorter.

Kellen Falkirk never spotted Bass when the marshal followed him to Charles Ward's offices. Whatever else the conversation was, it was brief. Falkirk left the law office only minutes after going in. He was frowning and spat tobacco at a dog lounging by the boardwalk.

Bass left the alley where he'd been standing across the street in the shade of a leather good shop. He scooped up a handful of dirt and rubbed it onto the dog's coat to help the animal get rid of the tobacco blob. Then he followed Falkirk.

The man returned to his hotel, got his saddle and gear, and checked out. Then he made for the stable.

Excited, Bass changed directions and headed for the Köhler Hotel. Alfred was catnapping in preparation for taking the night shift on Falkirk so Bass could sleep in a bed. Bass was going to miss that. He was sure he had a few days of traveling across the open country ahead of him.

He rapped on the hotel door and Alfred opened it a moment later.

"Falkirk's on the move," Bass said.

Alfred nodded and opened the door. Panniers loaded with food sat near the wall.

"I got all the supplies this morning while you were talking to the lawyer," Alfred said. "Grab your gear and meet me back here. I'll have everything ready to go."

Bass nodded. They'd known Falkirk would leave. It was just a matter of when, and when was now.

Bass and Alfred rode spread out and staggered along the trail leading out of Woodward. For a time, the narrow band of hard-packed earth ran alongside the railroad tracks, then it veered off and made its own way through more primitive country.

He scanned the ground for the telltale marking of Falkirk's bay. Bass had cut a divot into the horse's shoe last night, in case the man managed to get out of town without being seen.

"As long as we don't get a big rain," Alfred said, "we shouldn't have any problems keeping up with Falkirk."

"We know where he's going anyway," Bass replied. "More or less. He's headed out to the Cimarron Territory. To Bilodeau's ranch. We just have to make sure he doesn't spot us and decide to ambush us."

They kept riding, and Bass told himself they were good enough to keep themselves alive. They'd been through a lot together.

Walter Bilodeau's cattle ranch was situated on the west side of Clear Creek, a narrow waterway that broke up the flat land. Trees hugged the creek, but there was a lot of grazing land available for the large herd the rancher had.

Brief conversation with a general store shop clerk in the small community not far from Bilodeau's ranch had turned up that information. Walter Bilodeau had been one of the first men to put down roots in the area, and he was a major force in sending delegations to Washington, D. C. to get the lands released to the families living on them. So far they hadn't been successful, but all the locals were rooting for him.

Bass and Alfred tried to find a spot that would allow them to observe the ranch house and bunkhouse without being seen, but the Rocking B kept a lot of hands working the cattle.

"Okay," Bass said on the evening of the second day, "staying out here ain't gonna work."

"We could ride in," Alfred said.

"We don't know enough yet. Bilodeau is involved, but we don't know how much."

Bass trained his spyglass on the house and spotted who he believed was Jacob Martin on the porch. The young man fit the description Bass had gotten from Big Turtle. He was tall and gangly, with unruly straw-colored hair. He also had an attitude and didn't help around the ranch. Mostly he looked bored.

And trapped. He and Bilodeau argued twice out in the front yard. Both times were short, and once Bilodeau had knocked the young man to the ground.

"What do you think about Martin?" Bass asked.

"He's got too much free time on his hands," Alfred observed. "Would you let one of your boys sit around on his hands like that all day?"

"No, I would not. Idleness and boy-children are not good companions. That's devil's work just a step away."

"I think his stepfather is keeping him close to home," the posseman said. "Not letting him go anywhere and trying to keep him out of trouble. Or from getting into more trouble. Bilodeau doesn't like his stepson. He's trying to keep him tethered."

"Do you think Martin killed O'Malley?" Bass watched the young man through the spyglass.

"He could have, but I wouldn't bet on it. He might get into some foolishness, but I don't think he has enough spine to kill a man."

"Killing O'Malley have been an accident."

"That man was heart-shot. That's no accident."

"It could be."

"Paint it that way if you want," Alfred said, "but if you think that, I think you're wrong."

Bass sighed. "Me too." He studied Jacob Martin a moment longer. "What are the chances Walter Bilodeau would let us talk to his son?"

"His *step*son. I'd say that's not going to happen."

Bass agreed. He'd watched Walter Bilodeau ride out a few times. The man had been easy to recognize because the ranch hands deferred to him. He never had to tell anybody anything more than once either. He was in total control of his ranch. The man looked solid and formidable. His face was hard and sharp, like it had been cut out of stone, and he was well-groomed every day.

"Falkirk killed Hough," Bass said. "We're pretty sure of that, but we need to know why so we can get a handle on proving it. As far as we can tell, those two men didn't even know each other."

"If all of this ties together, and I agree with you that the lawyer says it does, it has to be over the missing dinosaur bone."

"Jacob Martin was in Woodward first. Falkirk came in later. We need to get to that young man."

That afternoon, Jacob Martin rode with a band of ranch hands and two buckboards toward the small community that had formed a few miles from the Rocking B. Falkirk rode with them.

Bass and Alfred gave them a head start, then followed.

Folks called the community Elmwood when they called it anything at all. It consisted of a general store, a lumber yard, a doctor's office, a stable and blacksmith's, and two no-name saloons because the Cimarron Territory wasn't kept dry like the Indian Territories were.

The ranch hands and Martin made for one of the saloons. Falkirk headed over to the general store. The buckboards were parked out front along with the big black bay Falkirk rode. Bass suspected the riders were in for the monthly supplies. Ranch hands ate a lot because the work was so demanding.

According to the same shop clerk Bass had talked to when he'd first arrived and was asking questions about Bilodeau, Falkirk was a gunman in the rancher's employee. He'd come down from Kansas with Bilodeau, but the clerk hadn't known more than that. A local man had braced Falkirk after insulting a woman in the gunman's presence and had gotten shot down in the street.

Bilodeau had paid for the funeral, and folks had gone back to their lives. But they gave Falkirk a wide berth.

Bass and Alfred halted outside of town. Bass took his good suit from his saddlebags and stripped out of his trail clothes.

"What are you going to do?" Alfred asked.

Bass smiled at the posseman and dressed. "I'm gonna go into town and buy me a dinosaur."

"You?" Alfred looked skeptical.

Bass brushed dust from his suitcoat and pocketed his marshal's star. He reached into the bag he kept that held extra things like rings, wigs, spirit gum, and an assortment of eye-patches to change his appearance. He slipped on a pair of spectacles. They made everything a little blurry and gave him a headache if he wore them too long, but they gave him a different look.

"Don't I look like somebody who could represent Cope or Marsh?" Bass asked.

"Which one?" Alfred asked. "Because you'll have to pick one."

Bass thought for only a moment. "Cope. He now lives in Haddonfield, New Jersey, and he's tramped around in Kansas looking for dinosaur bones with a man named Benjamin Mudge."

Bass had gleaned those facts from an extended talk with Russell Hull regarding the missing dinosaur bone. At the time the circus man had just been talking, but Bass tended to remember a lot of what he was told.

"Maybe you can pull that off," Alfred said. "Either way, we're not getting the job done sitting in the woods along Clear Creek and dodging ranch hands."

Bass reached into his jacket pocket and took out one of the business cards Hull had gotten from people Conall O'Malley had been in touch with regarding the dinosaur bone. He couldn't read it, so he showed it to Alfred.

"Tell me who I am."

Jacob Martin drank alone in a back corner of the saloon. The area was small, and business was slow. The other Rocking B ranch hands sat at a table and played cards. They rotated out to visit the two soiled doves working the upstairs rooms.

Bass scanned the room, walked to the bar, and ordered a beer from the tired-looking bartender who didn't even try to engage him in conversation. For a moment, Bass sipped his beer and studied the room.

The ranch hands were involved with playing cards, telling jokes and wild stories, and watching the doors to the upstairs rooms. They ignored Martin. The young man sat and looked sullen. A bruise showed on his cheek from where his father had hit him two days ago.

Bass knew he only had a brief opportunity and if he wasted it, he and Alfred would once more be camped along Clear Creek and fighting mosquitoes. He bought a fresh beer, stepped away from the bar, walked to Martin's table, and sat the beer down.

Martin looked up.

"I saw you were dry," Bass said. "Thought maybe you could use another."

Martin hesitated, and Bass knew the young man was highly aware of the marshal's skin color, then he gave a short nod.

"Much obliged." Martin slid the beer over and took a sip.

"You mind if I sit?" Bass asked.

"You bought me a beer. That buys you some time." Martin nodded.

Bass sat. "Not wanting to waste any of that time, Mr. Martin, I'll cut to the chase. I'd like to do some business with you, if I'm able."

The young man leaned back in his chair and narrowed his eyes in suspicion.

"I don't know you," Martin said.

"I don't know you neither," Bass admitted. "But I'm hoping we can change that. My name is Hercules Tweedy."

He plopped the business card on the table. Martin leaned forward, turned it around, and read it, moving his lips as he did so.

"I got your name from Russell Hull," Bass said.

Martin shook his head. "I don't know him."

"He worked for Dr. Conall O'Malley at Bishop and O'Malley's Traveling Circus of Amazing Enchantments."

"Why'd you get my name?"

"I'm buying dinosaur bones for Edward Cope. Maybe you've heard of him."

Martin hesitated. "I have."

"Good." Bass smiled. "Mr. Cope was in talks with Dr. O'Malley regarding the acquisition of the dinosaur bone Dr. O'Malley had."

"I heard that bone went missing," Martin said quickly. "I didn't have anything to do with that."

"I didn't suspect that you did," Bass replied. "But a man named Edward Hough sold Dr. O'Malley the bone. I wondered if you knew anything about that."

"No." Martin shook his head. "I didn't know anyone named Hough."

"He also went by the name Mademoiselle Vivienne DuMont and masqueraded as a women opera singer at the circus. I'm told he was quite good."

"*Mademoiselle DuMont?*" Martin looked like he was about ready to choke.

Bass nodded. "Hough was a career criminal."

"Vivienne DuMont was *not* a woman?" Martin seemed stuck on that.

"No."

Martin shook, looked like he was going to be sick, and took a deep drink of his beer. He wiped his lips with his shirt sleeve. He swore, but he kept his voice low so he wouldn't attract attention.

"Vivienne DuMont didn't look like a man," Martin said.

"Except for the beard," Bass pointed out.

Martin looked at Bass. "You sure about that?"

"I am."

Martin swore again.

"You had a fight with the circus barker while you were in Woodward," Bass said. "Over Vivienne DuMont."

Martin thought for a minute. "Me and her—*him*—had a deal. I found the bone and took it to the circus because I'd heard that old man looked for such things. I'd heard men got paid good money for finding bones like that, but I didn't trust anybody. I made the mistake of trusting her—*him*—and got double-crossed."

"How?"

"Vivienne DuMont…you said his name was Hough?"

"Yes."

"Well, I went to the circus to get the lay of the land and ended up talking to her, only she ain't a her, is she?"

Bass ignored the question. "Why her?"

Martin hesitated. "I like women. I've had a lot of women. But I never had one who had a beard. She was something different." He looked forlorn. "Only she wasn't really, was she?"

Bass stepped away from that subject. "Dr. O'Malley felt certain there were more bones where the one came from. I came here to find you and investigate that possibility."

Martin pointed to his beer glass. "I'm empty again."

Bass put on a false smile, returned to the bar, and came back with a fresh round.

"I don't know how much money you were hoping for with that first bone," Bass said, "but if there are more, Mr. Cope believes it could be the biggest find since the Hadrosaurus. If such a thing exists, Mr. Cope is willing to pay top dollar for the man who can point the way to them."

Martin narrowed his eyes in speculation. "How much?"

"Enough to change a man's life. *If* there are bones."

"Mr. Tweedy," Martin said, "there's a whole creature out there waiting to be collected, and I found it." He sat up straighter. "I want money, a whole lot of money, for it."

"I can get it for you," Bass promised.

Excitement burned in Martin's hazel eyes. Bass knew the young man was already spending the money he thought he was getting. Living under his stepfather's thumb had turned him hungry and desperate. Martin unconsciously massaged his bruised cheek.

"I don't have to fetch them bones?" Martin asked. "I can just lead you to them?"

"Yes. We'll take care of digging them up."

Martin chugged his beer. "I can do that. Tonight."

"Why tonight?" Bass asked.

"Because I ain't gonna be free until then." Martin glanced at the ranch hands at the other table and leaned forward. "Clear Creek runs up behind my pa's land. You lay in south along the creek tonight about midnight and I'll find you. Come alone. Just you and the money."

"I didn't bring the money with me," Bass said. "I wasn't going to ride out here just so I could get robbed."

Martin swore. "I already been snookered once."

"Do I look like a man who would snooker you?" Bass met the man's suspicious gaze and looked guileless. The only person who could see through that face was his wife, Nellie Jennie.

"You better hope not, Mr. Tweedy, because I ain't gonna be snookered twice."

Bass wanted to point out that Hough had already snookered him twice, once to beat him out of the money for the bone, and the second time about the fact that Vivienne DuMont wasn't a woman. But he didn't.

"Show me the bones," Bass said, "and I'll get you the money."

Martin nodded. "You will, or I'll take a pound of flesh, by God."

Alfred walked through the door and approached the bar. The posseman had remained outside to watch for Falkirk, who was the only man who might have recognized Bass. By coming in, he'd let Bass know the gunman was on his way.

"I've got to go, Mr. Martin." Bass stood. "I'll be looking for you at midnight."

"You do that," Martin said. "And come alone."

"I will." Bass headed out the back of the saloon.

"Could be he got scared and he's not going to show," Alfred said.

He leaned under a blackjack tree and was almost invisible in the darkness. At midnight, the creekbank was steeped in shadows. Woodsmoke from the Bilodeau ranch carried to them in faint traces.

"Maybe he did," Bass admitted, though he hoped not. If things didn't work out with the Jacob Martin angle he was playing, he wasn't sure what to do next.

Finding the bones of whatever creature was buried wherever it was buried wasn't going to tell him who killed Conall O'Malley, but it might put him closer to finding that out.

"That boy's mighty skittish," Alfred said.

"He's scared of his pa, and I don't blame him. The only things we have going for us is Martin's greedy and he wants to get away from Walter Bilodeau. I have to hope that's enough to bring him out here."

The ears on Bass's mare pricked forward. He waved a hand to Alfred and immediately felt foolish. The old man was just as alert as he was.

A few minutes later, a horse and rider pushed through the brush along the creekbank and stopped a few yards from Bass.

"Tweedy?" Martin whispered hoarsely.

"Yes," Bass responded.

"Come on out here where I can see you."

Bass stepped forward from the brush he'd used as cover. He went almost fearlessly because Alfred would have his rifle to shoulder and have a bead on Martin in case things went south.

"I thought maybe you weren't coming." Bass stood with his hands out to his sides.

"Took a minute to get away without nobody seeing me is all," Martin countered. "Get your horse and let's ride."

"How far are we going?"

"Three miles. It won't take long. You getting that money you're going to pay me will take longer."

Bass got his mare and joined the young man. Martin looked pale and nervous in the wan moonlight.

"I'm ready," Bass said.

Martin took the lead and headed out. Bass trailed behind him. Alfred would wait a short while, then follow.

"Do you know anything about my pa?" Martin asked.

"Only by reputation."

"The man is a tyrant," Martin said. He leaned into his horse as it headed up a small rise. "All he's interested in is his money. And making more money. He came out here to Cimarron Territory to start a cattle ranch because the land, as least in his mind, was free for the taking. He cut himself out that big spread before anybody knew he was there."

"Seems to have done all right by himself," Bass said.

"He's got himself a kingdom is what he has," Martin said. "He's making money and keeping it all to himself. He don't pass none of it along. My ma is happy to get what little he gives her because she's had to make do with less before she married him."

Bass wasn't going to argue that, though he felt certain Martin wanted to.

"I should get part of that," Martin said. "I've been working for him since I was a kid and he married my ma. Only that ain't the way he sees it. He keeps telling me that I should make my own money. So I finally find a way. And you know what that old skinflint does?"

"No," Bass said.

The countryside around them was thick with scrub trees. A coyote's eyes gleamed in the night a couple times, and an owl brushed by overhead on heavy wings.

"He takes that way of making money away from me is what he does," Martin said. "I found that bone and knew that old man who ran the circus bought such things because I'd seen the circus when it passed through Beaver City. At the time I was there moving a herd with the other hands. Had to pay for my own room at the Groves Hotel while my pa paid for the hands to say there. He told me it was a *business expense* and I should get used to having them."

Martin shook his head. He reached into his saddlebags and took out a whiskey bottle. He took a long drink, then returned the bottle to the bags. Bass took note of the fact the man was running on liquid courage.

"After we got back from pushing the herd," Martin went on, "I took that bone on down to Woodward and caught up with the circus. I was figuring out how best to approach O'Malley when I ran into Vivienne DuMont. Whatever *his* name was, may he rot in Hell. I wasn't thinking, so I let *him* take the bone. Later, I found out I wasn't getting none of the money that was paid for what *I* found. I went to see her—*him*—and got sideways with that barker fellah. Got myself arrested."

Martin got the bottle out and had another drink.

"I was locked up and had no choice but to send a telegram to my pa," the young man went on. "He come and his lawyer got me out, and he left Falkirk to take care of things."

"What things?"

Martin hesitated a moment, but he had a skinful of whiskey and a need to talk. "Falkirk killed O'Malley. He always does the killing Pa wants him to do. Pa sent him there to do that to shut things down."

"What things?"

"Pa was afraid if folks knew dinosaur bones could be found out in the Cimarron Territory, it might bring more attention to what he was doing out here, to his little empire he was building. He already hasn't had much luck getting the federal government to see things his way. He figures the dinosaur bones would make things worse on account of there being strangers traipsing through and digging around. If something was found on the land he claimed, they might come in and contest him over his property rights. He wasn't going to truck with that. Falkirk didn't find that bone, though."

Martin reined in his horse and pointed ahead.

Bass peered through the moonlit woods and spotted a narrow box canyon almost hidden from sight.

"You see that?" Martin asked.

"The box canyon?"

"Yeah." Martin took another pull from the whiskey bottle. "Ain't good for nothing. Covered in broken rock that can turn a horse's hoof in the blink of an eye and cost you a good animal. I went in there after some lost heifers. That's where I found them bones."

Bass knew he had Martin's confession about who killed O'Malley, and that might be enough to satisfy Judge Parker, but he was curious about what the young man had found that had gotten O'Malley and Hough killed.

"Show me," Bass said.

"Don't believe me?"

"I have to tell Cope and his people I saw the bones."

Martin turned in the saddle. "We come out here in the dark, and you're new to this country. It would be hard for you to find this canyon again on your own."

Bass nodded. "That it would be."

"I'll show you them bones and you'll get that money Cope is paying for them. That's how this is going to work."

"All right," Bass said.

Martin put spurs to his mount again.

On the eastern hillside inside the box canyon, Jacob Martin hauled away dead brush to reveal what lay beneath. Bass held a small lantern aloft and the soft golden glow played over the dirt, stone, and bone that was exposed.

"There it is," Martin declared proudly. "I only found a little bit of bone at first. Had to dig more of it out, but it looks to be all there."

The creature, whether it was an allosaurus or whatever it had been, only showed partially. But what was revealed looked complete. Bass thought Russell Hull would have been excited.

Horses' hooves echoed inside the box canyon as the animals approached. It was more than one, which told Bass that it wasn't Alfred. They'd left the pack animals at the stable in Elmwood.

Bass stepped over to his horse and pulled his Winchester from the saddle scabbard. He led the horse over to the side of the canyon, out of the way. There was no way he and Martin could hide their presence. Whoever had found them had come looking for them. He set the lantern on the ground a few feet away.

"Did you bring somebody?" Martin demanded. He reached down for the gun at his hip.

Bass grabbed the young man's wrist and kept him from drawing the revolver.

"Stop," he commanded.

"You're trying to rob me!"

"Those riders don't belong to me," Bass said.

Miller kept struggling to pull his pistol.

Unwilling to have his attention split or to fight a battle on two fronts, Bass lifted an elbow and slammed it into Martin's face. When the young man stumbled backward, surprised and bleeding from the nose, Bass followed up with a blow from the rifle's butt that left Martin stretched out unconscious on the rocky ground. Bass knelt, took the man's revolver, and stood to meet the riders just now entering the box canyon.

"Jacob!" a man yelled harshly. "Get out here and show yourself!"

Bass knew there was no other way than to face up to whatever was coming. He hoped he could keep things from turning violent.

"Is that you, Mr. Bilodeau?" Bass asked.

Bilodeau sat his horse and was barely revealed in the moonlight. He looked severe, like a man out of the Old Testament. Falkirk rode to his right, and other men formed a loose half-circle of shadows behind them.

"Who are you?" Bilodeau demanded. He raised the lantern he carried to the light crept into the box canyon.

"United States Deputy Marshal Bass Reeves."

"I've heard of you. You sure picked a bad night to show up here, but at least you got that fool boy to lead you to that stupid pile of bones that's threatening to cause such a fuss."

Bilodeau shifted the lantern light over to the semi-buried dinosaur skeleton.

"He wouldn't tell me where it was," the rancher said. "I couldn't even beat it out of him."

"He probably thought keeping it secret was the only way he'd ever get away from you," Bass said.

"Well, now that's downright unkind of you to say, Marshal." Bilodeau smiled, but there was no humor in the expression.

"You had Mr. Falkirk kill Dr. O'Malley," Bass said.

Bilodeau drew in a breath and let it out. "I did. Had him kill that fellah in the jail too, on account he finagled that bone from that sorry excuse of a stepson I got." He peered past Bass. "Did you kill him?"

"He's sleeping," Bass said.

"Well, good. At least he won't feel what's coming."

"What do you mean?"

"I mean now that I know where them bones are," Bilodeau said, "I'm going to destroy them and put an end to all this foolishness. I won't have those idiots climbing around out here drawing attention to this part of the world until I'm good and ready. I want our rights to this land settled first."

"You're under arrest," Bass said. He gripped his rifle tighter. "I'm taking you in for murder."

"Sure you are. You just wait right there." Bilodeau glanced over his shoulder and nodded. "Donnie, you just take that dynamite on up to them bones."

One of the men rode forward. He held a bundle of dynamite sticks under one arm.

Bass pointed his rifle at the man, but before he could fire or speak, Falkirk brought his rifle up smoothly to his shoulder. Bass swiveled, ducked, and dove into the rocks and scrub brush. Falkirk fired and the bullet cut the air over Bass's head.

Another shot cracked from somewhere overhead, then rifle shots cascaded into the box canyon and it became impossible to tell where they were coming from.

Bass settled in, aimed the Winchester, and moved the sights over the chest of the rider headed for the bones. He squeezed the trigger and Donnie slid backward over his horse's rear and dropped the dynamite bundle. Bass levered in another round. Bullets struck sparks and rock chips from the stones in front of him.

One of the saddles was empty and the riders milled around, temporarily confused. Bass tried to find Falkirk, knowing the man was going to be the deadliest killer among them, and spotted the big black bay nervously stamping its feet and rearing its head.

Unable to find Bilodeau, only the abandoned lantern on the ground, Bass put the sights over another of the rancher's men. Before he could squeeze the trigger, the man jerked to the side and tumbled to the ground.

"Somebody's on top of the canyon!" a man shouted.

"Kill him!"

The flare from a rifle muzzle blast lit the ridgeline of the wall and another rider fell. In the next instant bullets tore chunks from the ridgeline.

"Did you get him?" a man demanded.

"I don't know!"

"Somebody go see!" Bilodeau ordered.

Bass tried to track the man's voice and couldn't in all the thunder trapped in the box canyon. He sighted on another man, squeezed the trigger, and dropped him. He levered the rifle's action again.

The rest of the ranch hands deserted their horses and took refuge behind rocks, scrub brush, and the handful of trees that grew in the box canyon. The big black bay broke ranks and led the other horses on a wild scramble from the gunfight. Men shouted at the horses and some ran after them, but it was too late.

On the other side of the canyon, Donnie staggered to his feet and lurched back toward the ranch hands.

"Donnie!" Bilodeau shouted. "Get back and move that dynamite!"

The ranch hand ignored the order and kept running.

Bilodeau cursed and Bass finally got a fix on the man. Behind a tree, Bilodeau shifted his rifle.

Donnie managed two more steps before Bilodeau put another bullet into his chest. The man slid bonelessly to the ground. Bass was pretty sure he wouldn't be getting up again.

Bass laid his sights over Bilodeau and squeezed the trigger. The man's hat flew off, but he jerked back behind the tree under his own power.

Falkirk stepped out of the shadows and into the lantern light. Bass tried to swing his rifle around, but Falkirk moved swiftly. The killer grabbed the lantern and heaved it deeper into the canyon.

Turning end over end, the lantern flew in an arc, then smashed to pieces on the hard ground only a few feet shy of the dynamite stick bundle Donnie had dropped when Bass had shot him. Flames quickly spread across the dry scrub grass and raced for the dynamite.

"Get out of there!" Alfred shouted in Cherokee from the canyon wall.

Bass pushed himself to his feet but didn't head out of the canyon. He didn't want to desert his horse, Jacob Martin still lay there helpless, and the bones would be destroyed.

Bullets cut the air and dug into the ground around Bass as he ran. Aches and pains flared up within him, but he ignored them and grabbed the dynamite. He didn't have time to set himself. The spreading flames lit him up. Moving as quickly as he could, he heaved the dynamite into the canyon's mouth where the Rocking B riders had taken cover.

Bass threw himself behind a tree, brought the Winchester up, and watched the dynamite land within a few feet of Bilodeau and his men. Most of them broke cover and ran, doubtlessly thinking the explosive sticks were going to explode. Instead, the dynamite just hit the ground and disappeared behind grass, but Alfred picked off two more ranch hands before he was driven back by another fusillade of bullets.

Thinking quickly, Bass reloaded his rifle with cartridges from his belt, then ripped a sleeve from the shirt he wore. He picked up a fist-sized rock, wrapped it with the shirt sleeve, and thrust it down into the nearest flames long enough for the cotton material to catch.

Flames licked at Bass's fingers, but he held on long enough to throw the rock toward the dynamite. The fire-wrapped rock fell within a few feet of the dynamite. For a moment Bass feared the flames had gone out. Then a small conflagration sped from the rock in all directions, including toward the dynamite.

"Put that fire out!" Bilodeau squalled.

Two of the men ran for the stone. One of Alfred's shots put a man down. The other almost reached the explosive, but the flames caught the twisted fuses and they sputtered to life for a brief instant.

The explosion blew the remaining ranch hand to Kingdom Come, or gave him his first experience with the burning fires of Hell, and flattened the other Rocking B riders.

Ears ringing, Bass stood behind the tree where he'd sheltered and covered the area with the rifle.

Nothing moved.

"Alfred?" Bass called.

"I'm here. I didn't expect that."

"You see anybody moving?"

"Not yet, but some of them could be playing possum."

Bass didn't think that was likely, but he knew that it was possible. Grudgingly, he left the tree and stayed as much in cover as he could on his way to the canyon's mouth.

Broken dead men, lit by the firelight that danced around them, littered the ground.

Bilodeau lay partially behind the tree where he'd sheltered, but his staring eyes revealed that there was no life left in him.

Outside the fringe of dead men, a figure moved awkwardly and got to his feet.

Falkirk stood and reached for his pistol. Even dazed, he was so fast he got the Colt up and pointed before Bass could aim his rifle. Both weapons went off at the same time. Bass wasn't sure because his ears were ringing.

Falkirk's bullet went wide somewhere because Bass wasn't hit, but the gunman dropped his pistol and sank to his knees. He wrapped his arms around his stomach and slid back to his haunches.

Bass levered the Winchester, held the sights over Falkirk's chest, and walked toward the man.

Falkirk watched Bass but didn't say anything.

"As near as I can reckon," Bass said, "you killed a man who loved his daughter and only wanted to bring more understanding to the world, so I have no pity for you. If you lived, which you ain't gonna do gut-shot like that, Judge Parker would stretch your neck. If it's any consolation, I'll probably catch hell for letting you off so easy."

Falkirk released his last breath and fell over.

"The man who killed my father is dead?" Augustine O'Malley asked a few days later.

"Yes, ma'am," Bass said. He was still tired from the long ride. "As well as the man who sent him to do it. I've got Jacob Martin sitting in jail till Judge Parker decides if there's anything he wants to do to him. I know none of that will bring back your pa, but I hope it offers you some comfort."

"I'm sure it will. In time."

Bass stood a short way away from the Big Top with the young woman. Oliver Worth was overseeing the dismantling of the tent and its support ropes. Several townsfolk stood watching. All of them looked sad.

Bass had given Augustine a brief overview of everything that had transpired in Cimarron Territory. She appeared to have taken some solace in having everything settled, but it would never give back what had been lost.

"I appreciate everything you've done, Marshal," Augustine said. "Please thank Judge Parker for me when you see him."

"I'll do that."

The Big Top flattened, like all the air had been let out of it.

"What's next for you folks?" Bass asked.

"Another town," Augustine answered. "I'm not certain which one. Mr. Worthy knows. I'll figure it out." She gave him a brief smile. "After all, the show must go on. It's what my father would have wanted." She smiled gently. "I'm quite sure the same can be said for you and your endeavors."

"Yes, ma'am. Some days it seems like the work will never end."

"You be careful out there, Marshal. The West, particularly the Territories, needs a good man like you looking after it."

"Yes, ma'am."

"Good-bye and good luck."

Bass touched his hat brim and watched her walk away. He turned and looked at Alfred, who stood nearby.

"You hungry?" Bass asked. They'd eaten in the saddle that morning, and it hadn't been very filling.

"You're thinking about the peach pie over at the diner, aren't you?" Alfred asked.

"I am," Bass said. "I'm sure that one is gone by now, but I'm hoping they have another one just as good as that one was."

"I'm guessing they won't have it long after you get set up."

Bass grinned. "Probably not."

THE END

Cowboys and Dinosaurs?

No way, right?

And yet, it happened. Kind of.

I was thirteen or fourteen when I first saw *The Valley of Gwangi*, a film that featured stop-motion model animation effects by the great Ray Harryhausen, who had already blown my mind with *Jason and the Argonauts*.

In *Gwangi*, a rodeo owner is going under and a stuntman tries to help her out. Doesn't take long before they cross paths with a British paleontologist and end up looking for an *Allosaurus* that somehow survived the extinction event that killed all the dinosaurs. Well, *most* of them. There's a *Pteranodon* and a few other hangers-on to make it a party.

The *Allosaurus* dinosaur featured in my novella is just bones.

The movie isn't good, but it is Harryhausen, and if you can be five years old again, it can be fun. I watched it back when I was living in Seminole, Oklahoma, shortly after the moon landing. I figured if we could land on the moon and walk around, there were probably places on Earth we hadn't been to that had dinosaurs still lurking about.

I'd read Edgar Rice Burroughs's *The Land That Time Forgot*, Sir Arthur Conan Doyle's *The Lost World*, and Kenneth Robeson's (Lester Dent, also from Oklahoma for a short time) Doc Savage adventure, *The Land of Terror*, where Doc and his aides end up battling dinosaurs on an island.

None of these tales have ever left my thoughts.

But, I suppose you're asking yourselves, how did I ever imagine famous Oklahoma lawman Bass Reeves would be chasing dinosaurs in the Old West?

It really wasn't as hard as you would imagine.

In addition to being an English major in college, I was also a history major. Somewhere in there, can't remember where, I ended up crossing paths with some mention of the "Bone Wars" and "The Great Dinosaur Rush." The fact that Edward Drinker Cope and Othniel Charles Marsh actually duked it out collecting dinosaur bones in the Old West captivated my attention, but I didn't really know what to do with it.

The late Michael Crichton, who gave us dinosaurs in ways we had never seen before, wrote *Jurassic Park* and launched a movie franchise that is still ongoing. In fact, Crichton had a book that was published posthumously called *Dragon Teeth* that was set in the Old West and had the "Bone Wars" at its center. I haven't read that one, but I've got it on my TBR pile.

When the ever-gracious Ron Fortier agreed to take another Bass Reeves story from me, I wanted to give him something different, and I wanted to showcase the marshal in a way most people might not expect.

I started with Bass arresting a clown at a circus because I imagined him racing through sideshows as a bit of slapstick that would be fun. The dinosaur bone and the "Bone Wars" came along as the story gestated. I got caught up in that, thinking about ways to incorporate that bit of history in the background of a murder investigation.

The clown gave way to a bearded lady, which I thought was even more off-center. It certainly got Air Chief Ron's attention!

I had the kernel of an idea with the dinosaur bones, and I dug into the research. There were more dinosaur bones found in Oklahoma than I'd thought!

I learned that the *Acrocanthosaurus* is the state of Oklahoma's dinosaur, and one of the species is named after Atoka County in Oklahoma because that was where it was found. The name came into being in 1950, so Bass Reeves would never have heard of it. The dinosaur was named by J. Willis Stovall and Wann Langston, Jr.

There is a museum close to the University of Oklahoma where I teach writing that was once named the Stovall Museum. The museum is now the Sam Noble Museum of Natural History, but a lot of people still know it as the Stovall Museum. It originally began in the old campus geology building and had acquisitions from the 1904 St. Louis World's Fair, the Spiro Mounds, and the 1924 Sykes Expedition to Alaska and Canada. Dr. Stovall was the first to mount the fossils and build dioramas.

When my older boys were young, I took them to the Stovall Museum to look at the mastodon skeleton. As is usual in dinosaur mountings, not all the bones were originals, or even from similar species. This one had the head of an elephant, which was much smaller than the mastodon's body. They had a sign there that announced this.

Another famous dinosaur place in Oklahoma is the Black Mesa State Park & Nature Preserve that has 47 dinosaur prints that were discovered in the 1980s. The preserve is out near Kenton, Oklahoma.

Just this year, 2019, a man caught a 170-pound alligator gar that was almost 7 feet long. The gar is recognized as a prehistoric fish that's been around since the Early Cretaceous period over 100 million years ago.

Prehistoric sharks' teeth from Oklahoma still sell over internet commerce.

As it turns out, dinosaurs have never quite left the state of Oklahoma.

All of this swirled around in my head when I turned my attention to the new Bass Reeves story included in this volume. I enjoyed taking the marshal to the circus and propelling him into the adventures that ended up in a deadly box canyon ambush where the dinosaur's final resting place was.

So many people think of history as this episodic thing, like it's divided up into clean parts that stand aloof from the other parts. They forget that history is actually a blending agent and that one series of events tends to feed another, or at least to lay the groundwork for the events that come after.

Bass Reeves is that kind of history. His legend, though forgotten by many, lives on and has in these later years, swelled to new recognition. Though I haven't seen the HBO series *Watchmen*, I'm told Bass Reeves plays an important role in that story.

I hope you enjoy this tale I've crafted, and I hope you learn something as well. I enjoy writing the adventures Bass Reeves might have had, and I'm glad you're along for the ride.

MEL ODOM - grew up in southeastern Oklahoma, where diehard country boys still eat possums and soft-shelled turtles, but now lives in Moore, Oklahoma, a wonderful town that unfortunately attracts Pecos Bill riding a twister on a regular basis. He's lived through hog raising and F-5 tornados, surely two of the most dangerous things in the world.

Over the last twenty-plus years, he's written dozens of novels in many different genres, including some based on television shows like *Buffy the Vampire Slayer* and novelizations of *Blade, Tomb Raider,* and xXx. He's trekked through deadly forests and braved the Sword Coast in the Forgotten Realms, and written adventures of bioroid detectives in Fantasy Flight's Android game.

He teaches in the Professional Writing program at the University of

Oklahoma and writes all the time. He can be reached at mel@melodom.net, www.melodom.blogspot.com, @melodom on Twitter, and on Facebook.

His current military science fiction trilogy, *The Makaum War,* has been hitting bestseller lists.

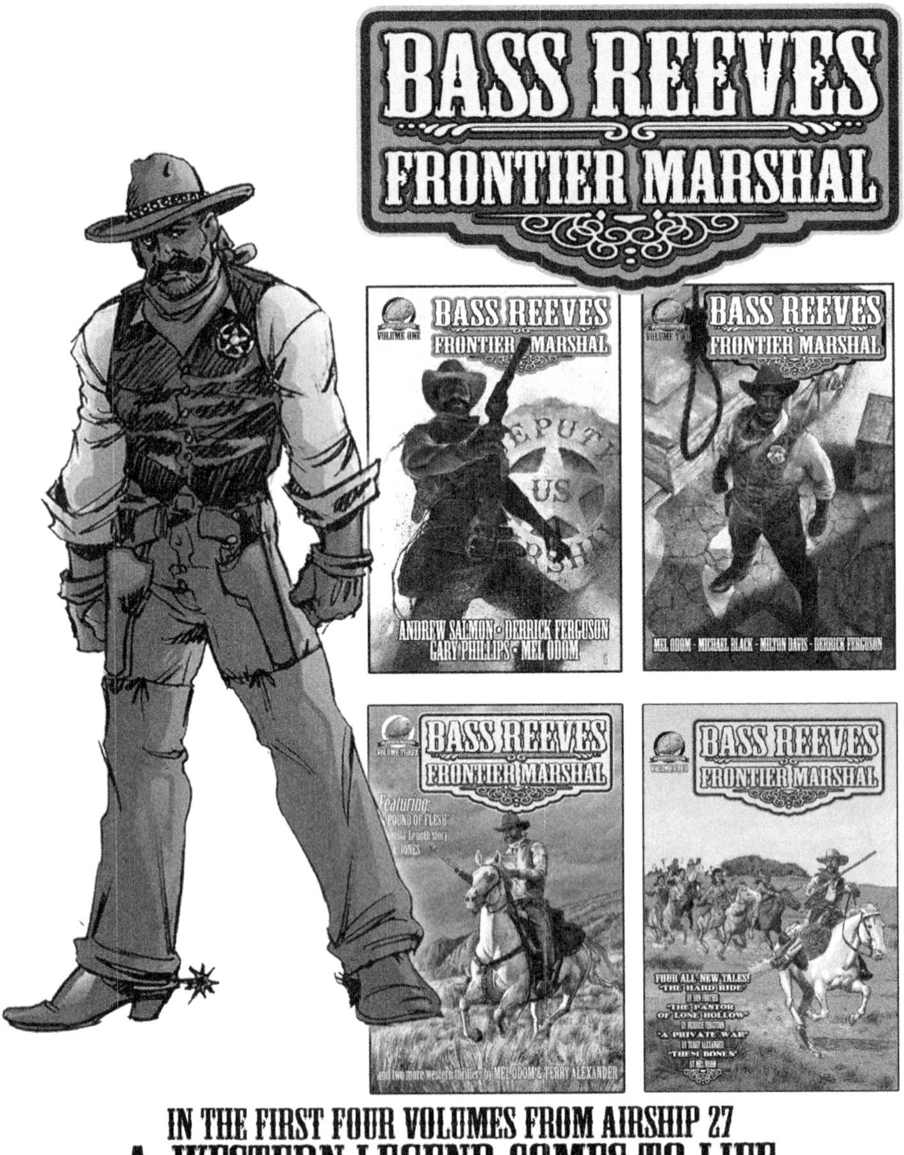

Printed in Great Britain
by Amazon